PUZZLE IN POPPLEFORD WOOD

A Churchill and Pemberley Mystery Book 3

EMILY ORGAN

Also by Emily Organ

Churchill & Pemberley Series:
Tragedy at Piddleton Hotel
Murder in Cold Mud
Puzzle in Poppleford Wood
Trouble in the Churchyard
Wheels of Peril
Christmas Calamity at the Vicarage - a novella

Penny Green Series:
Limelight
The Rookery
The Maid's Secret
The Inventor
Curse of the Poppy
The Bermondsey Poisoner
An Unwelcome Guest
Death at the Workhouse
The Gang of St Bride's

First published in 2019 by Emily Organ

emilyorgan.com

Edited by Joy Tibbs

ISBN 978-1-9993433-7-8

Chapter 1

"REMIND me never to visit the bank again on Compton Poppleford's market day, Pemberley," said Annabel Churchill as she sank down into the chair behind her desk. "It's complete mayhem! Countless yokels have crawled in from the countryside and blocked the roads with their rickety carts and animals, all of which have seen better days. I was trapped for fifteen minutes in a crowd of noisy, gap-teethed rustics with low-set ears. Most of them were wearing smocks. Smocks, I tell you! And I even saw a man in clogs. There's no excuse for clogs, Pembers. He'd be arrested for looking like that in Richmond-upon-Thames."

"How fortunate for him that he doesn't live there, then," replied Doris Pemberley, a thin, bespectacled lady with a mop of untidy grey hair.

"It's a different world altogether," said Churchill, adjusting her string of pearls. "I thought I'd adapted to Dorset life quite well, but every now and again one is reminded of the region's particular peculiarities."

"Don't they have market day in Richmond-upon-Thames?"

"They do, but it's a much more sophisticated affair up there. People unload their wares from shiny vans rather than carts riddled with woodworm. And the cows and sheep behave with much more decorum."

"No rustic types?"

"None. You get a few oiks from Hounslow, but no smocks. And definitely no clogs!"

Churchill smoothed down her silver helmet of lacquered hair. She was a large lady with a fondness for tweed skirts and woollen twinsets.

"But you only ever need one pair," said Pemberley.

"Of what?"

"Clogs. Because they're carved out of wood they go on forever; no need to ever replace them. They'll still be going strong even after you've died."

"Outlived by one's footwear. What a thought."

"And there's no need for any expenditure on new shoes."

"An advantage that should not be overlooked. Shoes are such poor quality these days, don't you find? A few bimbles along the riverbank and the soles are almost worn through. And the days of finding a decent cobbler on every high street are long gone."

"Clogs are the answer."

"Only if you're clinging to the bottom rung of the social ladder, Pembers. If one has any middle-class aspirations at all they're a distinct no-no."

"Well, don't worry, Mrs Churchill. The marketplace will soon be transformed for the unveiling of the statue of Sir Morris Buckle-Duffington next Tuesday."

"He sounds terribly important. Did he do anything particularly noteworthy?"

"He was an adventurer."

"That sounds rather vague to me. Have we eaten all of our custard tarts?"

"Yes."

"What about the iced fancies?"

"All gone. But the man has been to put the letters on the door."

"The door letter man! Oh, how exciting. I was so befuddled by the chaos of market day that I forgot to look closely at the door when I returned. Let's take a peek at his handiwork."

Churchill got up from her desk and walked over to the office door, the upper half of which was glazed with safety glass.

The words 'Atkins's Detective Agency' had once decorated the glass, but Pemberley had invested a great deal of time in scraping off the word 'Atkins's'. What Churchill saw in its place displeased her greatly.

"Have you seen what he's done here, Pembers?"

"No."

"Did you not check door letter man's work before you paid him?"

"No."

"Why ever not?"

"Because I didn't think I'd need to. What could be so difficult about putting the word '*Churchill's*' on the door?"

"My sentiments exactly, but he's still managed to make a hash of it."

"How so?"

"Get up off your chair and have a look, Pembers."

Pemberley did as she was told and quickly joined Churchill at the door.

"Oops!" she exclaimed.

"Since when did my surname become two separate words?"

"He did mutter something about it being quite a long name, and that there wasn't much space for it."

The lettering on the door read 'Church' and beneath it was the word 'Hills'.

"*Church Hills Detective Agency*," said Churchill scornfully. "And he's forgotten the apostrophe!"

"You often find that with sign makers," said Pemberley. "They put apostrophes in where they're not needed and forget them where they are."

"And that's acceptable, is it?"

"No, not at all. It's just what they do."

"And then get paid a tidy sum for it and go on their merry way. You'll have to telephone and get him back here."

"I can see myself that it would be quite tricky to fit the word '*Churchill's*' into that space."

"He'll just have to use smaller lettering. Shall I telephone and tell him exactly how he needs to do his job?"

"You might have to."

"It's ridiculous!" fumed Churchill, striding back into the office. "Why must one be required to supervise every single task? It's terribly draining, Pembers, and we have no cake to sustain us. Could you please fetch some from Simpkin the baker?"

"Any particular type?"

"Anything at all."

Churchill picked up the receiver of the telephone on Pemberley's desk, but didn't get as far as dialling.

"Oh hello, what's this?" The headline of the *Compton Poppleford Gazette* had caught her eye, swiftly prompting her to replace the receiver. "'*Mystery of Darcy Sprockett Solved*'. What mystery is that, then?"

"Let me fetch some cake, and then I shall elucidate."

Chapter 2

"WOULD you like to hear the long and the short of it?" Pemberley asked as she arranged six butterfly cakes neatly on a plate.

"Well, I've just read the write-up in the *Compton Poppleford Gazette*, but I imagine it's wildly inaccurate, as usual. Am I right in thinking that Miss Darcy Sprockett was a girl who went missing twenty years ago?"

"She was more of a young lady; about twenty years old. I'm hoping you've already put the kettle on the gas ring, Mrs Churchill."

"I most certainly have. It should be close to boiling by now."

Pemberley made a pot of tea and the pair sat down at her desk.

"Darcy Sprockett was the eldest daughter in the large Sprockett family, who lived in a tumbledown place at the edge of Poppleford Woods," explained Pemberley. "She made an excursion late one evening to fetch a basket of eggs from her great-aunt, Betsy, who lived in a cottage at the heart of the woods."

"Your tale concurs with the newspaper report so far. Do go on."

"She fetched the eggs from Great-aunt Betsy but was never seen again. The following morning her basket of broken eggs was found about fifty yards from Great-aunt Betsy's door."

"How terribly sad."

"And now, twenty years later, we have received news of the bones."

"Yes. The newspaper says they've just been discovered in a place called Todley Field, which is owned by one Farmer Jagford."

"That's right. And now the mystery has been solved."

"According to the *Compton Poppleford Gazette's* misleading headline, that is. Only it hasn't been solved, has it? How on earth did poor Miss Sprockett end up in that field?"

"Well, that remains a mystery."

"Exactly. What did the police do about poor Darcy's disappearance? Please don't tell me that hapless Inspector Mappin represented the constabulary back then."

"He did, actually."

Churchill groaned and bit into a butterfly cake.

"Inspector Mappin investigated but failed to uncover much," continued Pemberley.

"Why doesn't that surprise me?"

"The Sprocketts grew quite impatient with the lack of progress, so they instructed Mr Atkins to investigate."

Churchill raised an eyebrow. "Did they indeed? And how did my predecessor fare?"

"Not much better, I'm afraid. Everyone was left completely baffled."

"Oh dear… That's disappointing. What were the theories?"

"The only one anyone could think of was that the goblins got her."

Churchill gave a yelp as she bit her tongue. "Goblins?" she spat through a mouthful of cake crumbs.

"That's what Great-aunt Betsy claimed. After she discovered the basket of broken eggs she ran through the woods, shouting, '*The goblins have got her!*'"

"Let me just check that this was only twenty years ago, Pemberley, and not back in the dark ages?"

"Yes, just twenty years ago."

"Do people still believe in goblins in these parts?"

"A few. Old superstitions die hard."

Churchill shook her head. "Astonishing!"

"Darcy Sprockett has been known as 'The White Lady' since then."

"Why so?"

"Because she haunts the woods."

Churchill gave a start, causing her tea to slop into its saucer.

"People believe she's a ghost?"

"Yes. She's the White Lady of Poppleford Woods."

"Good grief, Pembers! Don't tell me you believe that yourself?"

"Only when I wake up at three in the morning and everything's rather dark and quiet and lonely. It seems very real to me then."

"Don't tell me that Atkins believed in all this goblin and ghost nonsense?"

"No, he didn't. He was the pragmatic type."

"Well, that's what you get with us detective types. Pragmatic to the bone, we are."

"He was dogmatic, too. In fact, I wrote a poem about him once and used both those words to make it rhyme."

"How lovely, Pembers. Do you mind if I have the last

butterfly cake? My last one was ruined when I bit my tongue."

"I think I saw the White Lady of Poppleford Woods once."

"Oh don't, Pemberley, I nearly bit my tongue again! What happened?"

"I was walking in Poppleford Woods a few years ago with a friend, and that's when we saw her."

"What was she doing?"

"Not a great deal. She was on the path up ahead of us, all dressed in white. Just as we were wondering who she was, she disappeared."

"Your friend also saw her?"

"Yes, Mrs Higginbath saw her as well."

"For a moment there I thought I heard you say '*Mrs Higginbath*'."

"I did."

"Your *friend* Mrs Higginbath?"

"Yes."

"The large, square-faced lady with all that long, grey, greasy hair?"

"Yes."

"The lady who runs the library and refuses to let me have a library ticket?"

"That's because you were rude about her nephew."

"I know *why*, Pembers, but that's beside the point. The point is that you consider Mrs Higginbath a friend."

"She was once a friend, but then we fell out."

"Oh, I see. Well, thank goodness for that. What was the reason for the falling out?"

"I lost a library book."

Churchill gave a tut. "Mrs Higginbath strikes me as the sort who would be willing to part ways with a friend over something as insignificant as a lost library book."

"She even threatened to send the bailiff around."

"She's the sort of person who would be obsessed with life's trivialities. Someone who's probably never had anything important or meaningful happen to her. She most likely has no idea at all what it's like to have real problems in life."

"I can't say that I do, either."

"But you're not like Mrs Higginbath, are you, Pembers? You're a nice person and she isn't. The difference is that simple. Anyway, this white lady you saw... Are you certain she was a ghost?"

"We couldn't think of any other explanation for it. And we couldn't think of anyone from the village who would be wandering around the woods dressed in white."

"A rogue bee keeper, perhaps?"

"Why would it have been?"

"Bee keepers wear those white suits, don't they?"

"But why a *rogue* bee keeper?"

"Because if they're roaming around the woods they're not by the hives, are they? They've gone a little *off piste*, so to speak. Perhaps it was someone in cricket whites."

"A cricketer?"

"Yes, searching for the ball. Perhaps it had just been hit for six, and a fielder was searching for it."

"I think there was a cricket match being played nearby at the time. It rings a bell."

"There you go. Case of the White Lady of Poppleford Woods solved."

"Except it isn't. Somehow Darcy Sprockett vanished twenty years ago and no one knows why."

"There's only one thing for it, then." Churchill drained her tea and brushed the cake crumbs from her ample bosom. "Do you have your stout walking shoes at the ready, Pembers?"

Chapter 3

"So this is Farmer Jagford's farm, is it?" Churchill asked her trusty assistant.

"Yes, Sponberry Farm."

"Does he grow sponberries here?"

"What are they?"

"I don't know. I wondered for a moment if they were a Dorset thing."

The two ladies stood on the crest of a hill, overlooking the farmhouse and barns nestled in the valley below. The mellifluous song of a skylark carried on the warm breeze.

"Where's the field, then?" asked Churchill.

"Todley Field? It's over the other side of the farm."

They continued on their way, and before long they saw a man approaching them.

"Looks like a farmhand up ahead, Pembers."

Churchill called out a greeting as they reached the young man, who was wearing a flat cap, a shabby waistcoat and stained trousers.

"Mornin'." He doffed his cap. "You 'ere to see the skellington?"

"We're interested, if that's what you mean," replied Churchill, noticing that the young man only had one eyebrow, which stretched across the entire width of his forehead.

"Bobby Jagford's went and found it while ploughin'! 'E's ploughed over it, and then when 'e's turned 'is tractor round to go over it again 'e's found a bone sticking out the dirt! 'E says 'e first thought as 'ow it were an animal. So 'e's got off of 'is tractor and then 'e's saw the 'ipbones."

"I'm sorry. Ipbones?"

"Yeah. In yer 'ips."

"Ah, *hip*bones. A pelvis, then. Is that what he saw?"

"I reckon so. Anyways, 'e's thought, 'I don't know no animal what 'as 'ipbones lookin' like that.' 'Cause they looked like 'uman 'ipbones, see. A dog ain't got no 'ipbones like that, as 'e? Nor no other animal neither. Then that's when he saw it."

"What? The hipbones?"

"No, 'e'd already seen the 'ipbones, 'adn't 'e? No, now he's gone and seen the skull! Ain't no mistakin' it's 'uman when yer see a skull like that."

"Indeed not."

"Anyways, 'e's gone diggin' around after that."

"Has he? Oh dear."

"'E's gone diggin' around, and 'e's found ribs! And then them little backbones an' all."

"Vertebrae?"

"Dunno. Then he's pulled up arm bones, leg bones, toe bones, finger bones, neck bones. You name it! All of it. The 'ole skellington!"

"It must be in rather a dismantled state by now, I imagine."

"'Spector Mappin says he's gonna put it back together." The young man wiped his nose on the back of his hand and hitched up his trousers.

"Is he really? That might be interesting to watch."

"They're all sayin' as it's '*er*!'"

"They are, are they?"

"The White Lady o' the Woods!"

"Indeed. Well, if you don't mind we'll proceed along this path and investigate a little further."

"Ev'ryone's been 'ere today," he said with a grin. "I told Farmer Jagford, I did. I told 'im as 'e needs ter go chargin' a sixpence to everyone what comes 'ere!"

"Let's hope he introduces the charge after our visit, in that case. Come along, Miss Pemberley."

Churchill and Pemberley walked through the farm and followed the lane that ran beyond it.

"Todley Field used to be two fields," said Pemberley. "Farmer Jagford cut the hedgerow down to make it into one."

"And the hedgerow is where the skeleton was buried, is that right?"

"That's what it says in the *Compton Poppleford Gazette*. And Bobby Jagford has ploughed it up."

Before long they reached a gate with a bicycle leaning against it. Hanging from the handlebars by its chin strap was a police inspector's hat.

"Oh no," groaned Churchill. "That's Inspector Mappin's bicycle."

She took a pair of field glasses out of her handbag and peered through them.

"Darn these things; it takes forever just to get them focused... Why can I see nothing but sky? Oh, hang on... No, that hasn't done it..."

"Would you like me to try?" asked Pemberley.

"No thank you. I'll be all right once I've got these things focused and pointing in the right direction. They're incredibly contrary… Oh, I've got something now."

Churchill found that if she squinted in a particular way she could just about discern two blurry figures standing in the middle of the field.

"It's Inspector Mappin and Farmer Jagford," said Pemberley.

"How on earth are you able to see what I'm seeing through my field glasses, Pembers?"

"I'm just using my normal eyes, aided slightly by my spectacles."

"Then you must have the vision of an eagle!"

"Not really, they're just over there. Look."

Churchill lowered the field glasses and saw that the two figures were, in fact, larger and clearer without them. "It's Mappin all right, isn't it?" she said. "We'll never get a chance to do anything with him knocking about; we'll have to wait for him to leave. Let's scurry along and pretend we're just passing by."

The two ladies continued on their walk.

"Hullo!" came a voice, drifting across the field. "Mrs Churchill? Miss Pemberley?"

"Pretend you haven't heard him, Pembers. Just keep walking. No, don't turn and look at him… Oh, Pembers! You turned and looked at him!"

"I'm sorry. I can't help but turn around when someone calls out my name."

"Tsk, Pemberley. Now we'll have to face that grumpy inspector."

The two ladies stopped and turned to watch Inspector Mappin as he attempted to stride across the field, continually stumbling over the newly ploughed furrows.

"Can you hear what he's saying, Pembers? He's muttering something rather angrily. I suppose we could make a pretty good guess as to what it might be."

"I'm quite sure he'll have used the word '*meddling*' by now."

"Without a doubt. He needs to expand his vocabulary when reprimanding us, doesn't he?" Churchill raised her voice. "What's that, Inspector? We can't quite hear you. Your voice is being carried away by the wind, more's the pity."

Inspector Mappin stumbled over another furrow, turning quite red in the face as he shouted something unintelligible, though his sentence finished with a word they heard quite clearly: "Snooping!"

"You're not accusing us of snooping, are you, Inspector?" asked Churchill as he neared the fence.

Inspector Mappin's gasping, crimson face was framed with bushy brown mutton-chop whiskers.

"That's rather rude of you," she continued. "I should think that half the village has tramped up here since the bones were found. Did you accuse everyone else of snooping?"

"They're different," retorted the inspector, leaning against a fencepost to catch his breath.

"Why are they different?"

"Because they're not trying to get involved in my case."

"And what makes you think that we are?"

"You always do."

"And is that such a bad thing?"

"Most of the time, yes."

"Well, I'm very sorry to hear that you feel that way. In actual fact, Miss Pemberley and I have no interest in this muddy old field at all. We were merely taking this path

14

down towards... Where does it lead again, Miss Pemberley?"

"South Bungerly."

"That's the one. I couldn't remember whether it was North or South."

"Poppycock!" retorted Inspector Mappin. "You're here to snoop!"

"I can't deny that we took a passing interest in the field as we strolled past it, didn't we, Miss Pemberley? I probably said something along the lines of, '*Oh look. There's the field where the skeleton was found.*'"

"And I think I said something like, '*Oh yes, so it is,*'" said Pemberley. "And then, '*I think that's Inspector Mappin in the middle of it doing his important investigating.*'"

"And then we moved on, didn't we, Miss Pemberley? On our way to South Bungerly."

Inspector Mappin folded his arms and regarded them with great scepticism. "Let's pretend for a moment that you really are on the way to South Bungerly. What do you intend to do once you're there?"

"It's not about the destination, Inspector," replied Churchill. "It's the journey that matters. Did no one ever teach you that piece of wisdom?"

The inspector snorted. "Wisdom, my eye! If you're not snooping, why do you have a pair of field glasses in your hand?"

"Bird spotting. I think I spied a lesser-spotted poppy-cock in the hedgerow."

"There's no such thing."

"I said that I *thought* I saw one, but then I realised it wasn't one."

"Because there's no such thing," added Pemberley.

"Exactly. Something I only realised when I saw that it wasn't there after all."

"What on earth are you two old ladies talking about?" asked Inspector Mappin.

"You're still gasping, Inspector. Please don't make matters worse for yourself by wasting your valuable breath scolding us. At least wait for your heart rate to return to normal."

"My heart rate is never normal when you're around, Mrs Churchill."

"Is that intended to be an insult or a compliment?"

"It's a fact, Mrs Churchill. You raise the pulse of everyone you cross paths with."

"I think it's a compliment," said Pemberley.

"Inspector, you flatter me," said Mrs Churchill, "but my trusty assistant and I must leave you to go about your business now."

"My comment was not intended to flatter!"

"Well, that's a shame. We'll leave you to solve the mystery of Darcy Sprockett all by yourself. All on your own, Inspector."

"Thank you."

"Never mind the fact that standing before you are two ladies with proven sleuthing skills. How many murder cases have we solved now, Miss Pemberley? Quite a number, I'd say."

"Four."

"It feels like more, somehow. And it's certainly four more than the Compton Poppleford constabulary have solved this year."

"You won't be able to help with this one, Mrs Churchill," retorted the inspector through clenched teeth.

"Clearly not. Anyway, enjoy doing all the hard work completely on your own, Inspector, with no help from anyone else whatsoever. We'll just get on with our lovely walk. Good luck with it!"

The two ladies continued on their way.

"How long must we keep going until we can stop and turn around, Pembers?" hissed Churchill from the side of her mouth.

"Until he's finished in the field, I suppose."

"But that might be ages!"

"I know."

"How far away is South Bungerly?"

"Three miles."

"Three miles?! That could take us all afternoon!"

"At a reasonable pace it should only take around an hour."

"I couldn't possibly keep walking for an entire hour, Pemberley! How ridiculous! And we'd have to walk back again, too. Isn't there a sneaky shortcut we could take back to the village?"

"Only through the field Inspector Mappin is standing in."

"Oh, darn it! How infuriating."

"We could go back that way and say that we forgot something."

"No, no, we couldn't possibly do that. He'll cotton on right away to the fact that we never had any intention of walking to South Bungerly. Perhaps there's some shrubbery we can hide behind until he's gone."

"I'd rather be walking than sitting around in shrubbery."

"Maybe you could walk on and I could sit in the shrubbery,"

"That wouldn't do us any good at all. We're supposed to be conducting an investigation! There's quite a nice bakery in South Bungerly, you know. It's a patisserie, in fact, and it's run by a French lady."

"Is that so? I must say that I'm rather partial to a croissant or two."

Chapter 4

"I'd COMPLETELY FORGOTTEN what it feels like to sit down," exclaimed Churchill as she collapsed into her chair back at the office. "Six miles, Pembers. Six miles! I haven't walked that far since the headmistress of Princess Alexandra's School for Young Ladies made us do a forced march as punishment for someone stuffing a sock into her ear trumpet."

"Why would someone do a thing like that?"

"So she couldn't hear anything. The sock was stuffed in quite well, actually, and it was about two weeks before she discovered it. In the meantime she thought she had gone completely deaf."

"Poor lady."

"She was a beast, Pembers! We were always wondering what she was cooking up in her cauldron."

"What was she cooking up?"

"Oh, nothing. She didn't really have a cauldron; it was just a joke we made about her being a witch. A joke that was amusing to people who were there at the time, but the context is arguably lost now. Anyway, that six-mile round trip almost finished me off."

"You did have a nice rest in a patisserie at the halfway mark."

"It was a medical necessity, Pembers. I would be quite dead by now if I hadn't eaten those eclairs. It's all Inspector Mappin's fault. If he hadn't been loitering in that field we would have been able to get a good look at the crime scene and conducted some investigations of our own."

"We could try again tomorrow."

"My legs have no juice left in them. I don't anticipate them being up to anything useful until next Tuesday at the earliest."

"Perhaps you could look at the case file in the meantime."

"The case file?" Churchill sat bolt upright in her chair. "Of course! Good old Atkins would have recorded the detail of his investigations, wouldn't he? Every minute minutiae, knowing him. Pembers, I could kiss you!"

Churchill sprang out of her chair and strode over to the row of filing cabinets that housed Atkins's files.

"And here it is! Under 'S' for 'Sprockett'. He was a marvellously organised man, wasn't he?"

"It was I who maintained the filing."

"And you were so wonderfully organised, too, Miss Pemberley. Putting the Sprockett file under 'S' makes my life so much easier."

"It's just a simple alphabetically arranged filing system, Mrs Churchill."

"I've always said that simple things are the best things."

"Have you?"

"Yes, of course! Anyway, let's see what's inside this file. It's reassuringly thick, I see."

Churchill carried the file back to her desk, sat down and eagerly turned to the first page.

"Were you working for Atkins twenty years ago, Pemberley?"

"No. I was still a companion to a lady of international travel back then. I was only in Dorset for a short while, but I remember hearing about poor Miss Sprockett's disappearance. Terrible, it was. However, most of my time that year was spent at Lake Como in Italy."

"How glamorous."

"My employer had suffered a mild yet persistent illness, and she chose to convalesce at a villa there."

"Well, if you're going to convalesce anywhere, a villa at Lake Como is the place to do it, isn't it? Now then, let's get on with this case. 'It was a dark and stormy night,'" she read aloud. "This is supposed to be a case file. Why does it read like the first line of a cheap novel?"

"Atkins had short-lived literary ambitions."

"'Miss Darcy Sprockett, aged twenty years old and the eldest child of fifteen…' Goodness! They breed like rabbits in these parts, Pembers! '…Left her family home to fetch some eggs from her great-aunt on the other side of Poppleford Wood.' Why fetch eggs on a dark and stormy night?"

"It will all be explained if you read on."

"'Mr Sprockett needed eggs for his breakfast but the Sprockett hens weren't laying.' Couldn't he have gone without eggs for just one morning? Why send his daughter out for them on a dark and stormy night?"

"She didn't mind, by all accounts. They breed them tough in these parts."

"Clearly."

"And she was probably happy just to have an excuse to leave the house. It was only small, and I imagine it must have been noisy and cramped with all those Sprocketts in it."

"'Miss Sprockett arrived at her great-aunt's home and collected the eggs before departing again. Her great-aunt, Betsy Earwold, was the last person to see Miss Sprockett alive.' Well, we know what they say about the last person to see a victim alive, don't we?"

"The same thing they say about the person who discovers the body."

"Both must be considered as suspects. Although in this case no one ever discovered a body."

"Just a skeleton twenty years later."

"Exactly! 'When Darcy failed to return home, the Sprockett family searched the woods for her at first light. Nothing was found aside from a basket of broken eggs. One or two remained intact.' I feel the need to plot this on a map, Pembers."

"Atkins drew a rudimentary map. It should be in the file."

"So it is. Right then, let's get this up on our incident board." Churchill got up and stood in front of the large map that hung on the wall beside the portrait of King George V. "We need a pin for the Sprocketts's house, a pin for Great-aunt Betsy Earwold's house and a pin for the basket of eggs."

The two ladies marked the locations on the map and stood back to admire it.

"Looking good, Pembers, looking good. I can see the path Darcy Sprockett would have taken through the woods now; it's clearly marked on here as a byway. What would you say the distance between the two houses might be?"

"About a mile and a half."

"And the basket was found only a short distance from Great-aunt Betsy's place, so poor Darcy didn't get far on her return journey. Where's Farmer Jagford's field on this map?"

"Over on the other side of the village," replied Pemberley, sticking a pin into it.

"Gosh. That looks to be about three miles from where the basket of eggs was found. How peculiar, Pembers. Someone must have transported her quite some distance."

"Or maybe she walked that way herself."

"But why would she? I could understand it on a pleasant summer's day, but on a dark and stormy night one is usually quite keen to return home. Let's carry on reading the file."

Churchill returned to her desk.

"'Interview with Miss Elizabeth Earwold, eighty-one years old, Borage Cottage.' So this is Darcy's Great-aunt Betsy. 'Darcy arrived at my home at half-past nine in the evening and we had a tot of brandy. I gave her a basket of eggs and she left at a quarter to ten, but no one ever saw her again. It was only a matter of time before the goblins in the woods got hold of someone.' There she goes again, Pembers. What a load of tummy-rot."

"Maybe Great-aunt Betsy had encountered them herself."

"Did she tell anyone she had?"

"Not that I'm aware of."

"If Great-aunt Betsy believed there were goblins in the woods, why did she allow her niece to walk through them? And at night?"

Pemberley shrugged.

"I have to say that Great-aunt Betsy seems to have been a trifle laissez-faire about the whole thing. Not only does she do nothing to protect her niece from the goblins in the woods, but she also seems to have regarded poor Darcy's demise as inevitable. '*It was only a matter of time,*' she writes. What sort of people are these Sprocketts, Pemberley?"

"Oh, they're one of those large families that cram themselves into a small house and shout at each other a lot."

"I know the sort; no need to explain any further. I feel the need for a restorative Eccles cake after digesting all that. Would you mind popping downstairs to Simpkin the baker?"

Pemberley did so while Churchill continued reading the case file. Before long, her ears pricked up as she heard footsteps on the stairs. They sounded like well-heeled shoes rather than the slippers Pemberley tended to shuffle about in.

A knock at the door announced the arrival of a tall, middle-aged lady in a large hat and fur-trimmed coat. She had finely drawn eyebrows and wore scarlet lipstick, and she carried a handbag that looked to have been purchased at an expensive London boutique.

Chapter 5

"Do I have the pleasure of addressing Mrs Churchill?" asked the well-dressed lady.

"You do indeed!"

"I'm Mrs Virginia Colthrop."

"What a delight to meet you, Mrs Colthrop! Do please take a seat." Churchill rearranged her pearls and smoothed down her hair.

Mrs Colthrop rested her handbag on her lap and cast her eyes around the office. "This was Atkins's business, wasn't it?"

"It was indeed."

"Terribly sad. A river in Africa, wasn't it?"

"The Zambezi."

"A crocodile?"

"Unfortunately, yes."

Mrs Colthrop gave a shudder. "Hopefully he wouldn't have known anything about it."

"I hope you don't mind me asking, Mrs Colthrop, but do you hail from the Home Counties? I know that part of the world quite well, and your accent isn't a Dorset one."

"It certainly isn't," she replied. "I hail from Surrey."

"A wonderful place. Whereabouts, may I ask? I spent many happy years in Richmond-upon-Thames."

"Did you now?" Mrs Colthrop cocked her head to one side with interest. "I'm an Epsom gal myself."

"Epsom! How delightful. And how lovely to meet you. How funny that we should both find ourselves down here in Dorset!"

"Why is that funny?"

"Well… I don't know, really. It's quite different down here, isn't it? So rustic and provincial."

"I moved here to be near my brother and his wife. I think Dorset is a beautiful place."

"Ah yes, it is that as well."

"I wouldn't live anywhere else."

"Oh, me neither," responded Churchill, desperately trying to establish a rapport. "What brings you here today, Mrs Colthrop?"

"My husband. Not physically, I should add. He hasn't taken me anywhere in a long time! In fact, he doesn't even know that I'm here."

"Oh, I see." Churchill lowered her voice and adopted a conspiratorial tone. "And what seems to be the problem with your husband?"

Mrs Colthrop was just about to reply when Pemberley returned from the bakery.

"Oh, allow me to introduce my aide-de-camp, my adjutant, Miss Pemberley. Miss Pemberley, please meet Mrs Colthrop."

"How lovely to meet you, Mrs Colthrop," said Pemberley. "I'm just in time with the Eccles cakes, it would seem."

Churchill winced. "Actually, Miss Pemberley, I think scones would be more appropriate."

"But you asked for Eccles cakes."

"I'll admit that they're my guilty pleasure, but one should always partake of a scone of an afternoon."

"What's wrong with Eccles cakes?"

"Nothing *per se*, Miss Pemberley, but I imagine Mrs Colthrop here is more of a scone lady."

"Please don't buy any scones on my account. I don't eat between meals anyway."

"You don't? How do you get from one meal to the next without a little sustenance along the way? Oh, please don't feel obliged to answer that. It's really none of my business! Well, thank you for the Eccles cakes, Miss Pemberley. I shall see to them later."

"Can I eat them all, then?"

"You'll ruin your dinner if you do, Miss Pemberley."

"I don't have anything in the house for dinner."

"Well, save one or two for our clients, if you please. A pot of tea would serve well, though. I do apologise for the interruption, Mrs Colthrop. You were about to explain the problem with your husband."

"Yes. His name is Peregrine and he's straying."

"Oh dear. I am sorry."

"Please don't show me any pity, Mrs Churchill, I'm quite used to his behaviour. I often find that this happens when the weather warms up. It puts a spring in his step, and then he simply cannot resist chasing after young things in summer dresses."

"In which case I feel quite sorry for the young things in summer dresses!"

"So do I. I've even considered putting him on a leash."

"Really?"

"Just a little joke of mine, Mrs Churchill. On a more serious note, I think he's finally found a damsel who recip-rocates his affections."

"Oh dear."

"I'd like to identify the woman in question so that a stop can be put to it all. It's rather embarrassing, and I can't abide having people gossip about our private life at dinner parties."

"A valid concern, if I may say so. Being the subject of gossip at dinner parties can greatly hinder one's proverbial ascent of the social ladder."

"You're exactly right, Mrs Churchill. You understand my predicament perfectly."

"A badly behaved husband is rather like a badly behaved dog. People are always so apt to point the finger at the owner."

"How right you are again, Mrs Churchill. And I won't tolerate any such stain on my reputation."

"Nor do you deserve it, Mrs Colthrop." Churchill picked up her pen and began to make notes on a sheet of paper. "Now, what can you tell me about your husband and his philandering? Have you witnessed him physically chasing after someone?"

"Not so far this summer, but he certainly has a roving eye."

"And what makes you suspect that he has found someone who reciprocates his affections?"

"The long periods of absence."

"What does he usually spend his time doing?"

"He likes to play golf."

Pemberley emitted a loud groan.

"Do excuse me, Mrs Colthrop," said Churchill. "Are you all right, Miss Pemberley? Aren't you supposed to be making the tea?"

"I've put the kettle on the gas ring and am waiting for it to boil."

"What were you groaning about?"

"I'm sorry, I couldn't help it. The sound emerges from me involuntarily whenever anyone mentions golf."

"I see."

"I simply cannot think of a duller way to spend one's time."

"Oh, there must be, Miss Pemberley. I'm sure of that."

"I'd rather extract my own teeth with a set of rusty pliers than play golf."

"Well, nobody's going to force you to play it, so there's no need to consider choosing between the two pursuits."

"Mrs Higginbath forced me to play it once."

"That's Mrs Higginbath for you. She's a different kettle of fish entirely. I apologise for the further interruption, Mrs Colthrop. You were telling me that your husband likes to play golf. What else does he enjoy doing?"

"Fishing."

Pemberley groaned again.

Churchill sighed. "What now, Miss Pemberley?"

"I've just been reminded of the only activity that is actually duller than golf."

"Fishing, by any chance?"

"Yes. And all those poor fish flapping around with hooks in their mouths. It's cruel!"

"But you eat fish, don't you?"

"No, I don't."

"I see."

"It's cruel."

"Miss Pemberley, will you please allow me to speak to Mrs Colthrop here without any interruption? It's important that she's able to give us all pertinent information about her philandering husband."

Pemberley gave Churchill a sulky look and said nothing more.

"I do apologise on behalf of my secretary, Mrs Colthrop," said Churchill. "Now, where were we? Ah yes, golf and fishing. Is there anything else Mr Colthrop likes to do?"

"He goes to the club and plays chess."

Churchill finished writing this down and then glanced back over her notes.

"The pastimes you've mentioned to me are all rather time-consuming. A gentleman might easily while away a day hitting balls on the golf course or casting his line into a river or lake, or wherever he does it. And chess games can be so interminably long that there ought to be a law against them. How do you know that his long periods of absence aren't simply the result of his languorous hobbies?"

"Because he's been whistling."

"Oh dear, that's always a bad sign. My late husband, Detective Chief Inspector Churchill of the Metropolitan Police, used to whistle when he'd been up to some mischief or other. It was that jaunty sort of whistle with no recognisable tune but with a merry, going-about-one's-business lilt to it."

"That's the one exactly!" said Mrs Colthrop.

"It was how I always knew when he'd had a little win on the horses. He wasn't permitted to bet on the horses, you see, but occasionally he went rogue, and on the rare occasions he won something he would whistle. He didn't even realise he was doing it, but it gave him away every time. That's when I would ask him to hand over his winnings."

"What did you do with them?"

"I donated them to the orphanage."

Mrs Colthrop gave a whoop of amusement. "Oh, Mrs Churchill. How ingenious!"

"I suppose it is, rather, isn't it?" She gave a proud smile.

"Anyway, I think we've determined that your husband's whistling is a subliminal sign that he's been having his cake and eating it."

"Without a doubt. I'd like him caught in flagrante."

"In where? Is that a restaurant?"

"*In flagrante delicto*, Mrs Churchill. Caught in the act."

"Of course. You'd like me and my trusty assistant, Miss Pemberley, to carry out some surveillance, would you?"

"Yes please. I have a photograph here to help you identify him. Please find out which damsel he's been wooing."

"Do you have any clues at all as to who it might be?"

"No, I'm afraid he's got me stumped this time. He gets cleverer at it as each year goes by."

"But not quite clever enough for you, Mrs Colthrop!"

Chapter 6

"What a charming lady," said Churchill after Mrs Colthrop had left.

"I don't like her eyebrows," said Pemberley.

"That's no reason to dislike her."

"I don't dislike *her*; I just dislike her eyebrows."

"Well, what of *Mr* Colthrop's eyebrows, Pembers? They're so large they must have their own grooming set."

Churchill was examining the photograph Mrs Colthrop had given them. Mr Colthrop had a wide, jovial face with large jowls and a short, thin moustache. "He's one of those men who grows his hair long above the ears and then arranges it over the top of his head to make it look as though he has more of it than he really does," she commented. "Then a little gust of wind comes along and whoomph! It's all blown off his balding pate. Do you recognise him, Pemberley?"

"Yes, I've seen him around the village all right. He goes about saying, '*What ho!*' and wears those baggy trousers that stop just below the knee and tuck into long socks."

"Plus fours, you mean?"

"Yes, those are the ones. Although his are so baggy I think they must be plus twenties!"

"Does the size of the number denote the bagginess of the trouser? No, that can't be right, Pembers. I think the four alludes to the fact that the trouser leg reaches to four inches below the knee. My husband explained that to me once. He used to wear them for golfing."

"Mr Colthrop often wears a pith helmet."

"Like our chaps wear in the tropics?"

"Yes."

"Well, it's fine in India and Rhodesia and places like that, but it's rather immoderate for Dorset, wouldn't you say?"

"He must wear it when he's feeling particularly jaunty."

"How very tiresome."

"It's one of the reasons I never married," said Pemberley.

"Not all husbands are like Mr Colthrop, Pembers. I should think very few of them are, in fact."

"It strikes me that a husband is just an extra thing to worry about."

"There is that, but they do have their uses, such as hammering nails into things, mowing the lawn and putting the milk bottles out."

"I can do all that myself."

"You clearly pride yourself on being an independent woman, Pembers."

"I don't even think of it that way. I'd simply prefer to do everything myself rather than having someone else getting under my feet."

"You should never underestimate the company of another human being, you know. It can be quite special."

Pemberley paused to consider this. "I'm trying to

imagine it," she said eventually, "but it's no good. I think I'm destined to be a loner."

"You must have come across a few men who could have been considered husband material while you were a companion to your lady of international travel."

"Oh, I did! Great swathes of husband material. A Prussian prince once asked me to elope with him."

"Pembers! What a different turn your life would have taken if you'd accepted!"

"Do you think so? I think it would have turned out much the same. I'd have tired of him very quickly and then, not knowing what to do, I'd have come back to Dorset."

"Like a homing pigeon."

"Yes, very much like that. It's no coincidence that the pigeon is my favourite animal."

"They're birds, not animals."

"Birds *are* animals."

"Are they? I thought they were separate. Like insects."

"Insects are also animals."

"Oh, but they're not, Pembers! They're an entirely different species of living thing!"

They heard footsteps on the stairs followed by a knock at the door.

"Come in!" chirped Churchill.

A cheerful, red-headed lady wearing a floral tea dress stepped into the room.

"Mrs Thonnings!"

"I didn't realise your name was spelt like that," said Mrs Thonnings.

"Like what?"

"The way it's written on the door."

"Oh, that. When's the door letter man coming to fix it, Pemberley?"

"Next Wednesday."

"It's a misspelling, Mrs Thonnings."

"So you're not *Church Hill* but *Churchill*, as in the family?"

"Yes."

"The Mr Winston Churchill family? Your husband was a relation, was he?"

"Not immediate, but it would be a great surprise to me if there didn't happen to be some shared lineage." Churchill proudly adjusted her pearls.

"What is he, then? A cousin of your husband's?"

"Maybe once removed or something."

"There was Lord Randolph Churchill as well, wasn't there? What an important family."

"Yes, the Spencer-Churchills and the Spencers, and the Dukes of Marlborough, of course. The family seat is Blenheim Palace in Oxfordshire, you know."

"Cor! Do you get to go there?"

"I haven't been invited yet, but there's still time."

"Not much time, though!" she said with a laugh.

Churchill felt her jaw clench.

"How lovely to be related to dukes and the suchlike," continued Mrs Thonnings. "Lord Randolph died of syphilis, didn't he?"

"That is mere rumour, Mrs Thonnings. Now, perhaps you can settle a dispute between myself and my second-in-command, Miss Pemberley. Are insects classed as animals?"

"No, of course not."

"Thank you."

"Or are they?" Mrs Thonnings put a finger up to her lips as she gave this some thought. "I reckon they must be, because they're living things, aren't they? They're not plants, so they must be animals. And I suppose large insects

35

must be animals because they're big, aren't they? If you think about it, a large, fluffy bumblebee isn't a great deal smaller than a little mouse."

"An interesting theory, Mrs Thonnings. I'm sure we'll make a zoologist of you yet."

"So, are they?"

"What?"

"Are insects animals?"

"It seems the jury is still out on that one. Anyway, what brings you all the way from your cosy haberdashery shop to our draughty offices?"

"Business is rather quiet today, so I've come to see whether you'd like any help. Do you remember how impressed I was when you solved the case of the murdered gardeners?"

Churchill nodded and forced a smile. The last thing she wanted was Mrs Thonnings trying to help with one of her cases.

"And I offered, didn't I? I offered my help on your next case. So here I am! I don't expect any payment; I'm happy to assist just for the thrill of it."

Churchill sighed and placed her pen down on her desk. "As I've explained to you before, Mrs Thonnings, there is no *thrill*, as you put it, or indeed any glamour about the way Miss Pemberley and I conduct our business."

"But surely it must be more interesting than selling buttons and bows."

"To be quite honest with you, I'm not sure that it is. My current task involves reading through this enormous file of papers, which was put together twenty years ago by my predecessor. It hardly makes for an entertaining read."

"Is it the Darcy Sprockett case?" Mrs Thonnings's eyes widened with excitement. "If you don't want to read those papers, I will!"

Churchill pulled the file a little closer, suddenly feeling quite protective of it. "It's not a matter of me not wanting to read them, Mrs Thonnings, but more the sense of duty I feel to my predecessor and to the poor Sprockett family."

"If it's boring, let me do it."

"It's not boring. It's merely a lot of work."

"Then let me help!"

"I'm quite content to plod on with it myself. I've always been a glutton for punishment, you see. In fact, I enjoy a good bit of hard work. That's why I bought this detective agency in the first place."

Mrs Thonnings sighed. "I can't help but feel that you don't want any assistance from me, Mrs Churchill."

"Oh, come now, Mrs Thonnings. It's not that we don't want your help, but more a case of it not actually being needed at this present time."

"I see." She gave a wounded sniff. "Well, I suppose I'd better go and reopen the shop."

"I need some new buttons for my yellow cardigan. I shall pop along for them later."

"Thank you, Mrs Churchill."

"Do you need some new buttons for your cardigan, Miss Pemberley?"

"This cardigan doesn't have any buttons."

"There you go. My assistant also needs a new set of buttons. We'll see you later, Mrs Thonnings."

Churchill began to sift through the case file as soon as Mrs Thonnings had left.

"There's a lot to read here, Pembers. I feel the need to take some air before I settle down to it."

"Are your legs up to it?"

"Of course. Why wouldn't they be?"

"I thought they weren't likely to be up to anything until next Tuesday at the earliest."

"You do have some funny notions about things, Pemberley. Anyway, I need to visit the Sprockett house. Do any of the Sprocketts still live there?"

"I don't know."

"I suppose there's only one way to find out."

Chapter 7

"This great expanse of boscage is commonly known as Poppleford Wood," announced Pemberley as the two ladies approached it on the stony path leading away from the duck pond.

"Boscage, Pembers?"

"Woodland."

"I see. Well, it's a lovely day for it, isn't it?"

Birdsong filled the air and fresh green beech leaves jiggled with the scampering of squirrels. A woodpecker was hammering away somewhere nearby, and the purple flowers of speedwell were scattered across the ground.

"Oh, how I love a stroll in the woods. We don't do it half enough, do we? There's something so restorative about all this green. It makes you want to pause and drink it all in. Let's drink it in, Pembers." Churchill stopped and took in a large breath of air before exhaling dramatically. "Doesn't that feel good? Nature is such a tonic. Doctors should prescribe it, don't you think?"

"Nature?"

"Yes. Forget bottles of pills; a healthy dose of nature is usually all that's needed. Ouch!"

"What's the matter?"

"A stinging nettle, that's what the matter is! It stung me through my stockings. And now I have a fly in my eye. Oh, darn it, Pembers!"

Churchill retrieved a handkerchief from her pocket and proceeded to extract the fly with it. "There's always something trying to ruin one's fun, whether it's a sting through one's stockings or a fly in the eye. Have you ever observed that?"

"It's all a healthy dose of nature, Mrs Churchill."

"If you say so. Now, whereabouts in these woods did you and Mrs Higginbath see the White Lady?"

"A little further down the path."

"I see."

"Besides, it can't really have been the White Lady. It was probably a bee-keeper or a cricketer as you suggested, Mrs Churchill."

"I suggested it while we were within the safe confines of the office, but now that we're out and about in the wood itself I'm feeling a little less sure." Churchill glanced around at the thick woodland and felt a prickling sensation at the back of her neck.

"Oh, don't say that! It was a cricketer!"

"Was it, Pemberley?"

"Yes!"

"Do you feel absolutely sure of it?"

"No, not really. But I have to be, otherwise I'll feel too frightened to walk on."

"It was a cricketer. Good. Now, where's this cottage we're supposed to be looking for?"

"Just over there. It doesn't look lived-in any more."

A track led up from the pathway to a small, crooked

gate. Beyond the gate was what had probably once been a well-tended garden, and the cottage had a thatched roof that had caved in on one side. No glass remained in the windows.

"All the Sprocketts used to live in there, did they?" Churchill asked.

"They certainly did."

Churchill and Pemberley walked down the track toward the cottage, battling their way through the overgrown garden.

"And it was from here that Darcy Sprockett left to fetch eggs from her great-aunt on a dark and stormy night," mused Churchill.

The little front door in front of them had once been painted red but was much faded, and most of the paint had peeled off.

"I wonder if she came through this door or whether there's another one round the back," said Churchill. "Let's have a look, shall we?"

They stepped over the remains of a wheelbarrow and made their way around the stone wall of the cottage to the rear.

"It looks as though there's another door here, Pembers. I wonder which she left by that night."

"The back one, probably. It's highly likely that the front door was reserved for visitors."

"I can't imagine the Sprocketts having many visitors trudge out to this little place," replied Churchill.

"Yer right, we don't," came a voice.

This unexpected remark startled Churchill so much that she dropped her handbag.

"Good grief! Who said that?"

41

"Me," came the voice again.

Churchill retrieved her handbag from the ground and looked up to see a small, bald, wrinkled head poking out of a window.

"Who are yer and what d'yer want?" asked the head, which was not unlike that of a tortoise.

"So sorry to bother you, we thought this cottage was uninhabited. Do you really live here?"

"Yer'd best answer my questions first, 'adn't yer?"

"Oh, righty-ho. I'm Mrs Annabel Churchill of Churchill's Detective Agency, and this is my aide-de-camp, Miss Pemberley. We're detectives."

"You ain't much younger 'an me."

"You can't beat years of wisdom and experience, can you, Mr...."

"Sprockett."

"The patriarch?"

"What's that?"

"The head of the family? Father of Darcy Sprockett?"

Mr Sprockett's face changed. "Oh, so that's why yer 'ere. Ever since they found that skellington in the field I've 'ad folks comin' round 'ere, botherin' me."

"Are you relieved that your daughter's final resting place has been discovered, Mr Sprockett?"

"Yeah, course I am. All them years wond'rin' what's 'appened. I still wonder what's 'appened, mind. Skellingtons can't speak, can they?"

"No indeed. If only they could." Churchill shivered at the thought. "What are your memories of the night she went missing, Mr Sprockett?"

"It were dark."

"So I've heard."

"And stormy."

"I've heard that, too."

"And I didn't know nuffink about 'er bein' missin' till first light. We 'ad so many of 'em runnin' round the place it's 'ard ter notice when one of 'em goes missin'."

"Who was the first to notice that she hadn't returned?"

"I don't fink none of us did, ter be fair. All I knew is that I didn't 'ave no eggs fer me breakfast. I shouted, *'Where's me eggs?'* but no one knowed where me eggs were, an' then Betsy come round talkin' 'bout goblins. Distraught, she was. Loved Darcy like 'er own daughter, she did."

"She'd found the basket of eggs Darcy had been carrying, I presume."

"Yeah. She'd brung the eggs with 'er and two of 'em weren't broke, so I 'ad 'em for me breakfast an' then we thought 'ow we might as well go alookin' for Darcy. Dunno where she got ter. Got 'erself lost, I s'pose."

"That's what you think happened to her? That she got lost?"

"Yeah."

"Aunt Betsy believed the goblins had got her, is that right?"

"None of us knowed what'd 'appened to 'er, so it were as good a guess as any."

"And you told the police she was missing."

"Yeah, but they couldn't find 'er."

'And my predecessor, Mr Atkins?"

"'E were the one what got eaten by a crocodile, weren't 'e? Yeah, the missis spoke to 'im. 'E went alookin' for 'er but never found 'er. No one did."

"A very sad tale indeed, Mr Sprockett. And now that her final resting place has been discovered, perhaps we can find out, once and for all, what really happened to Darcy that night, and whether someone was responsible for her death. If so, it's a secret that someone has been sitting on for twenty years. And more importantly, he or she should be arrested and face judgement in a court of law."

"I don't reckon no one done nuffink. She jus' got lost, simple as that. No one else would of been in Poppleford Woods on a night like that, 'specially with them goblins about."

"I see. Isn't your neck beginning to ache as a result of you poking your head out like that?"

"Nope, I often does it."

"Right. Well, Miss Pemberley and I have decided that we should like to finish the work Mr Atkins started and find out what really happened to your daughter, Mr Sprockett."

"Yer could do, I s'pose. It ain't gonna bring 'er back, though, is it?"

"No, I don't suppose it will," said Churchill, feeling saddened by the thought. "We'll just do the best we can, won't we, Miss Pemberley?"

"We certainly will."

"Can you recall exactly what happened the day your daughter went missing, Mr Sprockett?"

"Not really. Long time ago now, weren't it?"

"Well it was, yes. Can you remember whom she fraternised with that day?"

"Yer what?"

"Whom did she speak to? Whom was she seen with?"

"She done chores most o' the day. She went out fer a bit, then some lad come round with 'is trumpet."

"He was a friend of hers, was he?"

"Think so. Couldn't tell you 'is name. I didn't let 'im stay long, what with that trumpet blarin'."

"I don't blame you, Mr Sprockett, that sounds most unpleasant. What else?"

"I'm blowed if I can remember."

"Maybe your wife could tell me a little more, Mr Sprockett."

"Mebbe she could."

"Where is she?"

"I'm blowed if I know."

"When did you last see her?"

"Thirteen year ago."

"Oh, I see. There was a falling out between you, was there?"

"Nope."

"Then why did she leave?"

"I dunno."

"I see. You said that Great-aunt Betsy was fond of Darcy."

"Yeah. She was 'er favourite out the lot of 'em."

"That is very interesting indeed. And Darcy liked her?"

"Course she did. More than 'er own ma an' pa."

"She told you that?"

"More or less."

"That can't have been easy for you to hear."

"I ain't never worried too much about it. We got fourteen others."

"I suppose you have. Where are they all now?"

"The wife took 'em."

"I see. May I ask where?"

"Somewhere over round Blandford Forum way."

"Not far from here, then?"

"Could be the other side o' the world for all I knows."

"Do they not come to visit?"

"Nope. They don't like me."

"I'm sorry to hear that, Mr Sprockett. Have any of them returned to the village since the discovery of poor Darcy's…?"

"Skellington? Dunno. I dunno if they even knows

about it. That's all I got left now: a skellington. I'll get to burying 'er once they sends them bones back."

"From where?"

"The p'lice got the bones, 'cause they're lookin' at 'em. I'm gonna stick me 'ead back in now. Me neck's achin'."

"I thought it would, Mr Sprockett. Thank you for... Oh, he's withdrawn into his shell. Maybe we can come back and talk to him another time, Pembers. Let's be on our way for now."

"What an odd man Mr Sprockett is," said Churchill as they continued along the path through the wood. "He seems remarkably unaffected by the death of his daughter."

"The Sprocketts always were a strange lot. Perhaps he feels sad in his own way."

"Let's hope so, eh?"

Chapter 8

THE TWO LADIES arrived at another cottage about twenty minutes later. Painted white, and with a garden planted up with roses, it appeared well-looked-after.

"So this was Great-aunt Betsy's place, was it?" said Churchill. "How very nice indeed. Any idea who lives here now, Pembers?"

"A gentleman from Oxford is what I've heard," said Pemberley, "but I can't tell you anything more about him."

"Let's see if he's in."

"He won't know anything about Darcy Sprockett."

"Perhaps not, but I'm quite nosy, so let's knock him up anyway and find out who he is."

Churchill strode up the garden path and hammered on the shiny door. After a long pause it was opened, and a tall, dark-haired man with spectacles and a prominent Adam's apple peered out at them.

"Hello?" he said cautiously.

"Good afternoon. I'm Mrs Churchill of the eponymously named Churchill's Detective Agency, and this is my trusty assistant, Miss Pemberley."

"And?"

"And you are?"

"Oh, erm, I'm Mr Bingley." He pushed his spectacles up his nose with a long finger.

"It's a pleasure to meet you, Mr Bingley. You're from Oxford, I hear."

"Good gracious! How on earth do you know that?"

"Word travels fast in this part of the world. People don't have much else to talk about."

"Well, it's nice to meet you both, but I'd better be getting back to my work now."

"Work? What work could you possibly be doing in your nice little cottage here in the middle of the woods?"

"I'm hiding down here while I graft away at my thesis."

"At your what-did-you-say?"

"My thesis. For my doctorate."

"You're a doctor?"

"I'm studying to become a doctor of philosophy."

"I think it would be much more useful if you became a normal doctor, Mr Bingley. There's such a shortage of decent doctors these days, don't you find, Miss Pemberley?"

"What's the subject of your thesis, Mr Bingley?" asked Pemberley.

"Oh, it's about Leo Tolstoy and how his novels express his search for the meaning of life."

"Fascinating," replied Pemberley.

"What's that got to do with being a doctor?" asked Churchill.

"*Anna Karenina* is one of my favourite novels," said Pemberley.

"One of the best novels you could possibly read!" replied Mr Bingley with a smile. "*War and Peace* goes without saying, but may I suggest that you also try *The Death of Ivan Ilyich*? It really is a moving piece of work."

"It sounds rather miserable to me," said Churchill. "Who wants to read about the death of someone?"

"Which books do you like to read, Mrs Churchill?" asked Mr Bingley.

"Oh, well, I'm terribly busy most of the time. I quite like the books those sisters wrote... Their names escape me at the moment. Those ones who lived in that chilly vicarage up north somewhere and did a lot of romping about on the moors."

"The Brontë sisters," said Pemberley matter-of-factly. "Which university are you completing your studies at, Mr Bingley?"

"Balliol College."

"Oh, so not a proper university, then?" asked Churchill.

"Balliol is a college at the University of Oxford," Pemberley corrected her. "And one of the oldest, I believe. Isn't that right, Mr Bingley?"

"Yes. It was founded during the thirteenth century."

"Was it indeed?" exclaimed Churchill. "Well, it's almost as old as us then, isn't it? Anyway, Mr Bingley, we didn't come here to talk about doctors and universities and things. Did you realise that you are currently inhabiting a cottage that once belonged to a Miss Elizabeth Earwold?"

"Erm, yes, I did."

"Oh, jolly good. Then you are no doubt aware that this very same cottage was the last place young Darcy Sprockett was seen alive before she was snatched away twenty years ago."

"I've heard tell of that sad event."

"You know about the case?"

"Yes, I do."

"Do you recall who told you about it?"

"The lady who lived here before me. She never stopped talking about it, and even insisted on showing me where the basket of eggs was found."

"Ah yes, the basket of eggs! Could you please show us the spot, Mr Bingley?"

"May I ask why?"

"Because my predecessor, Mr Atkins, was appointed by the Sprockett family to find out what had happened to the poor unfortunate child. And now that her final resting place has been discovered I wish to complete the work that the late, great Mr Atkins began and solve the mystery of her disappearance. Now, where was the basket of eggs found?"

"On the path back there." He pointed toward the woods behind them.

"Yes, but where exactly? The location is extremely important. It's likely to give us a clue about the person who snatched her."

"They say that the goblins snatched her."

"And I say piffle to that, Mr Bingley! You seem like a sensible, intelligent man to me. Surely you don't believe this goblin theory?"

"I hadn't really given it a lot of thought. In fact, I assumed for a while that the whole story had been made up."

"We won't detain you any longer than it takes for you to show us where the basket of eggs was found."

"Do you promise to leave as soon as I've shown you?"

"We promise, Mr Bingley."

"Okey-dokey, then. Would you mind waiting here a moment while I take off my slippers and put on my shoes?"

"Not at all."

. . .

Mr Bingley joined the two ladies in his front garden a few moments later.

"It's just this way," he said, walking out through the garden gate.

They walked back along the path for a minute or two until Mr Bingley stopped abruptly.

"I think it was somewhere near here," he said, glancing down at the ground around him. "I recall there being a log nearby, but I can't remember what it looked like now."

"Was it brown in colour?" asked Churchill impatiently. "And covered with bark?"

"I think so, yes. Oh look! There it is over there."

They moved a few steps closer to the log.

"The lady who previously lived in your cottage showed you this spot, did she?" asked Churchill.

"Yes, she did. Quite recently, in fact, as I've only been in the cottage for five months. It looks a lot greener around here than it did then."

"On account of it now being summer, perhaps?" asked Churchill. "My educated guess would be that the lady who previously owned your cottage brought you here at the end of winter."

"Yes, it would have been about then. You're quite right."

"So where exactly was the basket of eggs found?"

"Just behind Miss Pemberley's feet."

Pemberley spun around to look behind her, as if the basket might still be there.

"So this is the spot," said Churchill, stooping low to examine the ground.

"We only have Mr Bingley's word for it," said Pemberley, "and he only has the word of the lady who lived in the cottage before him. Who knows where she heard it from? The location of the basket could have altered over the years... A bit like the way words tend to alter when you play Chinese whispers. Its exact location has likely been lost in the mists of time."

Churchill felt her heart sink. "Well, thank you for that, Miss Pemberley. You mean to imply that the basket could have been found anywhere in these woods, do you?"

"No, not just anywhere. It would have been somewhere on this path, I suppose, and fairly close to Mr Bingley's cottage. But what's to say that it wasn't three yards further down that way or five yards up that way?"

Churchill turned her head to look up and down the path, then sighed.

"The lady who lived in the cottage before me was quite adamant that it was here," said Mr Bingley.

"What's her name?" asked Churchill.

"Who?"

"The lady who lived in the cottage before you."

"I can't remember now."

Churchill felt her teeth clench with frustration.

"Do we need to know the *exact* location of the basket, Mrs Churchill?" asked Pemberley.

"I was hoping the location would give us some sort of a clue."

"Such as a smashed egg?" suggested Mr Bingley.

"A smashed egg would hardly have survived for twenty years, Mr Bingley! Anyway, thank you for all your help. It was very kind of you to go to the trouble of putting on your shoes and leading us out to this spot."

"I haven't really done anything."

"Your words, not mine, Mr Bingley."

"Well, good luck with the investigation, ladies. Have you done much of this sort of thing before?"

"Of course!" snapped Churchill. "I'm not as foolish as I look."

"Quoth Plato to his disciples," added Mr Bingley.

Pemberley laughed. "How witty!"

"What are you two talking about?" Churchill asked huffily.

"It's a quote from Joseph Conrad's *Heart of Darkness*," said Pemberley. "'I am not such a fool as I look, quoth Plato to his disciples.'"

"Well identified!" said Mr Bingley.

"Time-wasting nonsense, if you ask me," said Churchill. "Come along, Miss Pemberley, we have a crime to solve."

Chapter 9

"I CAN'T SAY that our little ramble was terribly edifying for me, Pembers," said Churchill once they had returned to the office. "Mr Bingley clearly has his head in the clouds."

"Mr Bingley is an intellectual."

"I feared as much. Clever people rather enjoy making other people feel ignorant with their quips about novel reading and Plato and suchlike."

"I don't think that was Mr Bingley's intention at all."

"Whether he intended it or not, it seems to be a common trait among people with oversized brains. All that cleverness and yet they're completely out of touch with the real world. Anyway, how have you found the time to read so many books in your lifetime, Pemberley?"

"During all the travelling I did. It was quite boring much of the time, so that's when I sat down to read. Hotels are marvellous places for picking up books; people just leave them there. And besides that, well, I suppose I've always had a little too much time on my hands."

"You've never had a husband to occupy every waking

moment, Pemberley. Husbands colonise an inordinate amount of one's time. I don't know how they manage it!"

"I consider myself quite fortunate in that respect."

"Whilst you were busy reading *War and Peace*, I was busy running around ensuring that Detective Chief Inspector Churchill had cleaned his golf clubs properly and remembered to fix the birdhouse. I wouldn't have had it any other way, but I always expected to take up reading once I was widowed."

"But instead of enjoying a quiet widowhood, you decided to buy a detective agency."

"Well yes, that was rather foolish of me. But it keeps us both out of mischief, doesn't it? Now then, what are we to do about this Darcy Sprockett business?"

"Why don't you get back to reading through Mr Atkins's file?"

Churchill glanced at the thick file sitting on her desk and sighed. "I could do, I suppose, but it seems like an awful lot of reading. Worse still, I could read the entire thing and still have no idea what happened to Darcy Sprockett twenty years ago."

"It's not like you to be so downhearted about a case, Mrs Churchill."

"No, it's not, but my initial enthusiasm has been rather dampened by the task in hand. I quite fancy a case that requires us to chase down a glamorous jewel thief instead. Would you fancy that, Pembers? "

"Atkins had a case like that once."

"Why doesn't that surprise me?"

"It took him to Monte Carlo."

"I imagine it would have done. My good friend, Lady Worthington, once told me that Monte Carlo was terribly overrated. Hark! I hear footsteps on the stairs. I hope this is our impending jewel thief case."

Churchill's heart sank as the brown-whiskered Inspector Mappin stepped into the room.

"Church Hills?" he said. "Sounds like one of those new housing estates they're building on the outskirts of Dorchester."

"Ha ha, Inspector. What do you want?"

Inspector Mappin removed his hat and made himself comfortable in the chair beside Churchill's desk.

"A little assistance, if you wouldn't mind, Mrs Churchill."

Although she felt flattered by the inspector's request for help, Churchill refused to show it. "How could two mere snoopers possibly be of service to an upstanding officer of the law, Inspector Mappin?"

"Two what-did-you-says? Snoopers?"

"You accused us of snooping when we were passing by Farmer Jagford's field the other day."

"Did I? I probably didn't mean *snooping*. Meddling, perhaps, but not snooping."

"You said snooping."

"I must have been having a rather difficult day, what with all this skeleton business and whatnot. Now then, I came here to speak to you about a bit of work your predecessor, Mr Atkins, assisted me with approximately twenty years ago."

"The mysterious disappearance of Darcy Sprockett? Why did Atkins help you with it?"

"The family had a poor understanding of the complexities involved in police work and grew somewhat impatient that my colleagues and I were not able to immediately ascertain the whereabouts of Miss Sprockett."

"You failed to find her, you mean, so the family asked Atkins to do it instead."

"He also failed to find her!"

"One of the few cases he didn't quite manage to crack," Pemberley chipped in.

"Anyway, here we are twenty years later with the discovery of a skeleton in Farmer Jagford's field," continued Inspector Mappin.

"May I respectfully enquire where the skeleton is now?" asked Churchill.

"Miss Sprockett's remains have been taken to Dorchester for analysis by a bone expert gentleman."

"An osteologist?" suggested Pemberley.

"Something like that. So the question is, how did the skeleton get into the field?" he said.

"The mind boggles," replied Churchill.

"Indeed it does. So I'd like to look at our file again, if you please, and pick up where we left off all those years ago."

"*Your* file?"

"Yes. The one Atkins and I worked on together."

"Did you really work on it together?" asked Churchill. "Or did the Sprockett family come here to see Atkins once they had become fed up with the sloth-like pace of your investigation?"

"We worked on it together!"

"So what's the file still doing in this office?"

"I suppose Atkins continued to look after it once the case had gone cold."

"He should have charged you rent in that case!"

"For space in a filing cabinet? It wouldn't even have made him a ha'penny a year."

"I should think it would have been at least a ha'penny a year in rent," she said, pulling the case file closer and leafing through its contents. "However, I can only see Atkins's distinctive handwriting here, Inspector, not yours. Are you sure you contributed anything to it?"

Inspector Mappin craned forward, desperate to take a peek at the papers. Churchill jealously folded the file shut again.

"Oh yes, there'll be some of my work in amongst that lot."

"But the bulk of it belongs to Atkins, does it not?"

"Belonged."

"Therefore, it now belongs to me."

He gave a dry laugh. "I'd say that was just a slight exaggeration."

"You are aware that my purchase of Atkins's private detective business included all fixtures and fittings, are you not?"

"I was one of them," Pemberley piped up.

"Indeed you were," said Churchill. "That came as quite a surprise at the time."

"A happy one, though," added Pemberley.

"A very happy one indeed."

"Mrs Churchill," the inspector forced a smile, "may I please request…?"

"Grinning doesn't suit you, Inspector. Please stop it."

He straightened his face. "With all due respect to your good self, Mrs Churchill, the mysterious disappearance of Darcy Sprockett occurred a full twenty years before you ever came to Compton Poppleford."

"And you consider that sufficient justification for me to just hand this file over, do you?"

"I suppose so, yes."

"You wish to take away Atkins's file, which he created and kept here in his office for two decades prior to his unfortunate demise on the Zambezi earlier this year?"

"The very same."

"A file which legally belongs to me now?"

"But you have no use for it, Mrs Churchill!"

"Have you forgotten the very nature of my profession, Inspector?"

"Don't you go investigating this case!" he retorted with a wagging finger.

"I'm perfectly entitled to do so. After all, it's an investigation my predecessor carried out at the express wish of the Sprockett family."

"But *he* was an experienced investigator and *you're…*"

"I'm what, Inspector? Careful what you say, now."

Inspector Mappin shifted uncomfortably in his chair, his eyes firmly fixed on the case file. "Erm, well, perhaps I can allow you to do a little investigation into the case if you'll agree to give me the file."

"It's not your place to either allow or disallow me, Inspector."

"Do you have no respect for the law, Mrs Churchill?"

"I have every respect for the law, Inspector Mappin, but I don't appreciate you accusing me of snooping one day and then demanding ownership of my property the next!"

"I merely asked for your assistance."

"Codswallop! All you want is my file."

"It's not your—"

"Ah ha, but it is. And you know it!"

The inspector sat back in his chair, folded his arms and glared at Churchill. She pressed the file up against her ample bosom and stared back at him.

"You do realise that what you're doing is illegal, don't you?" he said. "I could arrest you for… for not giving an item to me. And in not giving said item to me you are preventing me from going about my lawful business as an officer of the law."

"That's a charge you've just made up on the spot, Inspector. You'll need a warrant to seize this file from me."

"And he won't get one," Pemberley interjected, "on the basis that a search warrant can only be used to find and seize evidence of a crime. And we have committed no crime, Mrs Churchill."

"Exactly that, Miss Pemberley, thank you. I was just about to say the same thing."

Inspector Mappin emitted a loud harrumph.

"I'll have to subpoena it, then," he said sulkily.

"You intend to waste valuable funds from the public purse on a court summons for a bunch of old papers, do you?" asked Churchill disdainfully.

"It's not just a bunch of old papers."

"On this rare occasion I agree with you. It certainly isn't. This file here is the product of Mr Atkins's blood, sweat and tears, and as his loyal successor I shall continue with the case in his name."

"But I've been called upon to investigate a suspected murder, Mrs Churchill. I need all the help I can get!"

"If you need help there's only one thing you need do, Inspector."

"And what's that?"

"Treat us with a little more courtesy."

"Hehe. How nice it is to be a few steps ahead of Inspector Mappin," crowed Churchill once he had left the office.

"I felt a little sorry for him, actually."

"He called us snoopers, Pembers! *Snoopers!*"

"That was rather rude. But he is the local police officer, and he has been tasked with investigating the skeleton buried in Farmer Jagford's field. The poor man needs help."

"Tsk, Pemberley! He should have kept his own file; he's only got himself to blame. Perhaps if he'd worked more efficiently on the case twenty years ago the Sprocketts wouldn't have had to ask Atkins for assistance."

"We should still help him a little bit, though."

"All right, Pembers, we'll share the contents of this file with him. But only once we're several steps ahead. Now, it's getting quite late in the day, so I shall take this file home with me and read through it tonight. Then we can ease ourselves into some serious sleuthing tomorrow."

"But what about Mr Colthrop?"

"What about him?"

"Aren't we supposed to be conducting some sort of surveillance on him?"

"Oh darn it, I'd clean forgotten about him. All right, we'll do a bit of that first and then we'll get on with the meat and potatoes of the Sprockett case."

"The what?"

"Oh, don't worry about it. Get a good night's sleep, Pemberley, and I'll see you tomorrow."

Chapter 10

"So THAT's the Colthrop house, is it?"

"Yes. Oakley Manor," Pemberley replied.

Churchill gave a loud snort. "It's not quite a manor, is it? It's merely a large house."

"I think it's nice."

"It's nice all right, but definitely not a manor. Mrs Colthrop is terribly pleasant, but I fear that she is not without a few pretensions."

"The name Oakley comes from all the oak trees around here."

Churchill snorted again. "Hardly original, is it? I wonder whether Mr Colthrop came up with the name."

Oakley Manor was a pleasing Georgian-style house built from sandstone. It boasted large sash windows and an impressive columned porch.

"We've already seen Mrs Colthrop leave the house with her driver and given her the nod," said Churchill. "She seemed quite pleased to see us here, didn't she? Now we just need to wait for the husband to come crawling out of the woodwork."

"What if we have to wait all day?"

"The sun's shining, Pembers, and that always brings people outdoors. If it doesn't they must be vampires or something equally unpleasant."

"I don't think he's a *sanguisuge*."

"A what now? A sausage, did you say?"

"It's another word for bloodsucker."

"Ugh! What on earth are you talking about, Pemberley?"

"You mentioned vampires."

"I wish I hadn't now. I wonder how old this tree is." Churchill gazed up at the branches of the magnificent oak they were standing beneath. "It has quite a thick trunk. I'd wager it was planted here while King Henry the Eighth was merely a boy. Most of my childhood was spent climbing trees like this; I was practically arboreal. My mother used to have to stand at the foot of our tree and call up to me when supper was ready. There are two types of oak tree, aren't there?"

"English and sessile."

"Do you know how to tell the difference?"

"The acorns of the English oak are on stalks, whereas the sessile oak carries them directly on its twigs."

"Is that right? I wonder which method is most effective."

"An oak tree doesn't produce acorns until it's at least forty years old," continued Pemberley. "In fact, it produces its best acorns between the ages of eighty and one hundred and twenty."

"Is that so? Well, I think we're a bit like a pair of old oak trees ourselves, in that case. What do you think, Pembers? Our best years are ahead of us yet!"

"Despite the common image of a squirrel nibbling on an acorn—"

"And hiding them," Churchill interjected.

"Yes, and hiding them… Despite this common image, acorns are actually poisonous to many animals."

"Not squirrels, though."

"No, but they're poisonous to sheep."

"Is that so?"

"And horses."

"Really?"

"And goats."

"Goodness!"

"And dogs."

"Blimey!"

"Not forgetting cattle, either."

"It's about time Mr Colthrop came out of his house, don't you think? There's only so much chat one can endure beneath an oak tree. Mrs Colthrop left half an hour ago. You'd have thought he'd be champing at the bit to go and meet his lady friend, or whoever she is. Oh, look! Is this him?"

A man in tweed plus fours and a white pith helmet had emerged from Oakley Manor wheeling a bicycle.

"He's about to come this way along the lane, but if he gets on that bicycle we'll have no hope of keeping up with him."

"We could get on some bicycles ourselves."

"You know that bicycles and I don't get along, Pembers. I've told you before that I'll never ride one again. That's him all right, isn't it? I recognise him from the photograph. We'd better stop watching him as he's about to pass by. Let's pretend to be discussing this tree."

Churchill looked up at the branches again. "I wonder how old this tree is, Miss Pemberley. It's got quite a thick trunk. I'd wager it was planted here while King Henry the Eighth was merely a boy."

"There are two types of oak tree," added Pemberley.

"Yes, that's right. English and cecil. Cecil, is it? That can't be right."

"*Sessile.*"

"What ho!" Mr Colthrop called out as he passed them, doffing his pith helmet as he did so.

"Oh, good morning over there!" Churchill chirped in reply. "Lovely day for it, isn't it?"

"I'll say!" He replaced his helmet and walked on.

"A lovely day for what?" asked Pemberley.

"*It.*"

"But what is *it*?"

"Whatever you have planned for the day. It's just an expression."

"Rather a meaningless one, I'd say."

"Most expressions are rather meaningless, Pembers. We just say them to one another as platitudes in order to establish a general rapport. Now then, let's follow that man at a safe distance. Hopefully we'll catch him being delicately fragrant, or whatever it was that Mrs Colthrop said."

"What?"

"Catch him in the act."

"I don't think I want to *see* him in the act of anything, let alone *catch* him in it."

"It's not something I'm keeping at the top of my list either, Pembers, but it's our job. Come along!"

The two ladies followed Mr Colthrop along the lane, which eventually led into the village.

"What'll we do if he decides to play a game of chess?" Pemberley asked. "We can't exactly stand by and watch him for several hours."

"I should think it unlikely on a warm summer's day like today, Pembers. I imagine he'll choose an outdoor activity, such as fishing."

"Or golf," added Pemberley with a groan.

They followed Mr Colthrop as he wheeled his bicycle along the high street, stopping abruptly as he paused outside the antiques shop.

"Oh no, it looks as though he's about to pay a visit to that overpriced bric-a-brac shop, Pembers."

The two ladies watched as he peered in at the window display, leaned his bicycle against a wall and stepped inside.

"Perhaps his lady friend works in there," suggested Pemberley.

"That's a very good point. Come on! We'll have to go in and find out."

Chapter 11

"What ho!" said Mr Colthrop as soon as Churchill and Pemberley stepped inside the antiques shop. He doffed his pith helmet and then continued. "Just a minute... Aren't you the two ladies I saw not ten minutes ago beneath the oak tree?"

"I do believe we are!" chimed Churchill with a tinkling laugh. "It seems we all had the same idea this morning." She laughed again, inwardly cursing the antiques shop for not having a handy display that she and Pemberley could have hidden themselves behind.

"What can I help you ladies with this morning?" asked the shopkeeper, who had a small, mouse-like face and a head of fluffy white hair tucked beneath a felt cap.

"Oh, please don't worry about us," replied Churchill. "Do continue seeing to this good gentleman who arrived here before us. Miss Pemberley and I are merely here for a browse."

"Not too much browsing, I hope," replied the shop-keeper. "I like all my customers to make a purchase."

"Oh, I'm sure you do, Mr..."

"Purprend."

"Mr Purprend. How very nice to meet you. I'm Mrs Annabel Churchill and this is my assistant, Miss Pemberley. We were just looking for a... Remind me what it was again, Miss Pemberley."

"A what? A what did you say, Mrs Churchill?" Pemberley's eyes were wide and panicked.

"What did we come in here for, *la mia amica*?"

"Oh, in here? Oh yes. A, erm..." Pemberley's eyes rested on the item closest to hand. "A carriage clock."

"That's right, a carriage clock," said Churchill. "But perhaps not this particular one. It looks rather pricey."

"Everything in this shop is pricey," said Mr Purprend.

"I see. Anyway, please don't allow us to interrupt you any further. This good gentleman entered the shop before us and is no doubt impatient for your assistance."

"Oh, don't you worry about me!" replied Mr Colthrop, leaning jovially against the counter with one hand on his hip. "I have all the time in the world. I'm a gentleman of leisure, you see."

"How perfectly splendid," replied Churchill, her teeth clenching in frustration. "But we're probably in even less of a hurry than you are. What did you come in for?"

"A silver soup ladle. I collect them, you see, and during my last visit the good Mr Purprend here mentioned that he was expecting an interesting one in from the Netherlands. Has it arrived yet, Bernie?"

"I'm afraid it hasn't, Mr Colthrop," replied the shopkeeper.

Mr Colthrop gave a laugh and slapped his hand down on the counter. "Well, there you go then. That was over with quickly, wasn't it?"

"You could telephone me next time and save your shoe leather," said the shopkeeper.

"I suppose so, but I enjoy the walk to be completely frank with you. I find that a morning constitutional keeps everything moving just as it should." He patted his stomach. "And I have all the time in the world, you see."

"Because you're a gentleman of leisure," added the shopkeeper.

"Exactly that, Bernie, exactly that. Now, you get on and sell these fine ladies their carriage clock. I shall return later in the week." He turned to face Churchill and Pemberley. "Mr Peregrine Colthrop, by the way. It's a delight to meet you both."

"And you, Mr Colthrop," replied Churchill. "Do enjoy the rest of your day. Pray, what does a gentleman who has all the time in the world do with himself on a day like today?"

"That's a very good question, Mrs Churchill. I shall take a little amble beside the river and then work up an appetite for lunch at the club."

"The gentleman's club?"

"The very same. After lunch I shall nap in the club lounge in order to muster up enough strength for a game of tennis with the inspector. I believe it's his day off today."

"Inspector Mappin?"

"That's him all right."

"He has a day off?"

"So he tells me."

"What if he's needed to deal with a crime?"

"He has one of those constable chaps over from Bulchford to cover for him, I believe."

"Oh dear. No one's safe these days, are they?" commented Churchill.

"I'm afraid you're labouring under the misapprehension that we are any safer when Inspector Mappin is on duty," replied Mr Colthrop as he walked toward the shop door. "He's a thoroughly decent chap but a hopeless police officer."

Churchill couldn't help but laugh. "Oh goodness, Mr Colthrop, what a straight-talker you are!"

"I don't like to mince my words, that's for sure," he replied with a grin as he pulled the door open to step outside.

Churchill and Pemberley followed closely behind.

"Oh, you ladies are coming too, are you?"

"What about that carriage clock?" Mr Purprend called out.

"Well, do enjoy your day, ladies," said Mr Colthrop as he was reunited with his bicycle.

"Thank you, Mr Colthrop. Enjoy your day by the river, at the gentleman's club and playing tennis with Inspector Mappin."

"I shall do."

"Do you enjoy spending time at the gentleman's club?" Pemberley asked.

"Why, of course! One always finds good conversation, fine food and an extremely good selection of whiskies there, you see."

"But don't you miss the company of ladies?" Pemberley asked.

"Ladies? At a club?" he scoffed. "What nonsense! I enjoy the company of my good wife at home, and that is quite sufficient, thank you very much. Ladies at a club! Can you imagine the endless, mindless chatter? It would drive the chaps mad!"

"Mindless chatter?" asked Pemberley. "Is that all we women do?"

"Oh, I didn't quite mean it like that!" He gave an awkward laugh. "One couldn't possibly speak for present company, of course. Perhaps your minds are trained on more cerebral matters."

"They certainly are!" retorted Pemberley.

"Excellent. I shall bid you good day, then."

"He's quite an amusing chap, isn't he?" chuckled Churchill as they watched Mr Colthrop's retreating form.

"You're only saying that because he was so uncomplimentary about Inspector Mappin's policing skills."

"Clearly an astute gentleman."

"I can think of better words to describe him," replied Pemberley bitterly.

"Don't get upset about that *mindless chatter* nonsense, Pembers. If that's all he thinks women are capable of, he's simply underestimating us. There's nothing more powerful than being underestimated."

"You said that he was astute just a moment ago."

"Not so much when it comes to members of the fairer sex. Few men have any clue about us, with the exception of Detective Chief Inspector Churchill, of course."

"Was he a good judge of character?"

"Impeccable, Pemberley, quite impeccable. You would have liked him."

"He must have been a very special man indeed."

"Oh, he was. But enough of that now, I seem to have a bit of dust in my eye. The uncomfortable truth we find ourselves facing this morning is that our attempt to surveil Mr Colthrop has ended quite disastrously. Not only did he spot us twice but he engaged us in conversation, which means it'll be exceptionally difficult to keep an eye on him from now on."

"We could disguise ourselves."

"As what?"

"I don't know yet, but I'll give it some thought."

"Please do, Pembers. In the meantime, based on the description of his day there doesn't appear to be much time for associating with a fancy lady. She can hardly be admitted to the gentleman's club, and neither can I imagine her playing tennis with Inspector Mappin. Now then, I feel the need for some eatables from Simpkin and then a little research down at the library."

Chapter 12

"What is it you need to research, Mrs Churchill?" asked Pemberley as they walked down the cobbled high street toward Compton Poppleford Library.

Churchill was proudly carrying the Sprockett case file, which she had collected from the office on the way.

"You do know Mrs Higginbath will be in there, don't you?" Pemberley added.

"I do indeed, but I can't very well avoid the library for the rest of my days, can I? I'm hoping she'll leave her job before long and then I'll be able to get a long-awaited reading ticket from her successor."

The library was a small, crooked building leaning up against the town hall.

"No sign of her yet, Pembers," whispered Churchill as they entered. "She's probably lurking behind some shelving at the back."

"Or perhaps she's lost herself within the intricacies of the Dewey Decimal System."

"Oh yes. Let's hope that she's completely lost within that, never to find her way out again."

The two ladies tiptoed carefully toward a table at the far end of the library.

"Now then, we'll need a map from twenty years ago," whispered Churchill, "and a copy of the post office directory so we can look people up in it."

"I'll go and fetch them," said Pemberley in a hushed tone.

Churchill began leafing through the case file and writing down the names of all the people Mr Atkins had interviewed twenty years previously.

"I hope most of these people still live in the village," she whispered when Pemberley returned with the map and the directory.

Pemberley examined the list. "Yes, I think most of them do. Miss Agatha Byles is now Mrs Munion. I think I have her telephone number, so I'll telephone and ask when we can meet up."

"That would be wondrous, Pemberley, thank you. It says here that she was the sporting type."

"She was, and Darcy Sprockett was too. They were rivals in the Compton Poppleford May Day Fair All Girls' Triathlon."

"I can't say that I have much in common with sporting types. They're all rather serious, aren't they?"

"Only when they're training or competing. When they're not doing those things, they can be quite fun."

"I find that hard to believe."

"And the Compton Poppleford May Day Fair All Girls' Triathlon is quite an important tradition. I took part in it myself when I was a strip of a lass."

"Did you, Pembers? Well, I never would have thought it. A triathlon, you say? That's five events, is it not?"

"Three."

"Isn't that a decathlon?"

"No, that's ten events."

"So what's three events?"

"A triathlon."

"You're confusing me now."

"Oddly enough, Darcy Sprockett vanished the day after Mrs Munion beat her in the Compton Poppleford May Day Fair All Girls' Triathlon."

"Very intriguing indeed, Pembers, I shall make a note of that. Now, who else have we got? Barnaby Manners and Timothy Pentwhistle."

"He's a sailor now."

"Manners or Pentwhistle?"

"Pentwhistle. He went away to sea and was very successful at it."

"Good for him. Did he ever come back?"

"Oh yes. I know his mother from the Compton Poppleford Ladies' Philately Society."

"What on earth is that?"

"Stamp collecting."

"I didn't know you were the collecting type, Pembers."

"I'm not. I don't actually collect anything, but they invited me to join about fifteen years ago and I didn't have the heart to say no. Then I couldn't bring myself to leave because they don't have many members. Perhaps you could join, Mrs Churchill."

"I'm busy enough as it is, Pembers. Why don't you ask Mrs Thonnings?"

"She used to be a member but we had to ask her to leave."

"Why so?"

"It all began at the dinner party with the missing casserole—"

Churchill held a hand up to halt the conversation. "That's a story I would very much like to hear, Pembers, but let's do it another time. We must remain focused on the task at hand. Let's consult the post office directory and find out where these people live now, and then we can—"

"You can't bring that in here, you know," a loud voice announced, interrupting her.

Churchill reluctantly looked up to see a lady with a square face and long grey hair bearing down on her.

"Bring *what* in, Mrs Higginbath?"

"That book you've got there on the table."

"It's not a book, Mrs H, it's a case file. A very important case file, if you must know."

"Well, it's not allowed in here."

Churchill gave the case file a puzzled glance. "This harmless collection of paper? It's hardly likely to chew the shelving or do its business on the library carpet."

"Please don't try to make jokes in the library."

"I was merely trying to understand why I'm not permitted to bring this case file in here."

"It's too big."

"Too big for what?"

"For the library. Patrons must not bring bulky, oversized items into the library. It's stated in the rules."

"What about bulky, oversized patrons?"

"Are you trying to make another joke, Mrs Churchill?"

"Actually, it occurs to me that I'm not a patron because you won't allow me a reading ticket. Do the rules say anything about non-patrons bringing big things in?"

"I don't think so, no."

"There we go then, we're in the clear. I do so appreciate a little loophole, don't you, Miss Pemberley?"

"But Miss Pemberley is a patron," continued Mrs

Higginbath. "Therefore, she can't bring that bulky item in here."

"Ah, but she didn't bring it in, Mrs H. I did."

"She's looking at it."

"But she hasn't touched it. That has all been down to me."

"She's still associated with it."

"Surely the library rules don't explicitly state that a patron is forbidden from *associating* with a bulky, oversized item?"

"The rules state that non-patrons aren't even allowed in here, so that overrules everything." Mrs Higginbath folded her arms proudly.

"Which means what, Mrs H?"

"That it's time to sling your hook!"

Churchill calmly folded the case file shut and resisted the temptation to bring it crashing down on Mrs Higginbath's square head.

"You're quite rude for a librarian, Mrs Higginbath. Enormously rude, I should say. I wonder what the district librarian would make of it all."

"Mr Slatherington, I believe," added Pemberley.

"That's the chap," said Churchill. "He just happens to be a good friend of mine."

Mrs Higginbath's brow furrowed. "I didn't realise there was a district librarian."

"Oh yes," replied Churchill, rising to her feet. "An extremely important man, he is."

"He's also a magistrate," said Pemberley, "and an under-sheriff, too."

"What's that?" asked Mrs Higginbath, her brow creasing with concern.

"Yes, what is that, Miss Pemberley?"

"It means he is assistant to the high sheriff."

"Oh, then he's even more important than I realised," said Churchill, tucking the case file under her arm and picking up her handbag. "Well, we'd better be off now, Mrs Higginbath. I'm sure you won't mind if we borrow this map and directory."

"Borrowing is forbidden on those items," she replied weakly. "They're for reference only."

"Miss Pemberley will return them to you tomorrow, Mrs H. We have Mr Slatherington's blessing."

"What a stroke of luck that you know Mr Slatherington, Pembers," said Churchill as the two ladies ambled back to the office. "That put Mrs Higginbath on the back foot all right. Did you notice how I played along with your story and pretended that I knew him as well?"

"Oh, I don't know him at all."

"Really? You just happened to have heard his name, then?"

"Not at all. To my knowledge he doesn't even exist. He's a figment of our imaginations!"

Churchill stopped and gave her assistant a wide grin. "Pembers, I could kiss you. What a scream! Did you see how pale her face went? Next time Mrs Higginbath bullies us we can invent another important authority figure."

"It's only you she bullies. She doesn't bully me."

"True."

"It was very unwise of you to make an offensive comment about her nephew during the Piddleton Hotel investigation."

"Pembers, if I'd known back then that Mr Crumble was Mrs Higginbath's nephew I never would have mentioned his rude manners and gaudy suits in her presence, would I? It would be wonderful to travel back in time and correct one's mistakes, but as that option isn't currently available one must simply live with the consequences. And I still stand by what I said. It's no surprise to me that they're related."

Chapter 13

"GOOD MORNING, PEMBERS," said Churchill when her assistant arrived in the office the following Monday. "You've just caught me reading *Wuthering Heights*."

"I thought you didn't have much time for reading, Mrs Churchill."

"Oh, I don't really." She removed her reading glasses. "But now and again I like to lose myself in a little tome. I began this one at the weekend."

"What do you make of it so far?"

"I must say that they seem quite grouchy up there on the moors. All that wind, rain and general bleakness would be too much for anybody, I suppose. Why did they live so far away from everyone else? One should always be within walking distance of a decent general store, you know."

"But you're enjoying the book?"

"Oh yes. I like all the Brontë sisters' books, as I've already said."

"Then you've read *Wuthering Heights* before?"

"Yes, but a very long time ago. So long ago, in fact, that I've clean forgotten what happens in it."

"By the way, I telephoned Agatha Munion yesterday. She says she's very busy, but if we really need to speak to her we can join her for a game of tennis this afternoon."

"That suits me, Pembers, though I haven't worn my tennis whites since I left the Richmond-Upon-Thames Ladies' Lawn Tennis Club. How are you at tennis?"

"Not very good."

"Never mind. It's mostly in the wrist, you know. Once you've mastered the wrist you'll find that everything else naturally follows."

~

"You look quite the part, my second-in-command," said Churchill as she surveyed her assistant outside the Compton Poppleford Tennis Club House.

Pemberley was wearing a calf-length white skirt with an equally white blouse and plimsolls.

"I decided to buy myself a tennis outfit at lunchtime."

"I'm sure there was no need to go to all that expense. Any old clothes would have done."

"I've always been a believer in having the right tools for the job."

"I couldn't agree more, Pemberley."

"We need to present a professional image."

"We do indeed, and in recognition of your professionalism I shall allow you to claim back the expenses for your plimsolls. Are you ready to go?"

"I am. Have you had your tennis whites a while, Mrs Churchill?"

Churchill glanced down at her ankle-length skirt. "I have, actually. I'll admit that they're a little old-fashioned, and between you and me I can't quite do up the zip at the side, but the hem of my cardigan covers it nicely. Fortunately, the plimsolls are still a perfect fit." She adjusted her white headband. "Let's go get 'em!"

The only other people present on the tennis courts were a tall, broad-shouldered woman of about forty and a gangly girl who looked to be twelve or thirteen.

"Mrs Churchill, is it?" the woman called over as she slammed the ball across the court.

"It is, yes. Mrs Munion, I presume?"

"That's me. Hold it there, Phyllis."

Mrs Munion strode over to them, wiping the back of her hand across her brow. She wore a crisp white blouse, a pleated skirt and a white cap.

"Care to join us for a game of doubles?" she asked. My daughter and I will go easy on you given that you're in your latter years."

"Oh, there's no need!" laughed Churchill. "I'm quite a seasoned player. I was member of the Richmond-Upon-Thames Ladies' Lawn Tennis Club for many years."

"Good for you," replied Mrs Munion. "Come on, then. Let's see what you've got." She hurled a tennis ball at Churchill, who only just managed to catch it. "Phyllis, you're down this end with me."

The four ladies took up their positions on court.

"I'll serve, Pemberley," said Churchill. "You move back a bit and I'll move forward a bit. I think we get to use the fat and wide court for doubles."

"What do you mean 'fat and wide'?"

"The outer lines on either side but the inner line at the back."

"I've no idea what you're talking about."

"You'll pick it up, Pembers."

"Your serve, Mrs Churchill!" called Mrs Munion.

"Yes indeed! Here goes!"

Churchill threw the ball up into the air and felt a surge

of delight as she managed to hit it with her racquet. The ball sailed forward in a gentle arc and landed softly against the net.

"Second serve!" shouted Mrs Munion.

Churchill tried again, but the ball failed to get over the net once more.

"Love fifteen," shouted Mrs Munion. "Switch sides!"

"Which side?" asked Churchill. "Oh look, Pembers, they're swapping round. You stand here and I'll stand there. It's going to be rather difficult to have a conversation with Mrs Munion if we're expected to play tennis all the time, isn't it? I say, Mrs Munion!"

"Yes?"

"I wonder if we could spare a moment for a gentle warm-up."

"But Phyllis and I have already warmed up."

"Miss Pemberley and I haven't."

"Oh, all right. But we've only got the court booked for an hour, so get on with it."

She and her daughter left the court and lingered at the side.

"Go down there, Pembers, and I'll hit the ball to you."

"I still don't understand what the lines mean."

"Don't worry about the lines, we're just warming up."

Churchill and Pemberley began tapping the ball over the net to each other.

"Did Miss Pemberley mention that we wished to speak to you about Darcy Sprockett?" Churchill called over to Mrs Munion.

"Oh yes. What is it you want to know?"

"You were her main competitor in some sort of championship, is that right?"

"Yes. It was the Compton Poppleford May Day Fair All Girls' Triathlon."

"Five events?"

"Three. The pony scrumpy dash, arm-wrestling and scone-throwing."

"Mrs Churchill!" Pemberley called out. "All the balls are now on your side of the court."

"Oh, are they? Yes, so they are! Did you just hit one to me, Pembers?"

"Yes."

Churchill picked up a tennis ball and hit it back across the net.

"For a moment there I thought you said scone-throwing, Mrs Munion."

"I did. My record was forty-seven yards."

"You can throw a scone forty-seven yards?"

"At one time I could. I haven't done it for a while, but I still do a little coaching."

"You coach people on how to throw scones?"

"I coach on all three events."

"Mrs Churchill!"

"What is it, Pemberley?"

"Are you going to hit the ball back?"

"I will in a moment. I'm just having a chat with Mrs Munion."

Pemberley sighed and walked over to the net.

"What's the pony scrumpy dash?" Churchill asked Mrs Munion breathlessly.

"An eight-hundred-yard gallop on a pony with a tankard of scrumpy in one hand. The object is to complete it as quickly as you can while spilling as little of the scrumpy as possible."

"How do they decide who wins? The fastest pony or the least scrumpy spilt?"

"They work it out by means of an equation," replied

Pemberley. "Speed accounts for half the points and the amount of scrumpy spilt accounts for the other half. So if your pony covers the distance in a minute but you spill ten fluid ounces you'll be beaten by someone who covers the distance in one minute and three seconds but spills only five fluid ounces."

"I'm struggling to believe what I'm hearing," said Churchill. "Is this actually a sport?"

"It's a local tradition that dates back to the fourteenth century," replied Pemberley.

"And that makes it a sensible thing to do, does it? Because it's old?"

"Yes."

"Let's get to the point, Mrs Munion," said Churchill. "The day before Darcy Sprockett disappeared you beat her in the Compton Poppleford May Day Fair All Girls' Triathlon, is that right?"

"It all came down to the last event," she replied. "I'd won the pony dash and Darcy had won the arm-wrestling. There was a delay with the scone-throwing because some of them had to be weighted."

"What on earth does that mean?"

"Each scone has to weigh one-and-a-half ounces, and although Mrs Bramley did her best to bake each one to size, small weights had to be pushed into the centre of the undersized ones. The batch that day was particularly uneven, and Darcy wasn't happy about it. She claimed that some of her scones were overweight."

"Couldn't she just have nibbled a bit off?" asked Churchill.

"Eating any part of the scone results in an instant ban," replied Mrs Munion. "And sipping the scrumpy in the pony dash incurs the same punishment. The competitors may only consume the scones and scrumpy after the event. It's traditional for the winner of the competition to do so, in fact."

"Even the scones that have been hurled more than forty yards?"

"It's all part of the tradition, Mrs Churchill."

"People often assume that just because something is a tradition it must be a good idea."

"Generations of people can't be wrong."

"But they just might be in this case. In summary, then, you won the competition and the following day Darcy went missing."

"Yes. I thought she was sulking to begin with, but when they started talking about broken eggs and goblins I began to worry that it might be something more sinister."

"Which indeed it was. It's safe to say that Darcy Sprockett was in rather a foul mood after you beat her in the May Day Fair All Girls' Triathlon, is it?"

"Absolutely. She was a sore loser. Have you finished your warm-up now? We're running out of time for a game."

Mrs Munion and her daughter strode back onto the court.

"Your serve, Phyllis," said Mrs Munion, tossing a ball to her daughter.

Churchill felt relieved that she wouldn't be on the receiving end of a powerful serve from Mrs Munion.

"Are you ready, Miss Pemberley?" asked Churchill.

"Not really."

"You could ready yourself with your racquet, at least. Leaving it dangling by your side won't do us any good. Move back a bit and I'll move forward. The little girl's about to serve, but don't worry, I'll go easy on her."

The ball whistled past Churchill's ear.

"Fifteen love!" shouted Mrs Munion.

"Goodness, have we started?" asked Churchill.

She leapt back as the next ball headed straight for her, thumping into her thigh and losing itself in the voluminous folds of her skirt.

"Ouch! Where's it gone?"

"Thirty love!"

"I don't remember tennis being quite like… Hit it, Pembers!"

The next ball shot past Churchill and headed in Pemberley's direction. Pemberley made a surprisingly elegant leap toward it before hitting it far above their heads. Churchill was blinded by the sun as she watched the ball soar high above them. Then it fell again and landed with a frustrating bounce on their side of the net.

"Forty love!"

Churchill felt a snap of irritation. "It's rather hot. Are there any refreshments?"

The game was over a short minute later, and Churchill felt relieved to find herself recovering with a cold glass of lemonade.

"I'm a little out of practice," she explained to Mrs Munion and her daughter. "You serve very well for a little girl, Phyllis."

"She's been playing for eight years," replied Mrs Munion. "Anyway, well played Mrs Churchill and Miss Pemberley. It's nice to see two old ladies making an attempt to stay active."

"Oh, we're quite active, aren't we, Miss Pemberley? Bicycling is a particular favourite of mine."

She did her best to ignore Pemberley as she began choking on a mouthful of lemonade.

"You're clearly a fit lady, Mrs Munion," Churchill continued. Darcy Sprockett must have had similar physical abilities."

"Oh yes, she was a strong girl. Fast, too. She and I used to race each other in the hundred-yard dash, but we had to do so informally because women weren't allowed to run races against each other. She beat me most of the time."

"But somehow someone managed to overpower her in the woods the night she vanished. It must have been an individual of some considerable strength."

"It must have been," agreed Mrs Munion. "I'm sure Darcy would have put up a fight."

"And she was good at running, you say? I'm surprised she didn't manage to fight the culprit off and slip away, in that case."

"The element of surprise might have stunned her," said Pemberley.

"You may be right."

"Perhaps there was more than one culprit," suggested Mrs Munion.

"Yes, that could account for it," said Churchill. "But whom? And why? Can you think of anyone who would wish to harm Darcy Sprockett, Mrs Munion?"

"I can't, I'm afraid. She and I had a rivalry, and sometimes it was friendly and sometimes it wasn't. But I can't say that I was ever angry enough to consider murdering her."

"I read your interview with my predecessor, Mr Atkins."

"I remember him. He was a funny little man, wasn't he?"

"I never had the pleasure of meeting him myself. In your interview you stated that you went for a walk in Poppleford Woods the night that Darcy went missing."

"That's right, I did."

"Even though it was dark and stormy?"

"It was still light when I set out, but yes, it was stormy. I've always been drawn to stormy weather."

"And you returned home at what time?"

"I can't remember. What did I say in my original interview?"

"I can't remember either," lied Churchill.

"Possibly around ten o'clock," said Mrs Munion cautiously. "I get the impression you're testing me, Mrs Churchill."

"What do you mean by that?"

"You're trying to find out how much I remember of that day."

"Well, I am, but it's not a test."

"What is it, then? Are you trying to trip me up?"

"I have no intention of doing such a thing, Mrs Munion."

"You want me to incriminate myself."

"Not at all. I'm merely trying to establish the facts of the day."

"There's no denying that I was in the woods at the same time as Darcy Sprockett that evening, but I didn't know she was there and I certainly didn't see her."

"Very well, Mrs Munion."

"You do believe me, don't you?"

"Of course. Why wouldn't I?"

"You're giving me a suspicious look."

"Am I? I certainly didn't intend to. I'm concentrating, you see, and people do sometimes remark that I look suspicious when I'm concentrating. Don't they, Miss Pemberley?"

"Do they?"

"Yes, haven't you heard them? Oh, never mind."

"I didn't have anything to do with Darcy Sprockett's disappearance, Mrs Churchill," said Mrs Munion.

"I wouldn't dream of suggesting that you did, Mrs Munion. Did you happen to see anyone else while you were out walking in the woods that dark and stormy night?"

"Yes. I saw Timothy Pentwhistle."

"Ah yes, that name rings a bell. Isn't he the one who went off to sea?"

"He is."

"And what was Master Pentwhistle doing in the woods at that hour?"

"He walked past me, we bid each other a good evening and that was that."

"And how was his mood?"

"Normal."

"There was nothing about him that struck you as being out of character at all?"

"Nothing."

"Thank you, Mrs Munion. I do appreciate you answering my questions so frankly. What do you think happened to Darcy Sprockett?"

"She went off in a sulk and fell down an old well or ventilation shaft from one of the mines."

"There are mines beneath the woods?"

"Ancient mines, which I believe were dug by an ancient people who were hoping to find something worth mining but were disappointed when they found nothing."

"I see. How interesting."

"We only have five minutes left," Mrs Munion said, brandishing her racquet. "One more game?"

"Oh, must we?"

Chapter 14

"It's a terrible shame that only the dignitaries are given chairs, Pemberley," commented Churchill as they stood in the marketplace awaiting the unveiling of the statue of Sir Morris Buckle-Duffington. "My ankles are silently protesting after all the walking and tennis playing we've done recently. I bet those dignitaries haven't done an ounce of anything nearly as strenuous, yet they all have chairs. Wait a moment, isn't that Inspector Mappin? He's sitting on a *chair*! Why does *he* get a chair?"

"He's representing the constabulary."

"Pfft!"

"He's been a loyal, hardworking servant of the police force for many a year."

"Since when did you hold Inspector Mappin in such high regard, Pembers?"

"I don't. I'm just trying to explain why he has a chair and we don't."

"It's because of some quirky, old-fashioned logic steeped in rural tradition."

"You're right. And that's why Mrs Thonnings has a chair."

"Wait, *Mrs Thonnings* has a chair? *Why?!*"

"Because of that old-fashioned rural logic you mentioned."

"How ridiculous!"

"What ho!" came a voice from behind them.

Churchill turned to see a familiar figure doffing his pith helmet.

"Oh, hello Mr Colthrop. What brings you here?"

"I've come to see the statue of our local hero. Isn't that why we're all here?"

"I suppose it is."

"Unless you're following me again, Mrs Churchill." He gave a sly wink.

"*Again?* We haven't followed you for a first time, and we're certainly not following you today. How could we be when you're standing behind us?"

"That's a good point." He gave a laugh. "It would have to be quite a clever kind of following, that's for sure!"

"You don't get a chair either then, Mr Colthrop?"

"The wife's got it. We were only offered one between us, you see, so she's happily seated upon it. I have no need for a chair; I could stand up all day."

"Could you indeed?"

"Yes, I have the stamina of an ox."

"Good. Oh look, I think the mayor's going to speak now."

A small, wizened man clambered onto the stage that had been erected next to the statue, he appeared weighed down by the heavy gold chain around his neck. The statue itself had a velvet cloth draped over it. "Good morning, ladies and gentlemen." His voice was slow and dreary. "May I take the opportunity this morning to welcome you to the official unveiling of the bronze statue of Compton Poppleford's homegrown hero, Sir Morris Buckle-Duffington…"

"I already have the sense that this is going to drag a bit, Pembers," whispered Churchill. "Our time would probably be better spent elsewhere. What do you think?"

"Let's give it a few more minutes," whispered Pemberley in reply.

"Why do you suppose the Colthrops got a chair?"

"They only got one between them."

"One's better than none at all."

"Sir Morris left no descendants," continued the mayor. "However, we are graced this fine morning by the presence of his trusted valet, Mr Jones Sloanes."

He gestured toward an old man, who rose to his feet from the midst of the seated audience and gave a polite nod.

"Sir Morris deserves a better introduction than I could ever possibly give," continued the mayor. "So without further ado, I introduce to you the esteemed curator of the Compton Poppleford History Museum and chairman of the Compton Poppleford Local History Group, Mr Barnaby Manners!"

There was scattered applause as a tweed-jacketed man with thin brown hair and a large bow tie climbed onto the stage.

"Barnaby Manners," whispered Churchill to Pemberley. "He's in Atkins's case file, is he not?"

"Yes, he is."

"Then we need to speak to him."

"Sir Morris Frederick Charles Buckle-Duffington was born on the 17th of March 1824," Barnaby Manners read from a wad of papers. "He was the third son of Frederick Morris Buckle-Duffington, who was the eldest son of

Charles Morris Buckle-Duffington of Lower Compton Poppleford. Keen historians among you will know that Lower Compton Poppleford was the name of our esteemed village before it was moved half a mile to the east during the eighteenth century to improve the view from the manor house, Ashleigh Grange. The village retained the name Compton Poppleford following the relocation but dropped the word '*Lower*'. After all, the move resulted in the village sitting fifteen feet *higher* above sea level, so the word lower simply wouldn't do!"

He paused to allow a smattering of polite laughter.

"Charles Buckle-Duffington was an interesting character, having spent much of his childhood confined to his bed by a mysterious illness that caused his feet to swell…"

"I don't think I can endure this any longer," Churchill whispered. "It wouldn't be so bad if I had a chair, but my bunions are rather unforgiving at times like this. Shall we sidle away?"

"Let's."

The two ladies began to sneak away from the crowd.

"Leaving already, Mrs Churchill?" whispered Mr Colthrop.

"Indeed. Things to do, people to see and all that."

"I can't say that I'm looking forward to conversing with Barnaby Manners," said Churchill once they were back at the office. "What a dull man. Who could possibly be interested in the swollen feet of Sir Morris Buckle-Duffington's grandfather?"

"That's the problem with people who have absorbed a lot of information," replied Pemberley. "They assume everyone else wants to hear about it."

"I couldn't agree more, my second-in-command. Astute words indeed. Did I hear you put the kettle on?"

"You did."

"And do we have cake?"

"We do."

"Marvellous. Let's return to this case file, then."

The two ladies spent an enjoyable hour or so eating, drinking and reading through Mr Atkins's notes.

"Here's the summary of Darcy Sprockett's last day, Pembers," said Churchill. "She rose at six to feed the chickens and goats. Then she lit the fires, emptied the slops, prepared breakfast and scrubbed the scullery, while also ensuring that her younger siblings made it to school on time. Then she washed the family nightgowns, put them through the mangle and hung them out to dry. Good grief! It doesn't sound like her life was terribly fun.

"After lunch she bicycled to the recreation ground, where she was seen practising her scone-throwing by Miss Thora Gladstone and Miss Marjorie Ramekin. Isn't that a type of small dish, Pembers?"

"I think so."

"She left the recreation ground in the company of Master Timothy Pentwhistle, and witnesses described the two having a loud disagreement beside St Dustin's Well. They parted there, apparently, and Darcy continued on to her home, where she blackened the family boots before our favourite bore Master Barnaby Manners paid her a visit. According to Darcy's sister, Emmeline, Barnaby brought his trumpet with him. This was corroborated by old tortoisehead Mr Sprockett, wasn't it? Barnaby was thrown out of the house by Mr Sprockett when the trumping became unbearable. Shouldn't that be trumpeting rather than trumping?"

"Yes, I believe so."

"Trumping sounds better though, doesn't it? And he can't have been much good at it. In my experience the truly accomplished musicians are rather coy about their craft; it's the hopeless ones who are most determined to inflict their noise on everyone else. Anyway, let's continue… Darcy then prepared the family's evening meal of mutton and potatoes. What was wrong with everyone else in that household, Pembers? Didn't they ever lift a finger?"

"They must all have been doing other things."

"Clearly. So what does this mean for our incident board? We can put Mrs Munion, Mr Manners and Mr Pentwhistle up there now, I suppose. Where's St Dustin's Well?"

"Here." Pemberley stuck a pin in the map.

"And the recreation ground?"

"Just over here." Another pin went in.

"Marvellous." Churchill stood back and surveyed the wall. "There's one thing we do well, and that's incident boards. Don't you agree?"

"We do other things well, too."

"Yes, but I didn't want us getting too puffed up. One mustn't get too full of oneself, must one?"

Footsteps on the staircase alerted them to the presence of a visitor, and a moment later Mrs Colthrop stepped into the office. She wore a fur stole around her shoulders and held another expensive handbag in her right hand.

"Good afternoon, Mrs Colthrop!" Churchill gestured toward the seat opposite her. "Did you enjoy the unveiling of Sir Morris Buckle-Duffington's statue this morning?"

"I can't say that I did," she replied with a sigh. "Those chairs were dreadfully uncomfortable."

"Some of us didn't even get a chair!"

"So I gather. My husband was quite content to stand."

"He told us he has the stamina of an ox."

"That sounds like the sort of thing he'd say. You spoke to him, did you? That's why I'm here, in fact. I was wondering whether you'd uncovered the identity of this young thing he's been flitting about with."

"Not yet, Mrs Colthrop."

"Why not?"

"Well, we have been conducting some surveillance, and so far we have discovered that he likes to frequent the antiques shop."

"He'd better not be buying another one of those infernal soup ladles."

"I couldn't possibly pass comment on that. He has also been ambling along the river, visiting the gentleman's club and playing tennis with Inspector Mappin."

"No sign of him with another woman, then?"

"Not yet, Mrs Colthrop."

"And you spoke to him today, you say?"

"That's right. He was standing behind us at the unveiling of the statue. We didn't have chairs, sadly."

"So he knows who you are."

"He does, yes. Most people know who we are in this little village, don't they, Miss Pemberley?"

Her secretary gave a nod.

"But he hasn't twigged that you're carrying out surveillance on him?"

"Goodness me, no! We've exchanged pleasantries with him on a couple of occasions because that is quite unavoidable when one encounters a fellow in the course of one's daily activities."

"Has he seen you following him?"

"Not at all, Mrs Colthrop. We have merely encountered one another so far."

"I'm rather worried that he's going to become suspicious."

"Then let me allay your fears at once. My trusted second-in-command and I are often seen performing our errands around the village. Your husband hasn't the slightest ounce of suspicion that we might be interested in his daily activities."

"Good. That's a great relief."

"I'm pleased to be able to provide reassurance. Are you absolutely sure he has a lady friend? We certainly haven't seen any evidence of it so far."

'He's a secretive old goose, Mrs Churchill. I fear you'll have to work hard to catch him in the act."

"Oh, we'll catch him all right, don't you worry a jot. We have a plan."

"What's our plan?" asked Pemberley once Mrs Colthrop had left the office.

"We'll work something out."

"But you told Mrs Colthrop that we already had a plan."

"I bent the truth a little. It's the sort of thing you have to do when clients keep pestering you."

"Just like the way you didn't admit that Mr Colthrop already suspects that we're following him."

"Exactly. Mrs Colthrop doesn't need to hear operational details of that nature."

Churchill bit into an eclair she had found in her drawer.

"Do you intend to come up with a plan?"

"We both will, Pembers. Anyway, the woman's being rather impatient, isn't she? She only tasked us with this case a couple of days ago. These things take time."

"They certainly do."

"And besides, we have other very important cases to investigate. Tomorrow we must visit the Compton Poppleford History Museum and endure some sort of conversation with Barnaby Manners."

Chapter 15

"Tell me what Compton Poppleford History Museum contains, Pemberley," said Churchill as they approached a little red-brick building situated behind the town hall.

"It has a seventeenth-century plough."

"Is that so?"

"And a hundred-year-old milk churn."

"I fear I may be unable to contain my excitement."

"It's an important part of the dairy industry's history."

"I'm sure it is. But there's such a lot of history, isn't there? We don't need to know about all of it. I'm more interested in finding out what Mr Manners can tell us about Darcy Sprockett."

"The door letter man telephoned this morning and says he had a cancellation today so he can come and fix the door signage at four o'clock."

"That's marvellous. I'll be able to tear him off a strip for getting it so badly wrong in the first place."

"I wouldn't do that."

"Why not?"

"Because if you upset him too much he might not fix it properly."

"Oh, he'll fix it all right. I'll make sure of that."

Compton Poppleford History Museum was a dingy little place filled with glass-fronted cases. The air inside felt dusty and stale.

"Hullo?" echoed a voice from an unknown location. "Do we have visitors?"

"You do indeed," replied Churchill. "Where are you?"

"Here," said the tweed-jacketed Barnaby Manners as he stepped out from behind a display of old scrumpy jars. He wore a large paisley-patterned bow tie. "Welcome to the museum. You're the two ladies from the detective agency, aren't you?"

"We are indeed. Mrs Churchill and Miss Pemberley. Mr Manners, isn't it?"

"I am he. Have you visited the museum before?"

"I haven't," replied Churchill.

"I have," Pemberley interjected.

"Perhaps you'd like to purchase a guide to the museum, Mrs Churchill? They're only two shillings."

"No thank you, Mr Manners. My able assistant will be able to guide me."

"We do change our displays quite frequently, Mrs Churchill. The museum may not be exactly as Miss Pemberley recalls it."

"Oh, it's just as I recall it," replied Pemberley, glancing around. "The plough is definitely still here."

"Ah yes, the plough," said Mr Manners." You must come and see the seventeenth-century plough. It's remarkably well preserved for its age."

"Then the plough and I already have something in common."

He led them over to where the plough was enjoying pride of place on a rectangular podium.

"I'm surprised you haven't seen the plough before, Mrs Churchill. After all, our little museum is open every day of the week."

"Never a day off, Mr Manners?"

"Tuesdays and Thursdays are my days off. My wife fills in for me then. Now, the plough has an interesting history. We think it was originally in the hands of the Moldspit family, who lived in—"

"Actually, Mr Manners, we didn't really come here to see the museum," Churchill said, interrupting him in mid flow.

"You didn't?" His face fell.

"No. We came to speak to you about Miss Darcy Sprockett."

"Oh."

"I realise her disappearance isn't something you particularly wish to dwell on, but we're trying to find out who might have been behind her tragic demise."

"I see… Yes." He began to fidget with his bow tie.

"You saw her the day she went missing, is that right?"

"Well yes, I did." He glanced at his wristwatch. "I don't have a lot of time. I really must be—"

"How about you show us around your museum, Mr Manners, and then perhaps you could help in return by answering a few questions. I'll even buy a guide book if you're helpful enough."

"Really? You would?" His face brightened again.

"And make a donation toward the restoration of the hundred-year-old milk churn," added Pemberley.

"I have to do that as well, do I, Miss Pemberley?" asked Churchill through clenched teeth.

"Oh, it would be marvellous if you did!" beamed Mr Manners.

"Right then, let's get on with it. We've seen the plough, what next?"

"The Sir Morris Buckle-Duffington exhibition, of course!"

"Him again, is it?"

"Did you attend the unveiling of the statue yesterday?"

"We did indeed, Mr Manners. Or some of it, at least."

"Wonderful. Well, do come this way."

The two women followed him over to a portrait depicting a middle-aged man with a smug expression and a mop of grey hair. A curly-haired dog sat at his feet.

"The great Sir Morris Buckle-Duffington," announced Mr Manners. "This was painted in 1862 by an artist who—"

"He looks just like his statue."

"He does, doesn't he? Sir Morris was a wealthy man and had no descendants, so on his deathbed he declared that his treasures would be donated to the village. And so it was, with his patronage, that the Compton Poppleford History Museum was able to rent these wonderful new premises. All his personal papers, including letters and diaries, were also donated to the museum, but they are now locked away in the trunk that sits on the shelf below his portrait here, and no one is allowed to open it until 1962."

"Until 1962? Why, that's a lifetime away! Why can't the case be opened before then?"

"Sir Morris decreed that the chest could not be opened until fifty years after his death. The museum is its official guardian."

"But the chap's deceased. Surely it wouldn't do any harm to take a little peek at his papers?"

"We must honour his word."

"Aren't you tempted to take a little gander, Mr Manners? Just a surreptitious turn of the key in the lock and a quick look inside? You could leave everything just as you found it, lock the trunk again and no one would ever know."

"Absolutely not!"

"Oh come on, Mr Manners. Surely you've already done it."

"Never!"

"Isn't that the key hanging from that little hook just there?"

"It is indeed. It has hung there, untouched, for twenty years, and it shall hang there for another thirty."

"Well, there's a temptation if ever I saw it! Aren't you worried about it being stolen?"

"Why would it be? The trunk cannot be opened for another thirty years!"

"There's nothing to stop someone stealing it and opening the trunk, Mr Manners."

"It has been said that the key is cursed, and that anyone who touches it before the first hour of 1962 will suffer a terrible fate. I can't say that I care much for curses myself, but it has certainly kept any sticky fingers at bay for the last twenty years."

He led them over to a glass case situated beside the portrait.

"Here we see a ceremonial mask that Sir Morris took from a tribe in what is now the Southern Nigeria Protectorate. He first journeyed to Africa in 1841, and it was—"

"A very nice mask. What are those things next to it?"

"Oh, those are some bronze sculptures he took at the same time."

"Took?"

"Yes, for safekeeping. And in this neighbouring cabinet is a spear and shield from somewhere on the Malay Peninsula."

"He took those as well?"

"Yes, as a personal reward after a skirmish with the natives. If you know your history you will know that Singapore came into British possession in 1824, and—"

"Those things over there look Egyptian."

"That's because they are. Those are artefacts taken from various Egyptian tombs."

"Don't the Egyptians need those things for the afterlife?" asked Pemberley.

Barnaby Manners gave a wry laugh. "The ancient Egyptians believed so, yes. That's why they buried all those items with their dead. But we know that there's no truth in it."

"How do we know that it's not true?" she probed.

"Because we don't have that sort of thing in Christianity."

"But what if we're somehow mistaken? If these things are needed in the afterlife, keeping them inside a glass case in Compton Poppleford must be quite an inconvenience."

Mr Manners forced a smile. "They were donated to the museum, Miss Pemberley. They can hardly be returned to a tomb in the middle of the Egyptian desert."

"Well, I really think they should be!"

"Quite impossible. It was only right that Sir Morris brought them here for safekeeping. They'd only have been stolen by someone else if he hadn't."

"Two wrongs don't make a right," said Pemberley.

"If it wasn't for Sir Morris we would have no idea what these wonderful treasures even looked like."

"We could have looked them up in books," she replied.

"Only those whom Mrs Higginbath permitted to have a reading ticket could," said Churchill bitterly.

"Would you like to see some lovely watercolours of Compton Poppleford painted by a local artist?" asked Mr Manners.

"And then we're finished?" asked Churchill hopefully.

"The artist is really quite accomplished," he continued, leading them over to a set of artworks on the wall.

"Very nice indeed," said Churchill, "though I'm more of an oils person myself. I wonder if I could ask you about Darcy Sprockett, Mr Manners."

"Oh look, it's the field!" exclaimed Pemberley.

"Must you interrupt just as I'm finally getting to the purpose of our visit?" Churchill complained.

"Look!" Pemberley pointed to one of the watercolours, where land and sky were depicted in watery streaks of green and blue.

"That one is titled *Todley Fields Looking East*," said Mr Manners. "It was painted about twenty-five years ago by one of our best-known local artists, Mr Bertrand Hustings. He was born in—"

"Just a moment," interrupted Churchill. "Did you say Todley Fields?"

"Yes."

"That's the field where Darcy Sprockett's skeleton was found," said Churchill. "But why does it look so different?"

"Because it used to be divided into a number of fields," replied Pemberley. "Farmer Jagford cut down the hedges when he got a tractor so it would be easier to drive about in it."

"I see."

"A track used to run between the fields," said Mr Manners. "It was a quick way of getting from the piggery to the hay barns."

"One must always get from the piggery to the hay barns as quickly as possible," said Churchill.

"Why?"

"Don't worry, Mr Manners, I was having a little joke with you. In summary, then, Todley Field was once a number of fields until Farmer Jagford bought a tractor and made it into one big field."

"Yes, and he did it just last year," said Mr Manners.

"Interesting. Did you ever use the track across the fields, Mr Manners?"

"Oh yes, everyone did. Especially if they needed to take a shortcut to the piggery or the hay barn."

"Do you know whether Darcy Sprockett used the track?"

"Yes, everyone did."

"She was a sweetheart of yours, wasn't she?"

Mr Manners adjusted his bow tie. "I was led to believe that she was fond of me."

"Did she tell you that herself?"

"Not in so many words, no."

"In any words at all?"

"No words, actually, no. But apparently she told a friend and the news found its way to me."

"And did you act on this news?"

"I popped by the Sprockett cottage a few times."

"To what end?"

"To make conversation with her brothers, but I was really there to see Darcy."

"Were you fond of her?"

"Not quite so fond of her as she was of me, but moderately fond, yes."

"You must have been more than moderately fond if you decided to visit her."

"Well, there wasn't a great deal else to do in those days. After a bit of trout fishing and a game of cricket the only other thing to do was make eyes at a girl."

"This is the problem when one grows up in a rural area," said Churchill with a sigh. "It must stunt the minds of the youth."

"I played the trumpet, too. In fact, I took it with me to play Darcy a little something."

"Oh dear, really?"

"Yes. She was a little upset after a disagreement with that old sea dog, Pentwhistle. I was a good trumpet player, Mrs Churchill. I'm a little rusty these days, but back then I was quite decent. I played in the Compton Poppleford Roaming Cavaliers' Youth Brass Band, you know."

"Roaming Cavaliers?"

"That bit of the name didn't mean anything, but it sounds good, don't you think?"

"Which song did you inflict on poor young Darcy Sprockett that day?"

"'You've Been a Good Old Wagon But You Done Broke Down'."

"That doesn't make grammatical sense."

"It's American."

"That explains it, then."

"You mustn't be rude about American grammar, Mrs Churchill," said Pemberley. "America was my second home for a while."

"I must say that I'd quite like to go to America. I hear they give you very large portions there."

"Of what?"

"Food, of course. What else? Don't you find that food portions in England tend to be terribly measly? I was served such a miniscule sandwich last week it wouldn't have filled the stomach of a shrew."

"I'm concerned that we're straying from the matter at hand, Mrs Churchill."

"So we are, Miss Pemberley. I do apologise. So in summary, Mr Manners, you blasted poor Darcy Sprockett's eardrums with an ungrammatical American tune on your trumpet and then what?"

"Mr Sprockett had some objection about it, so I went home again."

"And what time was that?"

"I can't remember the exact time, but I was back in time for tea."

"Excellent. One must always time one's return home to coincide with the serving of tea. Did you go out again later that evening, Mr Manners?"

"No."

"What did you do?"

"I probably listened to *What a Lark with Tommy Briggins* on the wireless."

"No you didn't."

"Why yes, I did."

"You didn't, because a wireless wouldn't have been commonplace in the home twenty years ago. That was a time when Detective Chief Inspector Churchill and I had to make our own entertainment."

"I must have played on the old trumpet, then."

"You can't remember what you did that evening, can you? That makes me instantly suspicious, Mr Manners."

"Oh no, don't be! It's just that I enjoy Tommy Briggins so much I feel as though he must have been around forever."

"I agree that Tommy Briggins and his larks seem to have been irritating us over the wireless for an interminable length of time, but it can't have been more than ten years."

"Ten years of Tommy Briggins is enough for anybody," added Pemberley.

"What's wrong with Tommy Briggins?" protested Mr Manners.

"If you require a quick answer it would be better to ask what *isn't* wrong with Tommy Briggins," retorted Churchill.

"We've strayed from the topic again," said Pemberley.

"It seems you have a talent for distracting us, Mr Manners," said Churchill. "I wonder if it's a clever ploy – a ruse, if you like – so you can avoid explaining to us what you were really doing on the night that Darcy Sprockett went missing."

Chapter 16

"WHAT'S your view on that village bore, Manners?" Churchill asked Pemberley as they walked along the high street back to the office.

"He has poor taste in bow ties."

"Is he a murderer?"

"I suppose he could be. There's no doubt that he enjoyed making eyes at Darcy Sprockett."

"Rather evasive about his whereabouts that evening, wasn't he?"

"Either he was being evasive or he genuinely couldn't remember. It was twenty years ago, after all."

"The shock of her disappearance would have been enough to chisel the events from around that time into his mind. Convenient memory loss doesn't wash with me."

As she finished speaking Churchill noticed a familiar figure on the high street ahead of them.

"I'd recognise those plus fours and that pith helmet anywhere, Pembers. But who's that with him?"

"It's not Mrs Colthrop, that's for sure."

A lady in a floral skirt, pink jacket and summer hat was

holding Mr Colthrop's arm as the couple walked along the cobbled street ahead of them.

"How brazen!" Churchill exclaimed. "Can you believe it, Pemberley? He's parading along the busiest street in Compton Poppleford with his fancy lady. He cares not a jot!"

"At least we've caught him in the act now."

"We certainly have." Churchill felt a grin spread across her face. "Now, we mustn't lose sight of them. Dash over to the office and fetch the camera, Pemberley, then get back here as quickly as you can."

Churchill cautiously followed the couple along the high street, pausing to peer into shop windows whenever she drew too close. It wasn't long before Pemberley returned with the box camera.

"Take some photographs of them, Pembers."

"They're too far away."

"Get a little closer, then."

"They'll see me!"

"They've got their backs to us."

"They might turn around!"

"Just take some photographs! We need evidence!"

Pemberley trotted after the retreating forms of Mr Colthrop and his companion, then stopped to fidget with the camera. Churchill felt a snap of irritation as she watched her assistant wasting valuable time. She scampered after her.

"What are you doing?" she hissed.

"I had to wind it."

"They've turned the corner now. Come on, let's catch up with them again!"

The two ladies trotted around the corner, almost bumping into Mr Colthrop and his companion, who had stopped outside a cafe.

"And that over there is the path we need to take, Miss Pemberley," said Churchill, suddenly pointing toward a street in the distance. "Oh hello, Mr Colthrop! How are you today?"

"Never been better, Mrs Churchill!"

"Jolly good!"

Churchill nodded to his lady companion before she and Pemberley walked swiftly on by.

"I took a sneaky photograph of them," whispered Pemberley.

"Well done, Pembers," whispered Churchill in reply. "Good work! Let's hide along that little path there and wait for them to pass by."

"But they might go into the cafe."

"They might indeed. Let's just get out of sight, then we can wait and see."

"But we've already got a photograph of them."

"We need more."

"Really?"

"Yes. We need a photograph of them *caught in the act*."

"I thought we already had one."

"Actually *in the act*."

"What act?"

"An act of passion, Pembers. In the photograph you've taken they're merely standing side by side outside a cafe. Mr Colthrop could easily explain it away by saying that their acquaintance is purely platonic. But if we can catch them in an act of—"

"I don't want to catch them in an act of passion."

"I can't say that the thought rests easily in my mind either, but it's one's duty to tackle the unsavoury aspects of this job as well as the savoury."

"Which are the savoury aspects?"

"A good question, but let's discuss it another time. Here's the path I pointed out. Let's hide down there."

They turned down the path.

"Let's pop behind this shrubbery, Pembers, and hopefully we'll see Mr Colthrop and his lady friend as they walk past."

The two ladies hid and waited.

"Did you recognise his companion?" Churchill whispered.

"No, I've never seen her before."

"I must say that she was much older than I'd expected. After Mrs Colthrop's comments about young things in summer dresses I was expecting a young thing in a summer dress."

"She turned out to be an old thing in a summer skirt instead."

"She's certainly mature in years, isn't she? Of a similar age to Mr Colthrop, I'd say. Shush, here they come now."

Churchill peered between the leaves of the shrub and watched Mr Colthrop and his companion stroll by.

"Look at them both," she whispered. "Sharing a joke with not a care in the world. It makes you sick, doesn't it?"

"Does it?"

"Doesn't it?"

"I can't say that my feelings on the matter are quite as strong as yours, Mrs Churchill."

"That's probably because you were never married, Pemberley. All I can think is how I would have felt if Detective Chief Inspector Churchill had carried on like that, and I…" Churchill paused as she felt a lump in her throat.

"You what exactly, Mrs Churchill?"

"It doesn't matter. Come on, let's follow them again. I'll wager they're on their way to the manor."

. . .

Churchill and Pemberley surreptitiously watched as Mr Colthrop and his companion entered Oakley Manor through the front entrance.

"What a nerve that man has, Pemberley. He's invited that woman into his marital home while his wife is away! It's scandalous."

"Oh well, at least we managed to get a photograph of them so we can report back to Mrs Colthrop."

"It's still not enough, Pembers. We need something else to demonstrate how thorough our investigation has been. Perhaps one of us could call at the door about something."

"That wouldn't work at all. He'd realise we've been following him."

"We could come up with an excuse…"

"He would instantly be suspicious. I say that we've done all we can for today, and we need to get back for the door letter man, anyway."

"Oh yes, I'd almost forgotten about him. Oh hark! What's that, Pembers? I hear voices! Do you?"

"I think so."

"Let's get a bit closer to the house."

Churchill crept across the lawn of Oakley Manor, feeling quite sure that the voices were coming from Mr Colthrop's garden. She waved Pemberley over to join her.

"This is our chance!" she whispered.

"How so?"

"The oak trees provide the perfect vantage point."

"But how?"

"Just shin up that oak tree there, Pembers, and take a few photographs."

"I couldn't possibly."

"What do you mean you *couldn't possibly*? This is our

moment! We'll finally have the evidence we need to prove this man's errant ways, and Mrs Colthrop will be highly impressed by our work. Get up that tree now! This opportunity may never present itself again."

"But I'm afraid of heights."

"That's no height at all, Pembers. It's just a little hop up from the ground. Just enough to be able to see over the fence and take a few snaps."

"That's not a hop. It's about ten feet!"

"Not a bit of it, Pembers. I'd say four feet... or maybe six or eight. Ten at the absolute maximum. In fact, I'd take bets on it being nine."

"I'm not climbing nine feet!"

"It's only as high as your head."

"I'm not nine feet tall."

"Well, you are quite tall. I'm surprised you're even afraid of heights when your head is so used to being high up."

"I'm only five foot seven, Mrs Churchill."

"Practically a giantess compared with my diminutive five foot one. Now go ahead and hop up that tree."

"I can't, Mrs Churchill, really I can't. I already feel a rash breaking out." Pemberley pulled up her sleeve. "Look, can you see it there on my arm?"

"But you have to climb the tree, Pembers. I couldn't possibly do it, as I need to get back to the office in time for the door letter man. This really is our only chance to prove that Mr Colthrop is up to no good."

"Why don't *you* go up the tree while *I* meet the door letter man?"

"Me up a tree? Don't be ridiculous!"

"I thought you were practically arboreal when you were a girl."

"I was."

"But you've since lost the ability, I suppose."

"Lost it? I haven't *lost* it. I haven't lost anything at all. I'm still perfectly capable of climbing trees, thank you very much."

"But you don't want to climb this one?"

"I would happily climb this one, Pembers, but I have to go and meet the door letter man."

"As I said before, I can meet the door letter man while you climb the tree. After all, you did say that this may be the only chance we have to obtain concrete evidence of Mr Colthrop's secret liaison. Our only opportunity."

"You're right. Fine! Give me that camera, then. You go and meet the door letter man quick smart and I'll nip up this tree. It won't take me a minute, and afterwards I'll come and give the door letter man my twopenn'orth."

Churchill thought back to her childhood as she looped her handbag over one arm and the camera around her neck before tackling the trunk of the oak tree. The thick, woody knots provided useful footholds and the large sturdy branches above her head were easy to grasp.

She was just beginning to consider tree climbing a doddle when the strap of the camera got caught around a branch.

"Oh, bother!" she muttered, descending slightly to release the strap and then resuming her climb again.

The creak of a branch as it bent beneath her weight worried her a little, so she felt greatly reassured once she had managed to squeeze herself into a large V-shape between an upright branch and the tree trunk.

Churchill rested for a moment to recover her breath, then realised that she wasn't quite high enough to see over the Colthrops's fence. Above her, several sturdy branches seemed to provide an easy ascent into the crown of the tree, so she prepared to clamber on before realising that one foot was wedged firmly in the join between the branch and the trunk.

"Oh, bother again!" she muttered as she clung to the trunk and tried to pull her foot free. After several attempts she managed to dislodge her foot but unfortunately it parted ways with her shoe, which tumbled down and landed in the grass beneath her.

Churchill sighed. Having come this far she decided she would have to soldier on with just one shoe. She continued to climb, the bark prickling her foot through her stocking, and soon found herself a few feet higher.

"Good grief!" she heard a man call out. "Is that you, Mrs Churchill?"

She let out an exasperated sigh before turning to look into the Colthrops's manicured garden, where Mr Colthrop and his lady companion were sitting side by side on a wrought-iron bench, each holding a drink.

"Oh! Hello, Mr Colthrop!" she shouted as breezily as possible. "I didn't know this was your house."

"What on earth are you doing up in that tree?"

"Looking for birds' eggs to photograph."

"Really? Most birds have fledged by this time of year, you see. Which type in particular?"

"A… erm… A sparrow."

"Which type? House or tree?"

"Tree, I suppose. Given that I'm up in a tree!"

Mr Colthrop gave a hearty laugh. "Well, good luck with that. You're providing us with some super entertainment. We can just sit here and watch you!"

"Oh, there's no need for that. Do return to your conversation."

"We'd far sooner watch you. You'll need to be a little

higher up to have any hope of finding eggs, but I can't say that I'd recommend climbing any higher. It's not altogether safe, you see."

"Oh, I'm used to climbing trees. I was practically arboreal as a girl."

"No disrespect intended, Mrs Churchill, but I imagine that was some time ago now."

"The body is still willing, Mr Colthrop."

"Is it indeed?" He gave a saucy laugh. "Well, well!"

Churchill felt exceptionally irritated at being spotted by her target and his companion. And with both of them sitting facing her she realised it would not be a convenient time to take a photograph. She hoped the pair would soon forget about her and start talking among themselves once again.

She studied the branches above her head, wondering whether it was worth climbing any higher to keep up the pretence of looking for birds' eggs. The branches above her looked less capable of bearing her weight, and when she looked down she realised the branch she was standing on had started to bend rather precariously. Her knees began to feel weak.

"Are you all right up there, Mrs Churchill? Are you stuck?"

"Stuck?" she replied, focusing on Mr Colthrop again. "No, not at all." She forced a smile, her hands glued to the branch she was leaning against.

"Are you sure?"

"Perfectly sure, thank you. Do carry on with the rest of your afternoon."

A few minutes passed as Mr Colthrop and his lady friend chatted, and Churchill wondered how she was ever going to get herself out of the tree. She felt rather surprised that she had managed to climb so high in the first place. Whenever she looked down, her head began to spin.

"Found any nests yet, Mrs Churchill?" Mr Colthrop called out after a few minutes had elapsed.

"One or two!"

"Jolly good. We're adjourning indoors now." He rose up from the bench. "If you need our assistance at all just holler."

"Thank you, Mr Colthrop, but there really is no need for assistance of any sort whatsoever."

As Mr Colthrop and his lady guest turned their backs on her, Churchill realised this was her only chance to take a photograph of them. The camera around her neck was well supported by her bosom, so she manoeuvred her chest to face Mr Colthrop, tentatively removed one hand from the branch she was leaning against and managed to depress the shutter button.

"Aha! Gotcha!" she said to herself proudly as Mr Colthrop and his companion stepped back inside the house. "Just wait until Mrs Colthrop sees this!" she enthused.

Then she made the mistake of looking down again, which caused her to clutch the branch even tighter than before. Churchill knew she needed to follow the same route she had used to get up there, but which route was it? Everything looked so different from high up.

She clung to the branch for dear life and tried to muster enough courage to look at the branches beneath her in order to find her way down. As she finally managed to figure it out she saw the face of a small boy staring up at her.

"Haven't you got a home to go to, little fellow?" she asked impatiently.

He raised his hand and pointed up at her. "Look at this fat lady in the tree!" he yelled.

Within moments he was joined by several other boys.

Churchill did not appreciate this uninvited crowd of undersized onlookers.

"Where are your mothers and fathers?" she asked.

"'Ow'd you get up there?" questioned one of the boys.

"Never you mind. Go back to your homes!"

"Are yer stuck?"

"No. Go away!"

"Is this your shoe?"

"Yes! Put it down!"

A peal of boyish laughter rang out as an acorn bounced off her stomach. The boys began to gather as many acorns as they could find from beneath the tree and hurl them at Churchill. Before long she was being pelted from head to toe.

"Stop that now or I shall telephone the police!" she shouted. She glanced toward Mr Colthrop's home, hoping for the first time that he would reappear and help her, but there was no sign of him.

"'Ow you gonna call the police when yer stuck up a tree?" laughed one of the boys.

"I shall remember each and every one of your faces and will be speaking to your mothers!" she scolded, an acorn hitting her on the nose as she did so.

For the first time in a very long while, Churchill felt like crying. She was well and truly stuck in the tree, she had lost a shoe and there was no sign from the boys that they intended to put an end to their game. She felt completely helpless and put-upon.

Just as it was beginning to feel as though her luck would never change, it did.

"Oi!" came a manly shout.

The boys scampered off in different directions and Churchill breathed a large sigh of relief. With her taunters gone, all she had left to do was work out how to get down.

"Mrs Churchill?" came a voice from below.

She looked down to see the bushy-whiskered face of Inspector Mappin.

"Do you need some help?" he asked.

Her first thought was to refuse. The last person she wanted to accept assistance from was Inspector Mappin. But she realised that any further stubbornness would simply prolong her unhappy predicament.

"Yes please," she sniffed. "Thank you, Inspector."

Chapter 17

"I WASN'T EXPECTING to see you in the *Compton Poppleford Gazette* this morning, Mrs Churchill," said Pemberley as she arrived at the office the following day.

Churchill groaned. "I vaguely recall someone taking photographs now," she said glumly.

"'Inspector and Farmer in Heroic Tree Rescue'," Pemberley read from the newspaper in her hand. "'Two local heroes helped a damsel in distress yesterday when an elderly widow became stuck in the oak tree on Mucklebun Lane. Mrs Annabel Churchill had climbed into the tree to photograph birds' eggs when she found that she was unable to climb down again. "She was stuck in the tree that overlooks our garden," said Mr Peregrine Colthrop, a retired banker. "She was looking a tad wobbly, you see, so my sister and I repeatedly asked whether she wanted our help. She declined because she didn't want to make a fuss. It was all a bit silly, if you ask me."'"

"His *sister*?" queried Churchill.

"'Inspector Mappin discovered the hapless lady after stumbling upon a crowd of boys gathered around the base of the tree,'" continued Pemberley. "''First of all I thought they were throwing acorns at a cat," he said, "but then I realised it was Mrs Churchill. I considered it rather foolish for a lady of her advanced years to attempt to climb a tree, but to her credit she had managed to reach a fair height. I'm not sure how many photographs she managed to take, though!'''"

"Pffft!" said Churchill.

"'An attempt was made to rescue Mrs Churchill using a ladder, but its rungs were considered unreliable. Farmer Spicklehall subsequently offered the use of his cattle sling free of charge, and Mrs Churchill was successfully hoisted down from the tree in no time at all. The elderly lady was too distressed by the incident to provide any comment for our reporter.'"

"Yes, I can vouch for the fact that I had no interest in speaking to that slimy Smithy Miggins as I was being helped out of the cattle sling."

"'Mrs Churchill was, however, coherent enough to thank the inspector and farmer wholeheartedly for their heroic efforts. Inspector Mappin asked this newspaper to remind villagers not to go climbing trees unless it was "absolutely essential" and warned that "those of a certain age and build should not consider it at all".'"

"He truly is a fount of wisdom, that inspector, isn't he?" scoffed Churchill. "And quite the sanctimonious b——"

"But he did rescue you from the tree," interrupted Pemberley.

"Making sure he got a good pat on the back for doing so."

"Here's the photograph of you being hoisted down in the cattle sling."

"I really don't need to see it, thank you. Just being there

was enough. Now, what happened with the door letter man?"

"He didn't turn up."

"That explains why it still says *Church Hills Detective Agency* on the door, then. Completely hopeless. Has he been in contact to explain why he didn't put in an appearance?"

"He put a note through the door explaining that he'd had to make an emergency sign."

"What nonsense! How can anyone require a sign in an emergency situation?"

"When there are sheep in the road, perhaps?"

"You'd already know all about it if there were sheep in the road, Pembers. They'd stand out more than any sign."

The two ladies heard the door open downstairs and then footsteps sounded on the staircase.

"Oh no," groaned Churchill. "If that's Inspector Mappin here to berate me about trees, I shall... Oh! Good morning, Mrs Colthrop."

The lady's mouth was clenched into a tight, thin line and she remained standing, her shiny handbag clutched firmly in both hands.

"I assume you've seen the newspaper this morning, Mrs Churchill."

"I haven't. What of it?"

"How can you not have seen it? It's right there on your secretary's desk," she replied, pointing at Pemberley.

"Oh, *that* newspaper. I don't consider the *Compton Poppleford Gazette* an actual newspaper, you see. It's merely a selection of ill-informed gossip and tittle-tattle with no real news to speak of. In fact it's not even fit for wiping one's—"

"My brother edits that newspaper, Mrs Churchill."

Churchill felt her toes curl. "Mr Trollope? Interesting chap, isn't he? Do take a seat, Mrs Colthrop. I can only apologise for the clutter on my desk. Let me just move *Wuthering Heights* out of the way. There we go."

Mrs Colthrop gave her a withering stare as she sat down. "When I asked you to conduct surveillance on my husband, Mrs Churchill, I expected you to do so in a manner that would draw minimal attention to yourself. The whole idea was to do it secretly so that nobody knew you were doing it. I had foolishly assumed that, being a private detective as you purport to be, you would have known that."

"I know full well how to conduct surveillance, Mrs Colthrop. To date my work has been conducted in a highly professional manner at all times, with only one minor slip-up yesterday afternoon."

"You ended up stuck in a tree while spying on my husband, and the whole sorry episode has been plastered all over the front page of this morning's newspaper!"

"I agree that it was a sorry episode, Mrs Colthrop, and allow me to assure you that no one could be more remorseful than I am about it this morning. However, despite the unnecessary publicity surrounding my plight, I must state that your husband still harbours no suspicion that I have been surveilling him. He merely believes that I was photographing birds' eggs. That's what everyone believes, in fact, other than us three in the know. So there really isn't a problem here at all; just a minor embarrassment on my part. I will no doubt enjoy a good ribbing for the next day or two, and then everyone will forget about it and find themselves distracted by something else."

"I wouldn't be so sure of that, Mrs Churchill."

"The mental capacity of people in these rural parts is very limited, you know. They can only retain a small amount of information for a short amount of time."

"That's not true!" remonstrated Pemberley.

"Whose side are you on, Miss Pemberley?" retorted Churchill.

"Yours, of course, but not if you're going to say such beastly things about Compton Poppleforders."

"I apologise, in that case, but I'm sure you both see my point. Yesterday's little embarrassment will soon be silted over by the sands of time."

"That seems rather unlikely, Mrs Churchill. And what of my husband?"

"What of him?"

"He'll soon realise that you're spying on him if he hasn't realised already."

"He hasn't a clue, Mrs Colthrop, really he hasn't. He's completely clueless, in fact."

"I beg your pardon! That's my husband you're talking about."

"I apologise once again, Mrs Colthrop. There's no denying that my feelings have been rather bruised since the incident with the cattle sling, and perhaps I'm being a little blunt with my words. Do you wish me to continue with my surveillance of your husband?"

Mrs Colthrop's mouth puckered as she thought about this. "Well, I suppose he hasn't mentioned that he has any inkling you're following him."

"Jolly good."

"So I suppose you could continue with your work."

"Marvellous."

"But there must be no repeat of yesterday's incident, you understand."

"Do you think I have any appetite for being hoisted out of a tree again while having my photograph taken by the local rag?"

"No, of course not."

"You have my word, Mrs Colthrop. It would help if

you could inform me when Mr Colthrop's sister is visiting in future. I only climbed that tree in the first place because I saw the unaccompanied lady visiting his home with him and feared the worst."

"I understand. He has six sisters, all of whom visit him fairly often."

Churchill sighed. "Perhaps you could provide me with photographs of all six so I can work out who is a sister and who is not, Mrs Colthrop. I'm sure you are able to see how terribly confusing even the simplest of investigations can become."

Chapter 18

"I shall require extra cake today, Pembers," said Churchill once Mrs Colthrop had departed.

"We've already eaten the jam tarts and it's not even ten o'clock yet."

"They didn't quite hit the spot, did they? Oh no! I think I hear another visitor on the stairs."

A moment later Inspector Mappin poked his brown-whiskered face around the door.

Churchill felt a snap of irritation. "Inspector, if you so much as whisper the word '*tree*', even *once*, I shall personally escort you from the premises!"

"I have no intention of doing so." He raised his hands in a defensive manner.

"What do you want, then?"

"Erm, a little negotiation if possible." He removed his hat and placed it on the hatstand.

"In what regard?"

He took a seat opposite Churchill. "Well, I thought that perhaps seeing as I'd done you a favour you might return one for me."

"Which favour?"

"Rescuing you from the... Oh, erm. When you got stuck."

"In the tree?"

"Yes. I didn't want to say that word because——"

"I know, Inspector."

"I chased those little boys away, didn't I? The ones who were throwing acorns at you."

"You had acorns thrown at you, Mrs Churchill?" Pemberley cried out. "Oh, how horrid! How I hate little boys!"

"Yes. Thank you kindly for chasing them away, Inspector."

"And then I tried the ladder, but that didn't work because of the weak rungs and so on, and then there was the cattle sling——"

"I have no wish to be reminded of that again, Inspector. It's bad enough that it's all over the *Compton Poppleford Gazette* this morning."

"Ah yes, that is rather unfortunate. News reporters, eh? Can't live with 'em, can't live without 'em. Tsk."

"What do you actually *want*?"

"Well, I thought you might like to see your way to repaying the favour by sharing Atkins's case file with me. The file on Darcy Sprockett, that is."

"Oh, I see. This has been your plan all along, has it?"

"I don't know what you mean."

"You waited for an opportunity to be my knight in shining armour so you could demand the case file in return. I'm afraid it doesn't work like that, Inspector."

"He did rescue you, Mrs Churchill!" protested Pemberley. "If he hadn't arrived you'd still be up that tree now."

"Nonsense! I would have found my way down eventually."

"I wasn't waiting around to rescue you, Mrs Churchill," said the Inspector. "I was merely on my way home after clocking off."

"The moment you saw that I was in trouble you couldn't wait to help me out, could you?"

"Now, that's not strictly true."

"You rushed to my aid without further ado, ensuring that I got down from that tree swiftly and safely."

"Not at all. I was merely carrying out my civic duties. When I saw those boys throwing acorns at the tree I had no idea you were their intended target. I never imagined I would end up rescuing you from anywhere; the thought couldn't have been further from my mind."

"You said the word '*tree*', Inspector."

"Did I? I don't think I did."

"You did. You said, 'I saw those boys throwing acorns at the *tree*'."

"Oh yes, I suppose I did. Well, it's almost unavoidable when you consider the circumstances we found ourselves in yesterday."

"What did I say I'd do if you mentioned the word '*tree*'?"

"Oh, let him borrow the case file, Mrs Churchill!" Pemberley beseeched her. "I've always been a firm believer in one good deed begetting another."

"Really, Miss Pemberley?"

"Yes. Just give it to him, there'll be no harm done. It's not as if we've made much progress with the case, anyway."

"Haven't you?" asked Inspector Mappin.

"Shush, Miss Pemberley! Our progress on the case is strictly confidential."

"Even if you haven't made much progress, I must say

that your incident board looks quite impressive," said Inspector Mappin.

"Oh, thank you. We pride ourselves on our incident board, don't we, Miss Pemberley?"

"It's very good indeed," added the inspector.

"Well, thank you for saying so." Churchill gave a sigh. "I suppose I'm in no mood for arguing today, and I can't see what harm there might be in you borrowing the case file. I suppose it would be suitable recompense for your assistance yesterday. I expect it to be returned swiftly, Inspector, and I'll tell you now that there isn't much in it that will be of any great help, which is probably why the case has remained unsolved until now."

Churchill picked up her handbag as soon as the inspector had left. "Right, Pembers. Now that Mappin's got the case file we'd better get on with things, quick smart. Where does Timothy Pentwhistle live?"

"Let's consult the notes we made from the post office directory." Pemberley leafed through some papers on her desk. "Here we are. Apparently, he lives in Marigold Cottage on Hibiscus Lane."

"How very floral." Churchill got up and put on her hat. "Let's go."

"I thought you wanted more cake."

"You won't often hear me say this, Pembers, but the cake can wait."

Chapter 19

"Where is Hibiscus Lane, exactly?" asked Churchill as she and Pemberley strode down the high street.

"We turn left just after the library."

"Jolly good."

"Then left again."

"I see."

"Then another left, then right. And then up past the old bell foundry. Do you know where that is?"

"I don't think I do, Pembers. There's no need for such a detailed account. So long as you know where you're going I shall gladly follow."

"That's probably easier, otherwise I'd have to explain that it's right after the bell foundry and then——"

"No need to explain any further. I wholeheartedly delegate navigation to you, my unfailing adjutant."

They had just passed the library when they heard a shout from behind them. The two ladies turned to see Mrs Higginbath glaring at them, hands on hips.

"There's no such person as Mr Slatherington!" she fumed.

"Try telling that to Mr Slatherington," replied Churchill.

"I telephoned the county library in Dorchester, and Mrs Axbert had never heard of him."

Churchill gave a laugh. "Well of course she hadn't!"

"She certainly should have. She's the chief librarian at the county library!"

Churchill continued to laugh. "I realise that, but Mrs Axbert is small fry compared with Mr Slatherington. He hasn't the time to acquaint himself with little chief librarians at all the county libraries, has he, Miss Pemberley?"

"He certainly hasn't."

Mrs Higginbath folded her arms. "I can't help but think that you're both bluffing."

"Do we look like we have either the time or the inclination to go around inventing district librarians, Mrs H?"

"Yes."

"Well, I think Mr Slatherington and his superior, Sir Waffleton-Jones, would be interested to hear that, wouldn't they, Miss Pemberley?"

"Sir Waffleton-Jones?"

"Yes. We know him well, too, don't we?"

"Absolutely," replied Pemberley. "He enjoyed a distinguished career with the Royal Dorset Militia Artillery and was raised to the baronetage in 1917."

"He thoroughly deserved to be raised to the baronetage. Do you know any barons, Mrs Higginbath?"

The square-faced woman curled her lip.

"A revered philanthropist," continued Pemberley, "he donated a substantial amount of land to Heythrop Itching parish for the founding of Heythrop Itching Cricket Club."

"An extremely generous man," added Churchill, "and I say that as someone who has no interest in cricket whatsoever. I can't say that the crack of willow on leather does much for me."

"Sir Waffleton-Jones is incredibly generous, but he's also known for his quick temper," said Pemberley.

"Oh, yes. One wouldn't want to find oneself on the wrong side of Sir Waffleton-Jones, would one, Miss Pemberley?"

"One certainly wouldn't."

"Oh look, Mrs H has disappeared, Pembers."

The library door slammed shut.

"Do you think she believed us?" asked Churchill.

"I don't think she knows what to believe."

"Good, well that's sorted Mrs Higginbath out for the time being."

They turned down a lane to their left and continued on their way.

"So we're off to see the salty old sea dog now, Pembers."

"You're not going to call him that to his face, are you?"

"Would he not like it?"

"Of course he wouldn't!"

"I'm joking, Pemberley, I knew he wouldn't like it. Don't worry, I know how to be tactful."

"Besides, he's not particularly old. He's probably only about forty-two."

Sweet-scented honeysuckle clambered up the stone wall to their right and a delivery boy on a bicycle bade the two ladies good morning.

"Quite a pleasant place, Compton Poppleford, isn't it?" said Churchill.

"What makes you say that all of a sudden?"

"Oh, I don't know. Just the twittering of happy birds,

and the colourful flowers, and the sunshine, and the little white cottages straining beneath the weight of their thatched roofs, and a little silver tabby cat eying us from atop a postbox and the distant chime of a church bell. It's all so peaceful, and yet terribly civilised, too."

"Do you prefer it to London now?"

"Oh, it's impossible to compare the two places, Pembers. They're about as alike as chalk and cheese."

"As apples and oranges."

"As night and day."

"Here's Hibiscus Lane," said Pemberley. "Mr Pentwhistle lives down here."

"Aha! Midships astern!"

"Goodness, you startled me, Mrs Churchill! There was no need to say '*Aha!*' quite so loudly!"

"Isn't that what seafaring folk say?"

"I don't know."

"Aha! Starboard of the fo'c'sle!"

"Why are you talking like a pirate, Mrs Churchill?"

"I'm talking like a sailor. I can't help myself; I think there must be some brine in my blood. I feel quite sure that a great ancestor of mine had a maritime connection."

"A pirate, perhaps?"

"No, of course not! A senior naval captain who won a number of sea battles, I shouldn't wonder."

"Lord Nelson?"

"I like to think so, Pembers. Aha! Fore and aft! Climb the rigging and scrub the deck! Lock the cabin boy in the hold!"

"That's not very nice."

"It's just a nautical saying, Pemberley."

"Are you sure?" came a voice.

"Who said that?" asked Churchill, spinning around

and quickly deducing that the sound had come from the other side of the stone wall.

"I did," replied a man's voice.

She peered over the wall to see him standing in a little front garden surrounded by coils of rope. He was of an upright bearing with a broad moustache and neatly trimmed whiskers, which were flecked with grey.

"Hello, Mr Pentwhistle," said Pemberley.

"Yes, hello," said Churchill, her face reddening. "I was just having a little joke around with some seafaring phrases. I didn't intend for you to overhear."

"I can't say that I've ever locked a cabin boy in the hold," he said.

"I'm pleased to hear it. What a lot of rope."

"I'm just checking my lines. I'll be back at sea once this leg is fixed."

"We're quite fortunate to find that you're on land at present."

"Really? You're Mrs Churchill, aren't you? The lady who got stuck in the tree?"

"Oh, that! I wasn't stuck, as such. It was just taking me a while to find my way down again."

"It's just as well you weren't stuck up a mast in a fifty-foot swell!"

"Yes, I'd say that was indeed rather fortunate."

"There's one particular occasion that sticks in my mind when I was nearing Cape Horn, already scudding under bare poles—"

"Much as I would love to hear your tales of the sea, Mr Pentwhistle, perhaps we could save them for another time."

"Of course. When might that be?"

"When we've solved this case."

"Which case?"

"My secretary and I are investigating the sad and mysterious disappearance of Miss Darcy Sprockett."

"Oh yes. They found her skeleton in a field, didn't they?" He paused for a moment to pick up the end of a rope. "I'd always hoped Darcy would turn up again. I didn't want to believe that anything awful had happened to her."

"What did you want to believe?"

"I hoped she'd run away, but I suppose a dark and stormy night was not the night to do it if she'd wanted to. And she didn't take anything with her."

"What do you recall with regard to Darcy's disappearance twenty years ago?"

"I remember very little about it, I'm afraid. I've sailed around the globe by way of the Three Capes twelve times since then."

"But you must remember something. Darcy Sprockett was your sweetheart, was she not?"

He gave a shrug. "Not exactly, though I was informed that she was fond of me."

"Did she tell you that herself?"

"No, I heard it from other people. You know how it is. I was told that a few of the village girls were fond of me, truth be told. I didn't mind Darcy, though. I'd promised her we would sail away together one day. I sometimes wonder whether she went to Weymouth and waited for me there."

"Did you ever go to Weymouth to look for her?"

"I did, but she wasn't there."

"Maybe while she was waiting there she received an offer to sail away with someone else instead," suggested Pemberley.

"Another possibility," said Churchill, "but unfortunately, given that her skeleton has been found, we now know that Darcy Sprockett did not sail away with anybody."

"She would have loved the sea," said Mr Pentwhistle.

"What's this we've heard about an argument between you and Darcy?" Churchill asked.

"An argument?"

"Darcy Sprockett was practising her scone-throwing at the recreation ground after lunch on the day of her disappearance. Do you recall being present?"

"I remember being at the recreation ground a few times when she was training, so it's entirely possible that I was there on that particular day."

"Witnesses state that you left the recreation ground together and headed in the direction of the Sprockett home. However, you never got that far because you paused at St Dustin's Well."

"Did we?"

"Yes. You were seen arguing with Darcy Sprockett by the well, and then you parted ways and she journeyed on to her home. Where did you go?"

"I've no idea. Maybe I went trout fishing or played cricket. I can't think what else I might have done."

"Then you don't recall the argument beside St Dustin's Well?"

"No."

"Do you recall having any disagreements with Darcy Sprockett?"

"Oh yes, lots."

"What sort of things did you argue about?"

"I thought it was high time that she stopped doing the May Day Fair All Girls' Triathlon because it put her in such a terrible temper when she lost."

"Given that you were seen arguing the day after the May Day Fair All Girls' Triathlon, is it possible that the competition might have been the cause of your argument?"

"It might well have been."

"Because Darcy had been beaten the previous day by Mrs Munion, then known as Miss Agatha Byles."

"She was a beastly girl that Agatha, and poor Darcy would have been in a terrible mood about losing to her. I've no doubt that's what we argued about."

"But do you actually recall that day?"

"No, I can't say that I do. A lot has happened since then."

"You don't recall the argument beside St Dustin's Well at all?"

"I vaguely recall a bit of a to-do there, but I can't be sure whether it was that day or another."

"And after the argument you either went trout fishing or played cricket, but you don't specifically remember which."

"No."

"Because Mrs Munion, formerly Miss Agatha Biles, says that she saw you in the woods that evening."

"What on earth would I have been doing in the woods that evening?"

"I don't know. I don't really know what she was doing there, either. To confuse matters further, the case file I inherited from my predecessor, Mr Atkins, states that you went to the pictures in Dorchester on the evening that Darcy Sprockett went missing."

"Oh. Well that's what I did, then."

"Is your memory sufficiently jogged?"

"No, I can't say that it is. When you've been thrown about in the Southern Ocean as much as I have you find that your memory doesn't serve you as well as it used to."

"But we're talking about quite a significant event here, Mr Pentwhistle: the disappearance of a young woman."

"I agree that it is terribly significant and sad, but I've also seen men swept clean off the deck by waves as tall as a church spire."

"And that makes the loss of Darcy less significant, does it?"

"No, but it means that my mind is accustomed to such tragedies, Mrs Churchill. They don't chime as loudly in my head as they perhaps would to the likes of yourselves."

"Landlubbers, you mean?"

"Yes, if you choose to describe yourselves as such. I apologise if I seem rather unfeeling. It's what the sea does to you, I'm afraid.

"Clearly. So when you promised Darcy you would sail away together you didn't truly mean it?"

"I used to say it to all the girls."

"Did you sail away with any of them in the end?"

"No, I went by myself."

"I see. Well, I think we landlubbers have taken up enough of your time. Thank you for speaking to us, Mr Pentwhistle."

"I'm not sure I've been of much help."

"I'm not sure you have either, but never mind."

"Old salty Pentwhistle was rather off-hand, wasn't he?" said Churchill as they strolled back to the office. "He seems so unbothered by the whole affair that it seems quite suspicious. And I don't know why Mrs Munion would claim he was in the woods that evening when he claims he wasn't. Someone's telling us porky pies. I do remember reading in Atkins's notes that there was no witness to corroborate the fact that Pentwhistle was at the pictures that night."

Chapter 20

PEMBERLEY STRODE into the office the following morning with a scruffy brown dog at her heels.

Churchill looked up from her book. "A stray, flea-bitten mongrel appears to have followed you in, Pembers. Can you please shoo it out?"

Pemberley turned to look at the animal. "That's my pet dog."

"Pet dog? You don't have a pet dog!"

"I do now. Don't you remember me saying how much I wanted a dog?"

"No. I don't remember you saying that at all."

"I've been saying it for months!"

"I'm quite certain I have never once heard you say that you wanted a dog."

"I certainly thought it."

"Clearly."

"So this is Oswald."

"I see. And what breed is he, exactly?"

"He's a Spanish water dog."

"I'm not familiar with that particular variety."

"With a touch of terrier."

"Interesting."

"And a splash of spaniel. That's what Farmer Drumhead told me, anyhow."

"You got Oswald from Farmer Drumhead, did you?"

"Yes."

"Well you can't have him in here."

"Where else can he go?"

"I don't know. Elsewhere. Somewhere far away. Anywhere but here! This is our office, Pemberley; it's no place for a dog. Is he house trained?"

"Yes."

"That's interesting, because he's just produced something unpleasant down by the filing cabinets."

"That's because you're scowling at him, Mrs Churchill! Oswald hates being disapproved of. It upsets him very much."

"I don't disapprove of *him*, per se. I just disapprove of him being in our office. Does he have fleas?"

"Of course not!"

"Then why is he scratching himself?"

"He's nervous! Oswald is a very sensitive dog, you know. If you could see your way to being nice to him, Mrs Churchill, he won't keep indulging his nervous habits."

"We have a great deal of work to do, Pemberley, and Oswald will unavoidably get in our way. He'll be too much of a distraction."

"He can help us."

"Help us? How can a dumb, mangy, four-legged thing possibly help us?"

"He can be a dog detective!"

"Goodness me, Pembers, this is beginning to sound like

something out of a silly little children's story. The only thing dogs are useful for is guarding one's property, and I'm talking about large, fierce dogs, not little scrappy water spaniels or whatever he is."

"Spanish water dog."

"One of those."

"With a touch of terrier and a splash of spaniel."

"I shall need a touch of brandy and a splash of lovage in a moment, Pembers, and it's only nine o'clock. My patience has already been worn tissue thin. Now please remove that dog."

"Can't he just stay for the morning?"

"No."

"Until elevenses?"

"No."

"An hour, then?"

"One hour. In an hour's time he will need to be removed."

"Thank you, Mrs Churchill, I knew you'd come round. Look how happy his little face is now!"

Pemberley picked him up and he licked her nose.

"Are you going to clear up the little gift he left beside the filing cabinets?"

"Yes, of course." She put Oswald down again. "I'll fetch the borax."

"An interesting envelope was pushed through our door this morning."

"Oh? And what was it?" replied Pemberley as she scrubbed the floor.

In the meantime, Oswald trotted over to Churchill's desk and pushed his nose into her wastepaper bin.

"Get your face out of there, little doggy."

"What did you say was in the envelope?"

"I haven't divulged that information yet. I was just

asking Oswald to remove his face from the wastepaper basket. In all fairness, he seems to have listened to me."

The dog seated himself by Churchill's chair and looked up at her with his large brown eyes.

"Well, you know how to charm a lady who just happens to have a plate of custard tarts on her desk, don't you, little fellow?"

"What was in the envelope, Mrs Churchill?"

"Is Oswald allowed a custard tart?"

"No! He's only just had his breakfast. Is he distracting you?"

"No, not at all. He's quite sweet, really, isn't he?"

"What was in the envelope?"

"Oh yes, that. Mrs Colthrop popped it through our letterbox." Churchill picked up the envelope on her desk and opened it. "Behold the six sisters of Mr Peregrine Colthrop." She slid six photographs out of the envelope and arranged them on her desk.

Pemberley got up from the floor and stepped over to examine them.

"Mrs Colthrop has helpfully written their names on each picture," continued Churchill. "We have Caroline, Clarabelle, Christine, Colette, Candace and Cynthia."

Pemberley winced. "Oh no, I don't like Cynthia."

"What's wrong with her?"

"I don't know her at all. It's just the name; it doesn't fit."

"It begins with a 'C' like all the others."

"But it's pronounced differently from all the rest. Oh dear, poor lady. She must have felt like the odd one out when she was growing up."

"At least she had siblings, Pembers."

"I thought you didn't mind being an only child?"

"I didn't mind at all, but we're not talking about me.

Now, from looking at these photographs I'd say that it was Caroline we saw with Mr Colthrop. What do you think? There's something about the teeth, isn't there?"

"There's definitely something about the teeth."

"Let's pin these up on our incident board so we know what his sisters look like. Then we won't be carrying out needless surveillance thinking he's with a lady friend instead."

"Isn't that going to muddle the incident board? We've already got the Sprockett case pinned up there. It could get quite confusing."

"Ah, but we know what we mean, don't we? We may as well get a photograph of Mr Colthrop up there as well, so that when his wife pays her next visit she can see just how much work we're putting into this case."

"He was pictured in the *Compton Poppleford Gazette* recently for winning a dull fishing trophy, if I recall correctly."

"A nice recent photograph for us to use, then. Perfect."

Pemberley surveyed the incident board and sighed. "I suppose we could use some sort of colour coding for the cases. Sprockett could be red and Colthrop could be blue."

"I can always trust you to come up with an intelligent solution, my clever assistant."

"Did you just give Oswald a custard tart?"

"No."

"He's definitely eating something."

"I didn't *give* him a custard tart, but one may have fallen off my desk."

"How?"

"Things get knocked off very easily with these photographs and papers all over the place, not to mention my copy of *Wuthering Heights*. Now, let's make some tea and

146

get on with this incident board. After that, I suppose we should go and see what Mr Colthrop is up to today."

"But we must do it discreetly this time. We'll be in big trouble if he spots us again."

"He won't, Pembers. I'm not called Mrs Annabel *Subtle* Churchill for nothing."

Chapter 21

"Now, where do you think Mr Peregrine Colthrop would choose to hang about on a day like today, Pembers?" Churchill asked as they walked along the cobbled high street with Oswald trotting at their side.

"I suppose he could be on the golf course or strolling beside the river on such a nice sunny day."

"I agree."

"Shall we try the river first? There's a path that leads from there to the golf course."

"That sounds perfect, Pembers."

The two ladies turned off the high street and followed a path that led over a little hump-backed bridge and alongside the river.

A splash startled Churchill, and she gave a loud shriek when she saw Oswald floundering in the water.

"Quick, Pembers, get him out! He's drowning!" Panicked, she glanced around for a branch or rope to haul him out with. "Oh, poor little doggy! And you've only had him for one day!"

"He's just swimming, Mrs Churchill," replied Pemberley with a proud smile.

"He's what? He's… Oh…" Churchill rested a hand on her pounding heart as she watched the dog's happy bobbing head making its way toward a duck. "Oh, he's *swimming*! Isn't he clever, Pembers?"

"Not really. He is part Spanish water dog, after all."

"Well yes, I suppose he is, isn't he? That certainly helps."

The duck flew away and Oswald changed direction to follow a swan.

"Come on, Oswald!" called Pemberley. "We've no time for that today. Out you get!"

She gave a high-pitched whistle that pierced Churchill's eardrums, and the little dog clambered out of the river.

"Clever dog!" chimed Churchill. "Oh, I forgot that they do that," she added as he shook himself, spraying her stockings with water.

The ladies continued their pleasant stroll along the riverside.

"I must say that I haven't particularly warmed to any of our three suspects," commented Churchill. "Mrs Munion is rather brusque, Mr Manners is terribly boring and Mr Pentwhistle is a little imperious. Darcy Sprockett could have done with some nicer friends."

"If she'd had nicer friends she would most likely be still here with us now."

"Indeed she would. It's dreadfully sad. Which of them do you think did it, Pembers? My money's on the sailor. He seems to have conveniently forgotten much of what happened twenty years ago."

"Only because he's seen so much of the world since then."

"Apparently so. But I find it very odd that Mrs Munion

says he was in the woods that night while he seems certain that he wasn't."

"And he told Atkins he went to the pictures, but he has no witness to prove it."

"Either these people genuinely can't remember what they were doing twenty years ago or they've something to hide."

"What were you doing twenty years ago, Mrs Churchill?"

"Twenty years ago? Well, let me see... I was living in Richmond-upon-Thames, of course, and busying myself with the usual social activities that would entail: bridge, lawn tennis, art exhibitions, the theatre... that sort of thing. And actually, I was working myself up into quite a panic."

"Why?"

"Because Detective Chief Inspector Churchill was nearing retirement age and I wasn't quite sure how I would cope with him knocking around the house all day. It's all very civil when they head off for work at the usual time in the morning and return at a set hour in the evening; one can get on with the routine of one's own business then. Now and again he would be out for longer on an important investigation, of course. But when they're suddenly at home, just sitting there and making the front room look untidy with their newspapers, slippers, chewed pencils and the suchlike... You don't mind it so much when it's just the evenings and weekends, but weekdays too? That took a lot of getting accustomed to."

"So what happened when he retired?"

"Exactly what I'd feared. I was so keen for him to do something with his time that I encouraged him to write his memoirs. That kept him out of trouble for a few hours each day, at least."

"Did you ever read them?"

"I tried, but my dear husband never had much of a way with words. To think that he cut his teeth on the Jack the Ripper case and couldn't find a single interesting thing to say about it! He made one of the most terrible, shocking events of late-nineteenth-century London sound about as interesting as a game of cricket."

"Or golf."

"Exactly. Why do men enjoy hitting balls so much?"

"I'm not sure. You like tennis, though, don't you? That's hitting a ball."

"Yes, but you move around a little more with tennis, and it's usually all over in about ten minutes. That's as long as I can last at it, anyway. I've never understood these sports that take several days to reach a conclusion."

"Speaking of which, the golf course is just here. I wonder if Mr Colthrop is among the golfers."

"Now there's an interesting thought."

A hedge separated the golf course from the path beside the river. Churchill and Pemberley peered over it.

"I think I'll need my field glasses for this, Pembers."

Churchill pulled them out of her handbag and spent several minutes trying to focus them.

"I can see a huddle of men over there," said Pemberley, "but I don't think Mr Colthrop is among them."

"Nothing through the field glasses, either. Let's continue on our way."

The two ladies sauntered a little further along the path, regularly checking over the hedge for any sign of Mr Colthrop.

"What about that chap over there?" whispered Pemberley.

"He looks promising." Churchill tried to train her field

glasses on him. "The one in the voluminous pair of plus fours? It has to be him!"

"He certainly has Mr Colthrop's stature."

"He does indeed. Would you like to check using my field glasses?"

"I think I'll just use my normal eyes, thank you. It's him all right, and I think he's with Mr Higginbath."

"Is he any improvement on Mrs Higginbath?"

"No, he's worse."

Churchill peered through her field glasses again and managed to focus them quite well this time.

"Is that the putting green they're standing on? That flat bit at the end where the hole is?"

"Possibly. I don't know anything about golf."

"They've taken the flag out of the hole. Why have they done that?"

"So they can fit the ball inside it?"

"Why have the flag in the first place, then?"

"So they can see where the hole is when they're far away?"

"I see. Strange game, golf," whispered Churchill. "It's extremely important that he doesn't see us here, Pembers. If he sees us watching him Mrs Colthrop will be furious. Even worse, she might not pay us for our time."

"What do we do now, then? It's quite apparent that he's not with a lady friend."

"We'll wait for him to finish his game and see if he goes off to meet her."

"But how long will that take? Golf seems to last all day."

"True," replied Churchill with a sigh. Her stomach gave a rumble. "I'm hoping this is the last hole, but that may just be wishful thinking. I feel as though it's time for elevenses." She peered through her field glasses again.

"They've got a little dog with them. Are dogs allowed on the golf course?"

"I don't know."

Churchill lowered her field glasses and looked down around her feet.

"Where's Oswald?"

"I was beginning to wonder the same thing."

"Oh no, Pembers. That's him on the golf course!"

The two ladies watched as Mr Colthrop tried to shoo the dog away. Oswald picked up his golf ball and began to run back toward Churchill and Pemberley with the ball in his mouth.

"Oh, good grief! How embarrassing, Pembers. Tell him to take it back!"

"Take it back, Oswald!" hissed Pemberley over the hedge. "Take that ball back immediately!"

Oswald ignored her and ran through a gap in the hedge to join them, ball in mouth.

"Now Colthrop's coming this way! Oh help, Pembers, he's going to see us! We can't let him see us!" Churchill looked around for a place to hide. "Do you think it's safe to jump into the river?"

"Probably not."

Mr Colthrop was getting closer.

"Oh, this is bad luck indeed. Just quickly retrieve the ball from Oswald and hurl it over the hedge."

Pemberley did her best, but Oswald refused to let go. He skipped excitedly around the ladies' legs as they tried to catch him.

"Drop the ball!" shrilled Pemberley. "Come on, naughty doggy. The man needs his ball back!"

"He certainly does," added Mr Colthrop, his face appearing over the hedge. He had swapped his pith helmet for a plaid golfing cap. "Well, blow me down if Mrs

Churchill isn't behind this! What ho! Did you train your dog to steal my ball?" He grinned.

"Oh hello, Mr Colthrop. I didn't realise it was your ball, and no I didn't train him to do such a naughty thing. Besides, he's not even mine. We do apologise for ruining your game."

"Shame, really. I was about to finish that hole under par, you see."

"It wasn't going well, then?"

"No, that means it *was* going well. Oh look, the little fellow's in the river with it now."

Churchill turned in dismay to see Oswald swimming across the river with the golf ball still in his mouth.

Chapter 22

"Oh, Miss Pemberley, please do something about that dog! Call him back!"

Pemberley did as she was told but Oswald continued to ignore her. He climbed out onto the opposite riverbank and shook himself dry. The three of them watched as he burrowed into the earth and dropped the ball into the hole he had made.

"Do one of your whistles, Miss Pemberley."

Churchill covered her ears as Pemberley did so, and Oswald jumped straight back into the river once he had finished burying the ball.

Churchill sighed. "It doesn't look as though he intends to bring the ball back. What a naughty doggy. Where's the closest bridge to cross the river?"

"About half a mile away."

"So we need to walk a whole mile to retrieve the golf ball he's just buried on the opposite side? Don't you have a lead for that dog, Miss Pemberley?"

"No."

Oswald climbed out of the river and shook water all over their legs again.

"Perhaps if you had purchased one this whole sorry event could have been avoided."

"I didn't know that it was likely to happen."

Meanwhile, Oswald had scurried through the hedge again and was jumping up at Mr Colthrop, soiling his plus fours.

"It's hard to be cross with a little chap like this, isn't it?" chuckled Mr Colthrop. He bent down to pick the dog up and Oswald began to lick his face enthusiastically. "He's quite a little treasure, isn't he?"

"That's one way to describe him," Churchill said scornfully. "Mr Colthrop, we would be most grateful if you chose not to mention this incident to your wife."

"Why ever not? She'd love to hear about this funny little fellow burying my golf ball in the riverbank."

"I don't think she would. I think she would take rather a dim view of Miss Pemberley's questionable dog-owning skills."

"I'm sure she wouldn't."

"Yes she would. I believe she commented on someone else's dog-owning skills recently and was quite scathing about the woman in question. Miss Pemberley would be extremely upset if the same were to be said about her."

"Really?" Mr Colthrop put Oswald down again. "When did you speak to my wife?"

"We just happened to bump into her the other day, didn't we, Miss Pemberley?"

Her assistant nodded.

"She spoke terribly harshly of this particular person – I forget who it was now – and her inability to control her dog."

"That doesn't sound like my wife."

"Well, please don't mention it to her, anyway. You know how quickly rumours spread in this village."

"Oh, I certainly do. If you don't want me to mention to my wife that our paths crossed today I won't, Mrs Churchill." He grinned again and gave a knowing wink.

"Thank you, Mr Colthrop. Now, please excuse us while we go and retrieve your ball."

"Oh, don't worry about that. I've got spares."

"No, really we must. I insist."

"I won't hear of it. I shall retrieve the buried ball on my way home. I have plenty of time on my hands today. I'm a gentleman of leisure, you see."

"That's very kind of you, Mr Colthrop, and I do apologise for Oswald's behaviour."

"No need to apologise on his behalf. I know he'd say sorry himself if he could."

Churchill gave the dog a disapproving glance. "Actually, I don't think he would. I don't think Oswald has any conscience at all."

"Poor Oswald has been tainted by Mr Colthrop," complained Pemberley as they walked back along the riverbank.

"How so?"

"Oswald licked his face. And now I can't have Oswald licking my face ever again because it will be like Mr Colthrop licking my face."

"It won't at all, Pembers. What nonsense! Mr Colthrop didn't lick Oswald, did he? It was the other way around."

"I don't want to be licked by the same tongue that has licked Mr Colthrop's face."

"Believe me, Pembers, I've seen that dog lick far worse

things than Mr Colthrop's face. Stop worrying about it. What is far more concerning to me is the fact that we've overestimated our surveillance skills. We haven't been able to watch Mr Colthrop even once without him spotting us."

"We would have managed it today if Oswald hadn't ruined everything. All I need to do is buy him a lead and then we'll be fine."

"I hear what you're saying, my worthy assistant, but on previous occasions we didn't have Oswald with us and Mr Colthrop still noticed us. Therefore, I think the manner in which we have conducted our surveillance must be flawed in some way."

"Maybe we should wear disguises."

"That's a good idea in theory, Pemberley, but what could two old ladies like us possibly disguise themselves as?"

"Gypsies?"

"No thank you."

"Laundry women?"

"I'm not sure about that one."

"Nuns?"

"Is there a convent near here?"

"There must be."

"I quite like the idea of nuns."

"Wizened old watercress sellers? Mysterious and wise fortune-tellers?"

"We're heading back into gypsy territory again."

"Nurses?"

"I like that suggestion."

"School mistresses?"

"Good one."

"Ladies of the landed gentry?"

"That's my favourite one of all, Pembers."

"The challenge of a disguise is being able to blend in.

You don't often see ladies of the landed gentry strolling down Compton Poppleford high street. If we were to dress like that there's a possibility that we would merely end up drawing attention to ourselves."

"Which we already manage to do quite well. Did Atkins have disguises?"

"Oh yes, lots. He got his outfits from a good costumier in Dorchester."

"And what were his favourites?"

"He called himself Lord Petherick sometimes and donned a top hat."

"Very good."

"His Lawrence of Arabia costume was pretty decent. He was also adept at playing an army major, chef, cowboy, miner, solicitor, peasant, jockey, industrialist, vicar and a butcher from Yorkshire."

"Our Atkins sounds like quite the master of disguises, Pemberley."

"Oh, he was."

"Indeed. Well, I think you and I should visit that costumier in Dorchester to stock up on a few choice items."

Chapter 23

"I DON'T THINK READING novels is such a good idea after all, Pembers," commented Churchill the following Monday. "They have the propensity to give one such terrible dreams."

"Really, Mrs Churchill?"

"Yes. It's this business in *Wuthering Heights* where Cathy's supposed ghost has been wandering the moors for twenty years and then she's knocking on the window asking to be let in. It made my blood run cold as I read it, and blow me down if I didn't have a dream that the ghost of Darcy Sprockett was knocking on my window during the night! It felt so real I thought it actually *was* real. The thought of Darcy Sprockett wandering around for twenty years and wanting to come in at my window quite terrified me. I didn't sleep a wink for the rest of the night."

"That's what some people around here believe. It's why they call her the White Lady."

"Well, it seems as though I've been living here long enough to have my mind dragged into all these silly superstitions. This is clearly what these rural places do to you. Frightening, it is."

The door slammed downstairs.

"Oh, we have a visitor, Pemberley. Please don't let it be Mrs Colthrop. If she finds out about our latest failed surveillance attempt we're doomed."

There was a polite knock at the door.

"Come in!" sang Churchill.

A tall, dark-haired, bespectacled man cautiously stepped into the room.

"Mr Bingley!" said Churchill with relief. "Do come in."

"I didn't realise your name was spelled Church Hills," he said, removing his hat.

"It's not. That was down to the illiterate door letter man. I can't imagine he's read a book in his entire life. When's he coming to fix the letters, Miss Pemberley?"

"Wednesday week now."

Churchill tutted. "Typical. Anyway, do come and take a seat, Mr Bingley. To what do we owe the pleasure of your visit?"

He perched himself on the chair opposite Churchill and gave her an awkward smile. "I hope I'm not disturbing anything."

"Our door is always open, isn't it, Miss Pemberley?"

"It is indeed."

"I was just telling Miss Pemberley that my novel reading has been giving me bad dreams. Do you find that, Mr Bingley?"

"No, I can't say that I do. Have you been reading something particularly frightening?"

"*Wuthering Heights*."

"Not especially frightening, then. How do you think the theme of betrayal is addressed in the book?"

"I have a great deal to say on that subject, but it's probably best saved for another place and time. I try to concentrate on work while I'm in the office."

"Oh yes, of course. Pardon me. Oh, hello dog."

Oswald sniffed Mr Bingley's trousers, then gave himself a long scratch behind the ear.

"What a charming sextet," commented Mr Bingley, noticing the photographs of the Colthrop sisters up on the incident board.

"Pardon?" Churchill said.

"Sextet. Six people."

"Oh, those are the six sisters of Mr Colthrop."

"I see. Just one more and they'd be the Pleiades!"

He and Miss Pemberley laughed.

"What's that? Another Tolstoy thing?"

The pair laughed even louder.

"I can't see the joke there at all," muttered Churchill.

"Otherwise known as the Seven Sisters," clarified Pemberley. "The Pleiades is a star cluster in the constellation of Taurus."

"How on earth do you know so much about astrology, Miss Pemberley?"

"Astro*nomy*. I learned a little on a transatlantic steamship years ago. There was a keen gentleman astronomer on board, and on cloudless nights we would sit up on the ship's deck together and he would instruct me on the ways of the stars, planets and constellations."

"My mother warned me about men like him."

"What's wrong with astronomers?"

"One has to be suspicious of anyone who spends that much time lurking about in the dark."

"Even with a telescope?"

"*Especially* with a telescope. Tea, Mr Bingley?"

"Oh, thank you. Don't mind if I do."

"Tea for Mr Bingley please, Miss Pemberley."

"Of course."

"What did you come to see us about, Mr Bingley?"

"Firstly, I'd like to apologise for not having been much help when you visited me. I was deeply absorbed in a critique of *The Kreutzer Sonata* when you called round, and it takes me a while to swim back up to the surface, if you see what I mean."

"Not really, but do go on."

"Secondly, I received an interesting visitor."

"That was me, Mr Bingley!"

"Oh, er… I meant another one."

"I knew that was what you meant really. It was just a little joke of mine."

"Oh, right." He gave a gentle laugh. "I didn't immediately spot that one. Where was I? Oh yes, the visitor. It was an elderly lady by the name of Miss Elizabeth Earwold."

"Great-aunt Betsy? But I thought she was dead!"

"No, she is very much alive. She told me she's a hundred and one years old."

"That's wonderful news! Did you know that Great-aunt Betsy was still alive, Miss Pemberley?"

Her secretary placed the tea tray on the desk.

"No, I didn't," she replied. "What a hardy lady she must be."

"She must be as tough as old boots," added Churchill. "What did she have to say for herself?"

"She didn't like the decor in the cottage. I had to invite her in because I didn't think it would be fair to leave a centenarian standing on the doorstep."

"Are you saying that she had a soldier with her?"

"No, *she* is the centenarian. You're probably thinking of a centurion."

"Or a centaur, perhaps."

"Centaurs are mythical creatures."

"Great-aunt Betsy is pretty much a mythical creature herself, I'd say. Fancy her still being alive!"

"As I was saying," continued Mr Bingley, "Miss Earwold didn't like the decor. I told her that I hadn't done anything to the place; it was the lady who lived there before me who had put the gaudy wallpaper up."

"How did Great-aunt Betsy get to your cottage in the middle of the woods?"

"She had a driver. I didn't speak to him at all; he just sat in the car outside."

"How did a motor car even get down that lane?"

"I don't know, I'm afraid. All I know is that an extremely old lady somehow arrived at my door."

"Apart from criticising the decor, what else did she have to say for herself?"

"She was pleased that the cottage had a proper bathroom because she never liked the privy. It was too far for her to walk on a cold, dark night."

"But did she have anything useful to say? Anything about Darcy Sprockett, perhaps? It seems rather a coincidence for the aged aunt to turn up only a week after Darcy's body has been found."

"She did ask who had been sniffing around."

"Sniffing? You didn't tell her Miss Pemberley and I had been sniffing around, did you?"

"I did, actually. You and Inspector Mappin."

"And what did she make of that?"

"She called Inspector Mappin a word I have no wish to repeat in polite company, and when I explained that you'd bought Mr Atkins's business she also called Mr Atkins a rude name. In fact, she used a rather offensive name to describe you as well."

"Me? But she's never even met me!"

"I think she considered you to be part of the same

group of nosey, interfering cockalorums, to use her umbrella term."

"That's what I am, is it? Are you hearing this, Miss Pemberley? We've spent every waking moment trying to find out what happened to her poor great-niece and this is what the woman has to say about us!"

"She's very old," replied Pemberley. "She's reached the age at which she probably considers everyone around her to be an irritant of some sort."

"She was quite pleasant to me," said Mr Bingley.

"Did you hear that, Miss Pemberley? She was *quite pleasant* to Mr Bingley!"

"Yes, I did hear it. I'm only standing four feet away from you, Mrs Churchill. I don't think you should be offended by what Great-aunt Betsy said. She's never met you, as you so rightly point out, and therefore her opinion means nothing. I wouldn't waste another moment worrying about her."

"I don't like it when people form the wrong opinion before they've even met me, Miss Pemberley."

"Well, I'm afraid it can't be helped. Maybe one day she'll meet you and be pleasantly surprised."

"I'm sure she would be. In fact, I'd like to track her down and put her straight on a thing or two. Did she mention where she lives now, Mr Bingley?"

"Walton-on-Thames."

Churchill clapped her hands in surprise. "That's very near my old stomping ground of Richmond-upon-Thames! Very near indeed. I can't fathom them taking to her in Walton-on-Thames, though. Folk from rural provinces are generally regarded with great suspicion in that part of the world. I can't imagine her rustic ways going down well in their large parlours. She probably doesn't receive many invitations to lunch."

"She seemed to be quite a well-mannered lady to me," said Mr Bingley, "aside from the occasional crude word. But that was only because she was so upset about this whole business with her great-niece."

"Understandable," said Pemberley. "She'd probably hoped that Darcy Sprockett would be found safe and well one day."

"She's not alone in that hope," added Churchill, "but the rest of us aren't going about being offensive about people and calling them cockalorums and all the rest of it. Has the aged relative returned to Walton-on-Thames now, Mr Bingley?"

"Yes. I believe she was only visiting for the day."

"Pah! What else did she say?"

"She said that it was all a great shame, and that Darcy should be allowed to rest in peace."

"Did you tell her that we are very keen to find out who attacked her?"

"No, I didn't. I just expressed some general platitudes."

Churchill gave an exasperated sigh. "Doesn't she want to find out who did such an awful thing to her great-niece?"

"Perhaps she's the culprit," suggested Pemberley.

Churchill threw herself back in her chair and gasped. "Goodness, Miss Pemberley! That could explain her reluctant attitude, couldn't it? Yes, that's it! The old crone has no interest in finding out what happened to her great-niece that dark and stormy night because *she* is the guilty party!"

Chapter 24

"Are you sure?" asked Mr Bingley.

"Why else would Great-aunt Betsy be so lackadaisical about the whole affair?" replied Churchill.

"Besides, she was the last person to see Darcy Sprockett alive," said Pemberley.

"Yes, yes, yes! She was indeed! And she was suspiciously quick to blame the goblins too. I wonder how soon after the crime it was that she ran away to Walton-on-Thames."

"She didn't strike me as the murdering type," said Mr Bingley.

"Oh, they never do!" replied Churchill. "If one looked like the murdering type one would be routinely locked up in the police cells as a matter of course. One must look as little like the murdering type as possible, you understand."

"But an old lady murderer?" queried Mr Bingley.

"Old ladies are consistently underestimated," replied Churchill. "No one truly knows what we're capable of."

"But she would have been eighty-one when her great-niece disappeared. You're not trying to tell me that an eighty-one-year-old woman could be capable of something so dreadful, are you?"

"Consistently underestimated, as I say, Mr Bingley."

"What might her motive have been?"

"We may find that out once we're able to understand the inner workings of the strange Sprockett family."

"Maybe she was angry that Darcy broke the eggs," suggested Pemberley. "After all, Great-aunt Betsy had gone to the trouble of filling up the basket for her and then the clumsy great-niece went and dropped it."

"Rather an extreme response to a few broken eggs, isn't it?" said Mr Bingley.

"Did Miss Elizabeth Earworld strike you as someone who might have a short fuse?" Churchill asked.

"No."

"I suppose we also have the conundrum of how an eighty-one-year-old lady managed to carry the deceased Darcy Sprockett three miles to the place where her remains were found," said Pemberley.

"Now that is a puzzle," said Churchill.

"Maybe she persuaded Miss Sprockett to walk the three miles to the field with her," suggested Mr Bingley.

"On a dark and stormy night?" questioned Churchill. "And at eighty-one years of age?"

"How would the elderly aunt have persuaded her great-niece to undertake such a walk?" asked Pemberley.

"It doesn't seem very likely, does it?" said Mr Bingley.

Churchill sighed. "I'd got myself all excited about Miss Earwold being the culprit, but there are rather a lot of holes in this theory."

"Perhaps the aged lady had an accomplice," said Pemberley.

"Someone who scooped Darcy Sprockett up and placed her in Todley Field, you mean?" asked Churchill.

"Yes. I can't really imagine Miss Earwold doing it."

"What do you remember of Miss Earwold, Pemberley?"

"I didn't know her particularly well. Back then she was just one of those people who lived in the woods. There's always something rather odd about someone who chooses to live alone in the depths of the woods, isn't there?"

"What do you mean by that?" asked Mr Bingley indignantly.

"Oh, I do apologise, Mr Bingley!" said Pemberley, suddenly becoming flustered. "Present company excepted, of course. You have an excuse, though, don't you? You're busy writing your doctoral thesis on Tolstoy, and require the peace and quiet of the woods to complete it."

"Well, that was the plan until a couple of elderly ladies began hammering on my door and asking about some poor girl who went missing twenty years ago. I got more peace and quiet in Oxford, to be honest with you."

"It always pays to research the history of a house before deciding to live there," said Churchill. "You never know who might come calling at your door, otherwise."

"Did you research the history of the cottage you're currently renting from Farmer Drumhead before you moved in?" Pemberley asked.

"Now you come to mention it, I didn't."

Pemberley said nothing, but instead gave a visible shudder.

"Does it have a history I should be aware of, Miss Pemberley?"

"Let's not get distracted, Mrs Churchill."

"But I demand to know! I can't live in a place with a history I know nothing about!"

"It's too late now, Mrs Churchill. You're already living there."

"Come to think of it, the rent is rather cheap. Did no one else want to live there? Oh, do tell me, Miss Pemberley. Does it have a tragic history?"

"Now is not the time to discuss it, Mrs Churchill. We must concentrate on what Miss Earwold had to say for herself."

"She sounds like little more than a cranky old bat to me."

"But if she did have something to do with Darcy's disappearance someone must have assisted her," said Pemberley. "We must consider our suspects once again."

"I'm feeling quite bored with them all now," said Churchill. "I thought for a moment that we had a new suspect, and a definite one at that."

"She may have been the culprit," said Mr Bingley, "and perhaps her conscience has been bothering her for the past twenty years with a Raskolnikov-like torment."

"A whatty?"

"Dostoevsky," said Pemberley. "Raskolnikov is the main character in *Crime and Punishment*. He is tormented with regret after committing a murder."

"And so he should be. Anyway, much as I love literature, and particularly *Wuthering Heights* and the like, we mustn't stray from the point. I think what we have now is a situation in which Great-aunt Betsy must have colluded with one of our existing suspects. I've said it before and I'll say it again: I think Pentwhistle is our man. Mrs Munion saw him in the woods that night, and I'd conjecture that he was probably on his way to Mr Bingley's cottage."

"I didn't live there at the time, though."

"Thank you, Mr Bingley. I realise that."

"I just want to make sure that I'm not mistakenly included in this investigation."

"You won't be, please don't worry. You were no doubt

knee-high to a grasshopper twenty years ago. Now, we must look for evidence that the great-aunt and the salty sailor knew each other."

"It's a bit of an odd pairing, isn't it?" commented Pemberley.

"Maybe so, but it needs investigating all the same. I don't suppose Great-aunt Betsy left you any contact details, Mr Bingley? An address or telephone number, perhaps?"

"No."

"Darn it!"

Chapter 25

"Care to join us, Mrs Churchill?" puffed Mrs Munion as she volleyed a tennis ball in the direction of her daughter.

"I'm a little weary today, but thank you all the same."

Oswald gave a little bark as he strained on his lead, desperate to get hold of the ball.

"Down, boy!" instructed Churchill. She turned to face Mrs Munion again. "I don't suppose you have a minute to speak to us, do you?"

"Fire away," she replied. "Thirty-fifteen!"

"What do you know of the sailor, Mr Pentwhistle?"

"He's an upstart!"

"I see. You're quite adamant that you saw him in Poppleford Woods the night that Darcy Sprockett went missing, are you?"

"Yes. Forty-fifteen!"

"I don't suppose you could point to some key locations on a map of Poppleford Woods for us, could you?"

Mrs Munion sighed. "Just let me polish off this game."

Once she had won the game triumphantly, she

marched over to where Churchill and Pemberley were standing on the sidelines.

"Map, you say? What map?"

"Here," replied Pemberley, dropping Oswald's lead and holding out the map for Mrs Munion to look at. "Can you point to your location in Poppleford Woods when you encountered Timothy Pentwhistle that evening?"

"What an odd question," replied Mrs Munion, looking at the map one way up and then the other. "I can't honestly remember."

"Which path would you have taken?" asked Pemberley.

"This one here, which leads on from Mucklebun Lane."

"Can you remember the route you took?"

"Not that night, no."

"Did you often go into the woods for an evening walk?"

"Yes, quite often."

"Which route did you usually take?"

"I recall that it was a circular route, so I probably would have gone along here, up there and down here," she replied, tracing her finger along the map. "Although the weather was coming in that evening, so I may well have taken a shortcut through here."

"And where do you think you might have seen Mr Pentwhistle?"

"Oh, I don't know."

"Was it at the beginning of your walk or toward the end?"

"It wasn't at the beginning. It was probably about halfway through, as it wasn't yet dark and we both commented on how the weather was turning."

"About halfway would place him here," suggested Pemberley, pointing to a location near the centre of the map.

"Yes, that would have been about halfway."

"Assuming you took your usual route."

"I almost certainly would have done. I didn't often take any other route."

"Interesting indeed. Thank you, Mrs Munion," said Pemberley.

"Did you discuss anything else with Mr Pentwhistle that night besides the weather, Mrs Munion?" asked Churchill.

"Not really. He probably congratulated me on my Compton Poppleford May Day Fair All Girls' Triathlon win."

"Did he mention Darcy Sprockett at all?"

"I think he said something about her being disappointed to have come in second place."

"Anything else?"

"Not that I remember."

"How long did your conversation with him last?"

"I don't know. A minute or two, I should think."

"You didn't stop to talk for long, then?"

"No."

"How well did you know him at that time?"

"Quite well. We had all known each other since we'd been old enough to walk. That's just how it is in this village."

"Indeed," replied Churchill. "May I ask where you went after your perambulation in the woods?"

"Back home."

"Can you recall the hour?"

"No, but it was before sundown."

"Thank you for your time, Mrs Munion."

"Why do you ask?"

"Ask what?"

"All these questions."

"Oh, well we spoke to Mr Pentwhistle and he claimed he was at the pictures in Dorchester on the night of Darcy Sprockett's disappearance," Churchill explained. "He claims he didn't go anywhere near the woods at all."

Mrs Munion scowled. "He's lying!"

"He might be, or we could be a little more charitable about him and consider that his memory is simply unreliable. After all, we're talking about events that took place twenty years ago. Anyway, we mustn't keep you from your tennis any longer."

"Right." Mrs Munion paused to consider something for a moment. Then she called over to her daughter as she marched back onto the court. "Come on then, Phyllis! Your serve!"

"I can't, Mother."

"Why not?"

"There are no balls left."

Everyone glanced over at the scruffy dog, who was lying happily at the centre of the court chewing on a tennis ball. The remains of all the others were scattered around him.

"Pembers!" hissed Churchill. "That hound was supposed to be on a lead!"

"He is on a lead, but I had to drop it to show Mrs Munion the map!"

"You should have passed the lead to me."

"Hindsight is such a wonderful thing, Mrs Churchill."

Chapter 26

"Who do you think is fibbing? Mrs Munion or Mr Pentwhistle?" asked Churchill as they walked along the lane from the tennis club back toward the office.

"Well, on the face of it I would say Mr Pentwhistle, because he seemed to have forgotten that he'd told Mr Atkins he went to the pictures on the evening of Darcy Sprockett's disappearance. Mrs Munion, on the other hand, seems to have a more detailed recollection. A little too detailed, perhaps."

"Exactly what I was thinking, my trusty assistant. Mrs Munion was able to recall a spectacular amount of her walk that evening after some very basic prompting on our part, wasn't she? She seemed fairly certain about the route she took and about her conversation with Mr Pentwhistle. A little too certain. I wonder now whether she was simply telling us what she thought we wanted to hear."

"Perhaps my prompting was a little too prescriptive."

"Your prompting was perfect, Pembers. What we're really interested in is the way a suspect responds to such prompts. Mrs Munion seemed keen to speculate, didn't she? She could have been quite honest and told us she had no idea what she and Mr Pentwhistle talked about that night."

"Perhaps she's merely blessed with a good memory."

"Perhaps she is. Or perhaps she colluded with Great-aunt Betsy to make poor Darcy Sprockett disappear."

"And then there's Barnaby Manners, too."

"Yes indeed. We mustn't forget about him, either. I'd like to find out which of the terrible trio was on best terms with Great-aunt Betsy. Who would know?"

"You could ask Great-aunt Betsy that yourself."

"By telephoning her?"

"Yes. We could look in the telephone directory for Surrey at the library."

"Perhaps you could, Pembers. I think it's an excellent idea, but I'm not in the mood for Mrs Higginbath today. Would you mind popping over there by yourself?"

"Not at all."

"Let me take Oswald with me, and we'll see you back at the office. Mrs Higginbath will no doubt cast an evil spell on you if she sees him in the library."

"I shall take this little path to the left, then, as that will bring me out at the bottom of the high street right by the library."

"Very well, Pembers. Good luck with old Higginbath."

The two ladies parted company and Churchill made her way toward the other end of the high street.

Oswald gave a little bark.

"Don't worry, Oswald, you'll see your mummy again soon," Churchill said reassuringly.

He barked again.

"That's enough now."

He gave another bark, at which point Churchill stopped and wagged her finger at him. "Any more of that and you won't get a slice of Battenberg when we get back to the office."

Oswald licked his lips and said nothing further.

"Come on now."

The lane turned sharply to the right, and Churchill had been too busy looking at Oswald to notice anyone coming the other way.

"Oof!" she cried as her bosom squashed up against a man in a pith helmet.

"What ho!" he cried. "Goodness me! Mrs Churchill?"

"Oh dear. I am sorry, Mr Colthrop." She took a couple of steps back, embarrassed to have found herself in such close proximity to him.

"We must stop meeting like this," he said with a wink.

"I didn't see you there at all. I was talking to Oswald, here."

"There he is again, the little rascal!" He stooped down to say hello to the dog, who stood on his hind feet and licked Mr Colthrop's face once again. "You've got him on a lead this time, I see. Very sensible."

Churchill noticed two familiar-looking middle-aged women standing just behind him.

"Let me introduce two of my sisters," Mr Colthrop said, drawing himself up to full height again. "This is Clarabelle and this is Christine."

"I know."

"What?"

"Sorry, I meant *hello*! How lovely to meet you both. Well, Oswald and I must be on our way. Lots of work to do!"

"Indeed. Well, no doubt our paths will cross again soon, Mrs Churchill. They have a tendency to, don't they?"

"Not especially, Mr Colthrop," she said, growing flustered. "I bump into lots of people on a regular basis."

"Do you now? I can't say that I'm surprised after that great knock you just gave me. Perhaps you should look where you're going a little more carefully!"

He laughed as he turned to walk on, and his sisters smiled politely before following in his footsteps.

Churchill had been looking forward to a calming cup of tea and a slice of Battenberg on her return to the office, but instead she found Inspector Mappin seated at her desk.

He immediately rose to his feet. "I've returned the case file, Mrs Churchill."

"Oh, that's kind of you. Thank you, Inspector. Where's Miss Pemberley?"

"She's making me a cup of tea."

"You're a lucky man, then."

"You have a dog now, I see."

"Yes, this is Oswald."

The dog sniffed Inspector Mappin's leg, then began to lick his boot.

"I could do with a dog," he said as Churchill hung up her hat and took a seat behind her desk. "He could chase the criminals for me."

"How often do you have to chase criminals, Inspector Mappin?"

"Oh, once or twice."

"A week? A month?"

"I've done it once or twice."

"Ever?"

"That sounds about right, yes. I must admit that I've been sitting here admiring your incident board. It's rather good, isn't it?"

"We like to think so. Oh, hello, Miss Pemberley. Thank you for the tea."

Pemberley placed the tray on the desk.

"How did you get on with the case file, Inspector?" asked Churchill.

"It was pretty much as I remembered it, really. Baffling case. In truth, your incident board is proving more useful to me than the case file. It maps it all out just so, doesn't it? And the pins and string and photographs and suchlike link it all together rather nicely, don't they?"

"That's the general idea, Inspector Mappin. Don't you have your own incident board?"

"I do, but it's rather scrappy in comparison. I find that I have to keep moving the various elements around."

"But that's exactly what you're supposed to do. It shows that you're deep in thought about the case when you move a photograph here or a pin there, then tut and rearrange it. It's an essential aspect of a detective's work."

"Good to know, I suppose."

"Who's your chief suspect in the Darcy Sprockett case, Inspector?"

"I reckon it was that Bertrand Pockleswathe."

"Who on earth is he? Have we been looking at the same case file?"

"Yes, I should think so."

Churchill pulled the file toward her and hurriedly leafed through it. "Pockleswathe... Which one's he?"

"He was a well-known troublemaker."

"Was he? Did you know that, Miss Pemberley?"

"Oh yes. A terrible trouble-maker."

"And you didn't think to mention him to me?"

"I just assumed you'd read about him in the file."

"What sort of troublemaker was he?"

"A rabble-rouser," replied the inspector. "I felt his collar on many an occasion."

"But that doesn't necessarily mean that he was a murderer."

"He's already been detained for many years at His Majesty's pleasure."

"What was the nature of his crime?"

"He murdered someone."

"Really? Oh dear! Oh, there he is, I've found him in the file now. It says here that he set fire to a hay barn."

"That's how it always starts, Mrs Churchill. If a boy sets fire to a hay barn before the age of eight you can be certain that he'll go on to be a murderer."

"Is that so?"

"It's what my experience has taught me."

"Whom did he murder?"

"His cousin."

"How very tragic. But why would he want to harm Darcy Sprockett?"

"I don't know."

"Did he even know her?"

"Everyone knew everyone in the village back then."

"What would his motive for harming her have been?"

"I don't know, but a mere six months after her disappearance he murdered his cousin. The law of averages tells me you don't get two murderers at the same time in a village of this size."

"There couldn't possibly have been more than one, you feel?"

"No, it's impossible. Otherwise Compton Poppleford would have a murder rate to match Chicago or one of those other big cities they have in America."

"Rather an odd comparison if I may so, Inspector. Compton Poppleford is a world away from Chicago."

"Exactly. And that's why there couldn't possibly have been more than one murderer here at any given time, especially twenty years ago when the world was a simpler place."

"I don't disagree with that; it was certainly simpler. But I disagree with all the rest of it, I'm afraid. And Pockleswathe is already in prison, you say?"

"Yes, and may he rot there." He took a sip of tea.

"I see."

"So one could more or less consider the case to be closed."

"You're entirely convinced that Pockleswathe is behind Darcy Sprockett's disappearance, are you?"

"Indeed I am. No need for him to even be investigated any further."

"If he's guilty he should stand trial, Inspector!"

"But he's already in prison."

"Justice should still be served! What about the poor Sprockett family?"

"Do you see them clamouring for justice?"

"Not really."

"Well, then. Why do all that extra work?" He took another sip of tea. "Although I must say that your excellent incident board has set me thinking."

"Has it?"

"Yes. The laying out of facts in that way could encourage a person to put a different dimension on things."

"I suppose that's the main purpose of an incident board. You can't keep it all stored in your head, you know."

"Indeed you can't, Mrs Churchill." The inspector stood to his feet and put on his hat. "Thank you for the tea, Miss Pemberley."

"What do we do next, Inspector?"

"Leave that with me, Mrs Churchill." He tapped the side of his nose.

"What does that mean?"

"I've got it in hand. No need for you to go worrying about all this any more."

"You do realise that Mrs Munion and Mr Pentwhistle have given different versions of events for that fateful evening, don't you?"

"Who are they?"

"Didn't you read about them in the case file?"

"Probably."

"Come to think of it, you must have interviewed them at the time."

"I interviewed a lot of people back then, Mrs Churchill. I couldn't possibly recall all of them."

"Personally, I think Mrs Munion's and Mr Pentwhistle's conflicting accounts should be investigated further."

"Like I say, there's probably no need. In fact, it's best if you stay out of this as I launch the final stage of my investigation." He rubbed his hands together in anticipation.

"Which is what, exactly?"

"I'm afraid I can't say, but no more meddling, Mrs Churchill. You've done more than enough, and I shall ensure that your contribution is properly acknowledged this time."

"What contribution?"

"All will become clear, Mrs Churchill. Just leave me to get on with my job for now, if you please. Let's remember which of us is the official officer of the law, eh?"

Chapter 27

"That man hasn't a clue what he's doing, Pembers," said Churchill after Inspector Mappin had left. She looked through the case file again, pleased to have it back in her possession. Something interesting caught her eye.

"Goodness me, Pembers. Did you know this?"

"I'm unable to give an accurate response to your question until I know what 'this' is."

"Darcy Sprockett once worked as a maid for Sir Morris Buckle-Duffington."

"I didn't know that."

"There are notes from an interview here that Atkins conducted with Mr Jones Sloanes. Darcy was one of Sir Morris's favourites, apparently. Am I right in thinking that he died the same year she went missing?"

"Yes, I think he did."

"Interesting. How did you get on at the library? Did you track Great-aunt Betsy down in the Surrey telephone directory?"

"I certainly did."

"Wonderful. And how was Mrs Higginbath?"

"Rather meek. She's worried about Sir Waffleton-Jones, I believe."

"Why's she worried about him?"

"Oh, she worries about all authority figures, especially ones she wasn't previously aware of. Poor Mrs Higginbath. I think we've given her the willies!"

"She only got what was coming to her, Pemberley. The woman's a bully. Now what of Great-aunt Betsy?"

"I wrote the details down on this piece of paper here. Miss E. Earwold, Littleton Avenue, Walton-on-Thames." Pemberley got up from her desk to bring it over to Churchill.

"Oh no, I'd like *you* to telephone her, Pembers. She's already accused me of sniffing around and being a cockalorum or whatever it was before she's even met me!"

"She probably thinks the same of me."

"But more so of me. Let's telephone her and see what happens."

"What shall I say to her?"

"Ask her if she knows Mrs Munion, formerly Miss Byles, and whether she was acquainted with Mr Manners and Mr Pentwhistle."

"And what if she denies knowing any of them?"

"We can't predict what she'll say, but let's speak to her anyway and see where it gets us."

Churchill bit into a slice of Battenberg and sat back in her chair to listen as Pemberley dialled the telephone number.

"It's ringing," she mouthed to Churchill. "Still ringing," she added a moment later. "Oh, hello? Miss Earwold?"

Churchill listened as Pemberley introduced herself to Great-aunt Betsy and appeared to receive a lacklustre response.

"I can assure you that my little dog, Oswald, likes to sniff around, Miss Earwold, but it is not an activity I commonly undertake myself," said Pemberley. "We're merely trying to ensure that Miss Sprockett receives justice after all these years... I worked for the private detective Mr Atkins, do you remember him investigating?... Yes, he did... The Zambezi River, yes... That's right, a crocodile... Hilda... I will do... Embroidery, I remember now..." Pemberley gave a laugh. "Indeed, yes. Gooseberry pie!"

"What on earth are you talking about, Pembers?" hissed Churchill. "Get to the point!"

"He's a Spanish water dog with a sprinkling of spaniel and a tot of terrier... Yes... Oh, have you? Seven? Goodness!"

Churchill impatiently crammed another slice of Battenberg into her mouth as Pemberley discussed dogs with Great-aunt Betsy.

"Do you remember Agatha Byles?" Pemberley eventually asked. "Forearms like a farmhand, eh?... Noisy... What about Barnaby Manners?... Not a trombone, a trumpet... Freckles... And Timothy Pentwhistle?... The pictures?... Woods... Yes, I work for Mrs Churchill now... No, not at all. She's a terribly nice lady and very good at solving crimes... I can assure you that she knows exactly what she's doing... There's no need for insults, Miss Earwold... We're only trying to find out what happened that night... Well, she does mind her own business as a general rule, but in this case she's revisiting the investigation her predecessor, Mr Atkins, began but never managed to solve... If we left it to the police, Miss Earwold, we'd never get anywhere... Mappin, yes... He means well... Poop stick is taking things a little far, Miss Earwold... I beg your pardon?... Well, dunderhead yourself!"

Pemberley slammed the receiver down.

"It sounded like the conversation began well, Pembers."

"I managed to establish a rapport."

"Very important."

"But the rapport swiftly evaporated."

"She's a cranky old bat, isn't she? Did she call Inspector Mappin a poop stick?"

"Yes, and worse."

"And what about me?"

"I can't remember now."

"Yes you can, Pembers, it was only a few moments ago. What did she call me?"

"There's no need for me to repeat it."

"If that woman has insulted me I'd like to hear what she said!"

"I really don't want to tell you, Mrs Churchill."

"Why not?"

"Because you'll get all cross and angry."

"I'm already cross and angry!"

"It will agitate you even further."

"Tell me, Pembers!" Churchill slammed her fist down onto her desk.

"All right, but promise me you won't be angry."

"How can I possibly promise that? I'm growing steadily angrier by the second! Just tell me!"

"She called you a trout-faced blinkard."

"What on earth is that?"

"A blinkard is a dim-witted person who blinks slowly."

"Ridiculous! And how can she say that I have a trout face when she's never even set eyes on me?"

"Exactly! That's why her insults are best ignored."

"Do I have a face like a trout, Pembers?"

"No."

"Be honest if I have. I won't be offended!"

"I think you would."

"Nonsense! I can handle it. Do I have a face like a trout?"

"No."

"You're just saying that so as not to offend me!"

"More Battenberg, Mrs Churchill?"

"I've completely lost my appetite! Who does that woman think she is?"

"I think it was a bad idea to telephone her."

"It had to be done! A *blinkard*? What does she know about the way I blink?"

"She doesn't. It's just a saying, Mrs Churchill. Please calm down now; you're frightening poor Oswald."

"Oh no, where is he?"

"He's cowering under my desk."

"Oh dear." Churchill felt herself deflate like a balloon that had just been pricked with a pin. "I'm so sorry, Oswald. Come and have some cake!"

"He's not allowed cake."

"Says who?"

"Me. Who else? Dogs aren't supposed to eat cake. He had a nice pig's ear from the butcher's earlier."

"Great-aunt Betsy probably has pig ears."

"Can we forget about her now, please?"

"Did she have anything useful to say?"

"No."

"What did she say about our terrible trio?"

"She could recall each of them but gave no indication that she knew any of them particularly well."

"You'd think the woman would welcome an investigation into her poor great-niece's disappearance, wouldn't you? I don't understand her hostility and bad manners at all."

"Maybe she's going batty."

"She is a hundred and one, I suppose."

"She's probably lost all powers of logical thought."

"I think you may be right, Pembers. Let's call it a day, shall we? I'm feeling rather exhausted by it all."

Chapter 28

CHURCHILL AND PEMBERLEY locked up the office and went
their separate ways home. Churchill strolled along the high
street as the greengrocer folded up his awning and the
butcher took in his sign. Fat pigeons pecked at the crumbs
that had been shaken off the tablecloths at the tea shop.
She had just reached the statue of Sir Morris Buckle-Duffington when she heard a voice behind her.

"What ho, Mrs Churchill!"

She gave a sigh. *Not Mr Colthrop again,* she thought to
herself.

"Here we are," he said with a wink as she turned to
face him.

"Indeed we are. I'm just on my way home, Mr
Colthrop."

"So I see. There's a nice little French bistro on
Biddlingford Lane, you know."

"Is there now?"

"It's a little out of the way, if you get what I mean."

"Out of the way of what?"

"Prying eyes." He waggled his eyebrows.

"Well, enjoy your meal, Mr Colthrop. It's always nice to eat somewhere that's out of the way of prying eyes."

"Oh, it is." He smoothed his shirt and hitched up his plus fours. "Very nice indeed."

"Good. Well, I'd better be on my way."

"I wasn't thinking of dining there alone, you see," he added.

"No? I suppose it's always nice to have company when dining out."

"Oh, absolutely."

"Have a pleasant evening, Mr Colthrop."

"Call me Peregrine," he said with a bawdy wink. "There's no need for formality, Mrs Churchill. I was thinking that perhaps you might care to join me."

"Me?" She felt her stomach turn. "But why?"

"Why not?"

"Because I'm tired and it's probably best that you have dinner with your wife, Mr Colthrop."

"She's in Dorchester for the evening. While the cat's away—"

"Mr Colthrop! Are you suggesting what I think you're suggesting?"

He took a step closer, adjusted his collar and lowered his voice. "Let's not beat about the bush now, Mrs Churchill. I think we both know the real reason you climbed the tree that overlooks my garden."

"Do we?"

"Yes. You wanted to watch me."

"Oh, come now. I was photographing birds' eggs, Mr Colthrop."

"Still trying to fool me with that one, are you?" He gave a throaty chuckle. "And then we saw each other at the golf course, and again this morning in the lane. It's no coincidence that we keep bumping into each other, Mrs

Churchill. In fact, I could almost swear that you've been following me."

"Following you, Mr Colthrop? How preposterous! Why on earth would I do that?"

"Why on earth, eh? I suppose we've reached the point where we must both lay our cards on the table."

"Must we?"

"Oh, yes. I have no wish to cause you any embarrassment, Mrs Churchill, so I should like to clearly state that your feelings are not unreciprocated."

"Which feelings?"

"Ha ha. I see the game you're playing here, but I shan't mince my words." He paused to loosen his cravat. "Your comment about my not mentioning our last meeting to the wife didn't go unnoticed." He gave a wink. "There's something rather primitive about a deep attraction between two people, isn't there? Once one has stripped away the many layers of etiquette and protocol that society has laid down over centuries, one is left with a primeval urge, which has a raw, almost animal-like quality to it, don't you find?"

Churchill could feel the Battenberg beginning to repeat on her. "I can't say that I do find, Mr Colthrop."

"Oh come now, really? You're a full-blooded woman of the world, Mrs Churchill, and you've been about a bit. We both have. We're at the age where we know our own minds, you see. There is no longer any youthful caution or doubt. And no need for pretence, I say."

"Who's pretending?"

"We both have been, Mrs Churchill. Those stolen glances in the antiques shop, and from the boughs of the oak tree, and across the hedge of the golf course. We both knew what we were thinking. Or would you still prefer to leave it unspoken?"

"Not really. I've always firmly believed in speaking my mind."

"Ha ha. That's why I like you, Mrs Churchill."

"I see. Actually, I don't think I do."

"You're a lady, Mrs Churchill, and a fine example of one, too. Mature and well-seasoned."

"I'm not a piece of cheese, Mr Colthrop."

He let out a hearty laugh. "Oh, I do wish I could spend a bit more time in your company. I really do."

"I'm a busy woman."

"You most certainly are. And I'm a married man, I suppose. If Virginia were out of the picture... Well, who knows what might have happened, eh, Mrs Churchill?"

"The mind boggles, Mr Colthrop." Churchill suddenly felt mindful of the crochet hook she kept in her handbag, which could be used to poke him in the ribs should the need arise.

"You're one of the old breed, you see," he continued. "Stoic and steadfast. A true stalwart. Not like the younger generation with their flimsy, wearisome ways."

"I really should be getting on."

"I can't tempt you, then, to a little rendezvous at the bistro Français?"

"No thank you. In actual fact, I'm not feeling particularly well now. I must be on my way."

"Sorry to hear it. I do hope you feel better soon. Would you like a bit of company on your walk?"

"No."

"I see. Well, I shall always think fondly of you, Mrs Churchill. You will never be far from my thoughts."

"Are you planning on going away, Mr Colthrop?"

"No. Why do you ask?"

"Your words were beginning to sound like a speech one

might make if one were about to depart on a long journey."

"I have no plans to go anywhere."

"In that case I expect I shall see you around, Mr Colthrop. Goodbye."

Chapter 29

"I HAD the misfortune of being propositioned by Mr Colthrop yesterday evening, Pembers," said Churchill as they walked through Poppleford Woods toward Mr Sprockett's cottage.

"Oh, no! How distasteful!"

"It was, rather. The man has no scruples at all. Still, I suppose it settles the case as far as Mrs Colthrop's concerned."

"What do you mean by that?"

"Well, we can simply tell her that he propositioned me and then she can have her divorce."

"No, no, you mustn't do that!"

"Why not?"

"Because she'll get all upset about it."

"But she has to know what he's really like."

"And she will in due course, just as soon as we've managed to take a photograph of him with his lady friend."

"We're not having a great deal of luck with that, Pembers."

"Patience, Mrs Churchill, patience. If you tell Mrs Colthrop about her husband's amorous advances he'll deny that any of it ever happened. It will be your word against his, and she'll probably choose him because he's been her husband for so many years."

"She wouldn't believe me? The private detective she hired?"

"Probably not, I'm afraid. But if he's propositioned you, Mrs Churchill, I imagine that he propositions a lot of ladies."

"What exactly do you mean by that, Pembers?" she snapped.

"I didn't mean to cause any offence. What I meant to suggest was that men who do that sort of thing tend to go about it a great deal. It'll only be a matter of time before we catch him doing it to someone else."

"I wish I shared your patience, Pembers, but I'd like to be rid of the case once and for all."

"I don't blame you, Mrs Churchill. An amorous word from Mr Colthrop would truly sicken me."

"One needs to be built of strong stuff to do this job."

"That's why you're so perfect for it, Mrs Churchill."

"Do you think so? Why thank you, Pembers. I can't wait to get the old toad off our hands."

"I'm sure we'll catch him out sooner rather than later."

They approached the Sprockett cottage, stepped over the remains of the wheelbarrow and made their way to the back of the house, where they had last seen Mr Sprockett's head poking out of a window.

"Hello?" Churchill called out. "Mr Sprockett?"

Oswald chased away some chickens that were pecking at the ground.

"I think you should put the old hound on his lead,

Pembers. We don't want to give the aged Sprockett any further reason to be grumpy with us. Helloeeee?"

"What's that noise?" The familiar head appeared from an upstairs window and surveyed them with a scowl. "Oh, it's you again."

"We've come to speak to you about Great-aunt Betsy, Mr Sprockett. Do you have a moment?"

"Not ter speak ter yous about 'er, I don't."

"Is she your aunt?"

"The wife's aunt. Is that your dog?"

"It's Miss Pemberley's dog."

"'E's botherin' me chickens."

Pemberley called Oswald, but once again he chose to ignore her.

"Get 'im away frum me chickens."

"I don't think he'll do them any harm, Mr Sprockett."

"'E will too. 'E's got a wicked look in 'is eye."

Churchill marched over to Oswald and picked him up. "Here you are, Miss Pemberley. Perhaps you can hold your dog for a while to stop him completely distracting us from proceedings. Are you in touch with your estranged wife's Aunt Betsy, Mr Sprockett?"

"No."

"My trusty assistant, Miss Pemberley, spoke to her on the telephone yesterday. Sadly, Miss Earwold was quite short with her."

"She's still alive?"

"Yes, didn't you know? In fact, she visited her former home just a few days ago."

Mr Sprockett sniffed. "I ain't never liked 'er."

"It turns out she isn't keen on us asking questions about Darcy. She's been quite rude about all the investigators, truth be told."

"She's rude about ev'rybody."

"I thought she'd want to find out what had happened to Darcy, but she seems to want everyone to forget about the case altogether. Have you any idea why that might be, Mr Sprockett?"

"Nope."

"I find it rather suspicious. I think the reason she's being so unhelpful is that she had something to do with Darcy's disappearance."

"She wouldn't 'ave 'ad nuffink to do wi' that."

"Why not?"

"Why would she? Gimme a reason why she would."

"I don't honestly know, Mr Sprockett. I was hoping you could tell me."

"There ain't none. She were always fond of our Darcy. She wouldn't never 'ave let no 'arm come to 'er."

"Have any other members of your family visited the village recently?"

"You've asked me that afore. I dunno, do I?"

"Oh, I see. I just wondered whether there had been any change."

"Nope. No change."

"Right. And there's nothing more you can tell us about Great-aunt Betsy, I suppose."

"Nope. Bye."

Mr Sprockett's head disappeared again.

"We're no more enlightened now than we were first thing this morning, are we, Pembers? How very tiresome this whole business is becoming. I wonder what Inspector Mappin has up his sleeve. He appeared to have something up it when he returned the case file, didn't he?"

"He just assumed the murderer was that Bertrand Pockleswathe fellow."

"Yes, but then he suggested he had an inkling about someone else being involved. I'm extremely keen to find out who that might be, aren't you?"

Chapter 30

"You do realise you've been carrying that dog for about a mile and a half now, Pembers," said Churchill when they reached Compton Poppleford high street.

"Oh, so I have! I'd quite forgotten about him. He seems to like it, doesn't he? And it helps to keep him out of trouble."

"It does, but he must still make use of his own legs. We don't want him to become one of those fat little doggies you see waddling about the place. Oh no! Is that Mrs Colthrop waiting outside our door?"

"I do believe it is."

Mrs Colthrop wore a large hat and a fur stole, and she appeared to be wringing her hands in distress.

"Oh, there you are!" she cried. "Finally! I've been trying to find you!"

"What's the emergency, Mrs Colthrop?"

"It's Peregrine. He's been arrested!"

"Really? Whatever for?"

"Murder!"

"Murder? That's quite impossible, Mrs Colthrop. There must have been some sort of misunderstanding."

"There hasn't at all. Inspector Mappin has him down at the station and I'm not allowed to see him. Oh, it's awful! So terribly awful!"

"Who is he accused of murdering?"

"That girl they found in the field."

"Darcy Sprockett?"

"Yes, her."

"Did he know her?"

"No! But Inspector Mappin seems to think he did."

"Was your husband even living here twenty years ago?"

"No, we were up in Epsom. We've often visited my brother here over the years, though."

"Mr Trollope."

"Yes, and his delightful wife. We've always been regular visitors of theirs, and now that hopeless inspector thinks my husband somehow committed a murder while we were staying with them! Why on earth would he do such a thing? He's as harmless as a turtle dove."

"Is he, by Jove? Well, let's go up to the office and make you a nice cup of tea, Mrs Colthrop. Things always feel better after a nice cup of tea and a sliver of cake."

"How could I possibly feel better about my husband being arrested for murder?"

"I'll have a chat with the inspector shortly and find out what sort of evidence he has."

"Thank you, Mrs Churchill."

Once Mrs Colthrop had been consoled with a generous helping of tea and cake, Churchill and Pemberley made their way down to the police station.

"No entry, I'm afraid," said Inspector Mappin through the gap in the door.

"Why ever not? This is our local police station."

"I've got the chief inspector here from Dorchester, and we're busy questioning a murder suspect. You'll have to come back another time."

"Is your murder suspect Mr Colthrop?"

"I'm neither at liberty to confirm nor deny the name of a person or persons who may or may not have been arrested at the present time."

"But how could Mr Colthrop possibly be responsible for Darcy Sprockett's disappearance? He wasn't even living here twenty years ago!"

"He was a regular visitor to the village back then, but I shall say no more on the matter given that I'm not at liberty to confirm or deny whether he is the person or among the number of persons who may or may not have been arrested at this time."

"You're using that strange police language, Inspector Mappin. We shall leave you to it for the time being, but when you've finished with your suspect perhaps you'd like to explain to poor Mrs Colthrop the reasons behind her husband's untimely arrest. The poor lady has been inconsolable over in our offices this afternoon, and even more worryingly she's eaten practically all of our walnut cake."

"Any next of kin will be contacted forthwith."

"I take that as a confirmation that you'll speak with her, in that case. And may I just add what a dreadful mistake I think you're making here? Mr Colthrop may be many things, but I'm quite certain he's not a murderer."

"I suppose our investigation into the love affairs of Mr Colthrop will have to be put on hold for the foreseeable,

Pembers," said Churchill once they had returned to the office. "And there's only one slice of cake left. I should bill Mrs Colthrop for it!"

"Please don't. She was in such a distressed state."

Churchill opened the Darcy Sprockett case file and leafed through the pages once again. "This case is truly baffling, Pembers. Could Mr Colthrop really have been responsible for Darcy's disappearance? Do you think Mappin has gone and solved the blasted thing?"

"I hope not, or we'll have no work to be getting on with at all."

"And that would be terribly tedious," added Churchill. She flicked through the pages of the file one way and then the other. "But what are we to do now?"

"I still say that Timothy Pentwhistle is a slippery fish."

"He is, isn't he?"

"I think we need to ask him why his version of events differs so much from Mrs Munion's."

"We could, but he's not likely to own up to anything, is he? He's just going to confuddle us with tales of his seafaring and claim that the brine has somehow washed away all his long-term memories. Goodness, Pembers! Have you seen what that dog has done to the leg of your desk?"

Pemberley peered down to where Oswald lay resting on the floor, quietly chewing the leg of her desk. He had worked almost halfway through it.

"It's going to snap!" said Churchill.

"It won't," replied Pemberley, "it's mahogany. But I think he's bored. I'll take him for a little stroll along the high street."

"What a good idea. I think I'll join you both, actually. A little constitutional will set things right in my head."

. . .

The two old ladies and the dog walked in the opposite direction of the police station, where several press reporters and photographers had gathered. They made their way along the high street to where the statue of Sir Morris Buckle-Duffington stood. Churchill felt nauseous as she recalled Mr Colthrop's unwanted advances beneath Sir Morris's cool gaze. It was then that an interesting thought occurred to her.

"Who's that old fool who once worked for Sir Morris?" she asked Pemberley.

"Which one?"

"The old cove who stood up at the unveiling of the statue. What was he? A valet or something, wasn't he? Had a strange name."

"Ah yes, the valet. Mr Jones Sloanes."

"That's the one. I suppose he would have known Darcy Sprockett when she worked for Sir Morris, wouldn't he?"

"I suppose so."

"Any idea where he lives?"

"No, but I've seen him visiting the Wagon and Carrot a few times. Someone might know something if we ask in there."

"Why are you carrying Oswald again, Pembers?"

"He likes it."

"But it's not exactly exercising him, is it? I thought the whole point of taking a little walk was to exercise the dog."

"So it was. I'd forgotten." She put him down on the ground. "It's just that I quite like cuddling him. Oh, look at his little face! He's saying, 'Don't put me down here, Human Mother! I want to be carried!'"

"No he's not, Pembers. Come on, now. Let's go and find this Jones Sloanes character."

Chapter 31

A FEW BRIEF enquiries at the Wagon and Carrot led to Churchill and Pemberley knocking on the door of a small but smart little cottage tucked away down a lane beside the churchyard. A slender, stooped man with high cheekbones and pale green eyes answered the door. He regarded Churchill coolly as she introduced yourself.

"I suppose you'd better come in," was his response.

"Should we leave the dog outside?" asked Churchill.

"Is he well-behaved?"

"Of course."

He showed them into an impeccable parlour, where several fine pieces of china adorned the polished mantelpiece.

"Thank you so much for agreeing to see us, Mr Sloanes," said Churchill. "My aide-de-camp Miss Pemberley and I are seeking some assistance with a case we're working on. You were once valet to Sir Morris Buckle-Duffington, I understand."

"I was indeed."

"What do you make of his statue?"

"I think it flatters him."

"In what way?"

"I'd hoped for a more honest representation of his pot belly."

"Goodness, really? I must ensure that the same statue-maker is employed to create a bronze likeness of myself when the time comes!" laughed Churchill, patting her generous stomach.

If Mr Sloanes was amused by this he chose not to show it. Oswald sat himself down on the oriental-style hearthrug with his tongue hanging out.

"How long did you work for Sir Morris?" Churchill asked him.

"Almost forty years."

"Did you travel with him?"

"Of course."

"You saw a good deal of the world, then, just like Miss Pemberley here in her travelling days."

"Indeed. I recall that we bumped into one another in Yangon, in fact," replied Mr Sloanes.

"Wherever that is."

"Burma."

"I suppose I should have guessed that. It sounded distinctly Chinese."

"Burma is an entirely different country to China."

"I realise that, but it's in roughly the same part of the world, isn't it?"

"But it's still quite different," said Mr Sloanes.

"Yes, I get your point. What are the portions like there?"

"In terms of food, you mean?"

"Yes."

"They're quite generous at the governor's residence,

but I imagine they'd be fairly paltry for the everyday Burmese."

"Did you ever visit the governor's residence, Miss Pemberley?" asked Churchill.

"Oh yes."

"I see." Churchill felt a pang of envy. "Well, perhaps I should leave the two of you to discuss the merits of Burmese governors and residences and suchlike."

"There's no need, Mrs Churchill," replied Pemberley. "After all, we came to speak to Mr Sloanes about another matter altogether, didn't we?"

"If you say so, Miss Pemberley. We happen to be investigating the sad disappearance of Miss Darcy Sprockett, Mr Sloanes."

"A terribly tragic affair."

"You knew her when you both worked for Sir Morris, did you not? Excuse me a moment." Churchill lowered her voice to a whisper. "Can't you stop him doing that, Pembers?"

"I'm sorry?"

"That dog. Look what he's licking!"

"Dogs do that."

"There's a time and a place for him to tend to his intimate cleaning, and an expensive hearthrug in the parlour of Mr Jones Sloanes is neither!"

"Oswald doesn't know that."

"Just give him a poke. It's embarrassing."

Pemberley got up to distract Oswald while Churchill turned to face Mr Sloanes once again. "I do apologise. Dogs have some terribly dirty habits, don't they?"

"I've seen humans do worse."

"Really, Mr Sloanes? *Really?* Good grief, well perhaps I've led rather a sheltered life. Anyway, let's resume. You knew Darcy Sprockett when she worked for Sir Morris, is that right?"

"I did indeed."

"Was she well thought of?"

"Very much so."

"By whom?"

"By all of us, and especially by the master himself."

"He stated as much?"

"Oh yes. He was always talking about '*my little Darcy this*' and '*my little Darcy that*'. He had no progeny, you see, so he more or less viewed her as a daughter."

"A daughter who was in service to him?"

"Yes. A little odd, isn't it? However, it was no odder than she was used to, by the sound of things. She told me how much work she had to do for her family when she was at home. She never stopped, the poor love."

"But Sir Morris was kind to her, was he?"

"Oh yes. Very much so."

"And she was a general maid?"

"Yes. She didn't have to do anything unpleasant, such as scrubbing in the scullery or emptying slops. She did quite well out of the whole affair, really. Working in service wouldn't have been her first choice of employment, but then there wasn't a lot of choice in Compton Poppleford twenty years ago. It was either service or farm work."

"Is there more choice in Compton Poppleford these days?"

"Probably not, now I come to think of it. One could become a shopkeeper, I suppose."

"And you all lost your jobs when Sir Morris died, did you?"

"Yes, we did. I was nearing pension age, so it didn't matter too much to me. But poor Darcy and a number of others lost their source of work."

"What did she do after that?"

"She took up waitressing in the French bistro, I believe. Do you know it?"

"No, but I've heard of it. Miss Pemberley, the dog's doing that thing again!"

"He must have an itch."

"It's more than an itch; I'm concerned that it's becoming a habit. Just distract him with something, will you?"

"Would a biscuit suffice?" asked Mr Sloanes.

"It would be a great help. Thank you, Mr Sloanes. I do apologise on behalf of the dog. How very embarrassing."

Mr Sloanes gave Oswald a digestive biscuit, which the dog gratefully gulped down.

"I understand that Sir Morris was a man of considerable means," Churchill continued.

"Of course."

"And what happened to his means after he died? We know that Compton Poppleford History Museum benefitted, but what about his staff?"

"We all got a little something. Some of the ornaments you see over there were once his."

"But the little somethings wouldn't necessarily add up to a big something. Where did the bulk of his means end up? Was there an heir? I realise he didn't have children, but perhaps there was a brother or a nephew, or maybe a cousin once removed."

"I couldn't tell you who got hold of his money. I know that he had cousins, so perhaps they inherited it all."

"There must have been talk of all that as his day of reckoning drew near. After all, he was an extremely old and wealthy man. Were the vultures beginning to circle?"

"Not that I noticed. I did occasionally wonder about the inheritance, and as I say I got a little something. But a good deal would have been unaccounted for. Perhaps it went to a distant cousin or to charitable causes. I couldn't tell you for sure, Mrs Churchill."

"Who was the executor of his estate?"

"His solicitor."

"And who might that have been?"

"Mr Verney."

"Is he the only solicitor in Compton Poppleford?"

"I don't know. Is he?"

"Everyone seems to avail themselves of his services to manage their affairs."

"Perhaps he's a particularly good solicitor."

"He strikes me as a rather dour and dull individual, which may well mean that he's a good solicitor. Thank you for your time, Mr Sloanes. I think Miss Pemberley and I had better call on Mr Verney next. Come along, Oswald!"

Chapter 32

MR VERNEY SAT IN A WINGED, buttoned leather chair behind an oversized mahogany desk in an austere-looking office with red-and-gold striped wallpaper. He was a short, dusty-looking man wearing a pinstriped suit. Churchill and Pemberley had met him several times before while investigating the death of Mrs Furzgate.

"I can hear a dog barking," he said. "Is it yours?"

"Yes, it's Oswald," replied Pemberley. "We thought it best to leave him outside as this doesn't seem like a particularly suitable place for dogs."

"It certainly isn't," he replied.

"He doesn't like being left on his own," added Pemberley.

"A good reason to make your visit swift, then. How may I be of assistance?"

"We believe that the late, great Sir Morris Buckle-Duffington was one of your clients," said Churchill.

"That's correct."

"My distinguished assistant Miss Pemberley and I are

investigating the tragic case of Miss Darcy Sprockett and have learned that she was in the employ of Sir Morris."

"That's correct."

"We have also learnt that she was a favourite of his."

"She was."

"We also learned that he left quite a fortune behind, and we were wondering where that fortune might have ended up."

"May I ask why you were wondering such a thing?"

"Because if Miss Sprockett came into a large fortune at that time, someone may have wished to acquire it from her. They could have taken out a life insurance policy on her, then done away with the poor girl."

The solicitor winkled his nose. "What a terrible thought."

"It is indeed, but it has happened on many a sad occasion."

"Do you know if anyone purchased such a policy?" he asked.

"Not yet, but if we can establish whether or not she was the beneficiary of Sir Morris's fortune we can start making enquiries."

"I see."

"Do please tell us, Mr Verney. Did she receive the lion's share?"

"It's not for me to say, Mrs Churchill."

"Presumably you administered Sir Morris's affairs after his death."

"I did indeed."

"So you must know whether he handed it over to Miss Sprockett or not."

"His wealth was distributed between a number of beneficiaries and good causes."

"And what of Miss Sprockett?"

"Confidentiality forbids me from being any more specific than that."

"But Sir Morris has been dead for twenty years!"

"That may be so, but I am bound by a moratorium that forbids public access to his private papers for fifty years."

"Oh no. Not that old thing again."

"*Thing?*"

"Mr Manners was carrying on about it when we visited the museum, wasn't he, Miss Pemberley?"

Her assistant nodded.

"All of his important documents appear to have been locked up in that fusty old trunk at the museum," added Churchill.

Mr Verney shrugged. "There's nothing more I can do for you ladies, I'm afraid. You'd better fetch your barking dog."

"What was so interesting about Sir Morris's papers that he banned anyone from looking at them for fifty years?" Churchill asked.

"I honestly couldn't tell you."

"Oh, come on, Mr Verney. You must know."

"Really I don't. I only administered his estate when he died, then I placed everything inside the trunk. I couldn't tell you what else is in there."

"The key hangs on the wall right above that trunk," said Churchill. "Haven't you ever felt tempted to unlock it and take a little peek?"

"Not at all."

"Young Manners must have had a look, mustn't he?"

"Oh no, he certainly wouldn't have done. He takes the moratorium and the museum's role as the guardian of the trunk extremely seriously."

"He doesn't sound like much fun. Can you not sympathise with our pressing need for information, Mr Verney? If we could just find out whether Sir Morris left his fortune to Miss Sprockett we might be able to establish a possible motive for her tragic demise. You must surely hold this vital information in that grey matter of yours, without the need to wait another thirty years to open up an old trunk. Did he leave her anything? Aye or nay?"

"The moratorium applies to my mouth as well as to the papers, Mrs Churchill."

"Goodness, does it? You poor fellow. In all my years you're the first person I've ever met with a moratorium attached to a body part."

"Hadn't you and your assistant better be on your way?"

"Well, yes, I suppose we should," retorted Churchill, rising to her feet. "You're clearly not about to tell us anything useful, Mr Verney. Thank you all the same."

The two ladies stepped out of the lawyer's front door and rescued Oswald, who was overjoyed to see them.

"Oh, how delightful, Pembers! Your dog has left one of his little gifts on Mr Verney's front step."

The two ladies stopped at the bakery and bought half a dozen fruit buns before retiring to the office.

"Now then, Pembers. How good are you at forging letters from people?"

"Such as?"

"Sir Digby Waffleton-Jones."

"That chap we threatened Mrs Higginbath with?"

"That's right."

"He's a Digby, is he?"

"He certainly is. And proud of it, too."

"And he's planning to write a letter?"

"That's right. Addressed to Mr Manners of the

Compton Poppleford History Museum. It will be a notification that a number of dusty exhibits have been reported to him, and that an authorised clean of the museum is to take place this Thursday morning. He expects the cleaning team to arrive at half-past eight on the dot."

Chapter 33

"I've got some lovely new embroidery threads in stock," announced Mrs Thonnings as they entered the haberdashery shop. "You enjoy a bit of embroidery, don't you, Miss Pemberley?"

"I used to, but then I pricked my finger."

"One little prick was enough to stop you forever, was it?" commented Churchill. "Goodness! You do give up on things rather quickly, don't you?"

"The trouble was, my finger became infected," replied Pemberley, "and then they had to lop the top off it."

She showed Churchill and Mrs Thonnings her disfigured right forefinger. Mrs Thonnings gave a yelp and Churchill reeled back against the shop counter.

"Good grief, Pembers, I had no idea!" Churchill exclaimed. "You should have told me sooner! You manage to type quite well with it... Or *without* it, to be more accurate. The tip of your finger, I mean. Are you all right, Mrs Thonnings?"

Mrs Thonnings's face was ashen pale beneath her mop of artificially red hair.

216

"I think so, Mrs Churchill, thank you for asking. It was just a bit of a shock, that's all. I didn't expect to see a finger without its tip today."

"Oh, it happened about eight years ago," said Pemberley. "I'd quite forgotten about it until you mentioned embroidery."

"Can I interest you in any embroidery threads, in that case?" ventured Mrs Thonnings.

"I suspect not," said Churchill.

Mrs Thonnings looked beyond Churchill and gave an angry scowl. "Let me just fetch my broom and shoo that mangy dog out of here," she said. "He's been in here once before. I've been meaning to telephone the dogcatcher ever since."

"That's Oswald!" protested Pemberley.

"Do you mean to say that he's yours?"

"Yes."

"Oh, I didn't realise. I do apologise, Miss Pemberley. I didn't know you had a dog."

"He's a recent addition to our detective agency," added Churchill. "We'll make sure he doesn't wander in here again, won't we, Miss Pemberley?"

"The first time must have been the other morning when he trotted off without me for about twenty minutes."

"Yes, it must have been," Churchill agreed.

"Terrible news about Mr Colthrop, isn't it?" said Mrs Thonnings.

"Oh yes. Well, not so terrible if he's actually a murderer, but if he's innocent, which I suspect he is, then it's very terrible indeed," concluded Churchill.

"Such a pleasant chap, isn't he?"

"I can't say that I know him awfully well."

"He's a thoroughly decent old soul, and he doesn't deserve to have been arrested at all," continued Mrs

Thonnings. "I hope Inspector Mappin is mistaken once again."

"I have every confidence that he is."

"Do you indeed? That is most reassuring."

"It's not reassuring at all, Mrs Thonnings, as it means that the only member of the constabulary in this locality is completely hopeless at his job."

"I think he's quite good at solving minor incidents, such as missing bicycles and lost sheep. He's just not so good at the murder cases."

"Which is where we come in."

"Oh indeed, Mrs Churchill!" A grin spread across Mrs Thonnings's face. "I do wish I could help you with your murder investigations! They're so much more exciting than selling embroidery threads and half-dying from boredom after a visit from the button company sales representative. He was here for three hours yesterday afternoon trying to convince me to buy five thousand blazer buttons. I told him I couldn't expect to sell that many in a whole lifetime! There's such limited demand in a little village like ours, but he didn't seem to understand that. He's from Westbury, you see. You could probably sell a lot of buttons in a busy metropolis like that."

"I'm sure you could. Now you mention it, you may be able to assist us after all, Mrs Thonnings."

"With one of your murder investigations? Really?"

"Yes."

"Oh, just tell me what you need me to do!" She clapped her hands together with glee.

"Well, we're rather keen to uncover who the culprit behind Darcy Sprockett's tragic demise might be, and we're quite sure that it isn't Mr Colthrop."

"Are you going to prove his innocence, Mrs Churchill?"

"In a roundabout way, yes."

"How exciting! Just tell me what you need from me."

"Would you mind watching Oswald for us tomorrow morning?"

Mrs Thonnings's face fell. "Oh, I see. You want me to look after the dog?"

"I did warn you that solving murders is rarely a glamorous and exciting business, Mrs Thonnings."

"Ah yes, I understand. Tomorrow morning is fine with me, Mrs Churchill."

"Also, I can't help but notice your rather useful-looking haberdashery trolley over there. May we commandeer it? We're going undercover tomorrow morning."

"Undercover? Golly! How thoroughly exhilarating, Mrs Churchill! How I wish I could go undercover!"

"Well, if you lend us your trolley, Mrs Thonnings, your trolley can go undercover with us."

"Oh gosh! What fun!"

"Are you quite sure about this plan, Mrs Churchill?" Pemberley asked once they had left the haberdashery shop and were strolling back down the high street.

"I'm quite sure, Pembers. First we need to confirm that Darcy Sprockett was Sir Morris's main beneficiary, and once we've done that we will know that our suspected motive was the correct one."

"But what if it goes wrong?"

"We've planned it too well for anything to go wrong, Pembers. Just have a little faith."

They passed the police station.

"I wonder how Mr Colthrop enjoyed his night in the cells," commented Pemberley. "He won't have coped with it well, I suspect."

"No, he won't."

"I feel rather sorry for him."

"Oh, don't. It's high time he was taken down a peg or two."

"But what if Inspector Mappin decides to press charges? Mr Colthrop could end up in a proper jail. Proper jail is a dreadful place. I hated it!"

"When were you ever in jail, Pembers?"

"I spent a week in Holloway Prison for knocking a policeman's helmet off."

"Why on earth did you do that?"

"He was trying to stop me from chaining myself to the railings outside the Houses of Parliament."

"You weren't one of those suffragette types, were you?"

"I was indeed. When I had the time, that is. I didn't get many days off while I was a lady's companion."

"Your employer must have taken rather a dim view of you being imprisoned for a week."

"She never knew! She would have been terribly disapproving if she had. I asked a friend to tell her I had scarlet fever."

"Well, I certainly remember Detective Chief Inspector Churchill having a tricky time grappling with those ladies, not to mention their placards. He supported their cause but was obliged to carry out orders from above. One cannot allow one's emotions to come before one's duty."

"I don't think I'd arrest a lady for knocking my helmet off if I were a police officer."

"Different measures for different times, Pembers. Anyhow, we seem to have digressed. I'm sure old Colthrop will be released shortly. Mappin will see sense in a day or two, and I can't imagine that he has any viable evidence against him. I really don't understand why he's arrested the man at all. It's certainly scuppered our surveillance attempts."

"Perhaps Mr Colthrop's scarlet woman will attempt to visit him while he's in the cells."

"That's a thought, Pembers. Perhaps we can quiz Mappin about any visitors who have been in. We'd have to do it tactfully, though. We don't want anyone to know that we've been surveilling Mr Colthrop."

Chapter 34

EARLY THE FOLLOWING MORNING, two cleaning ladies bumped their trolley over the cobblestones to Compton Poppleford History Museum. They wore identical dresses of blue-and-white ticking with full-length aprons tied over the top. Floppy cotton bonnets covered their heads.

"Did we really need to bring the trolley?" shouted Pemberley over the deafening rattle. "We're drawing rather a lot of attention to ourselves!"

Churchill noticed the greengrocer giving them a quizzical look as he arranged his potato display.

"Don't worry about it, Pembers. Just stay in character."

"It's not built for cobbles. The wheels are about to come off!"

"It's sturdier than it looks. Onwards!"

The cleaning ladies paused for breath outside the museum.

Churchill adjusted her bonnet and smoothed down her apron. "Now, what do you think of our outfits, Pemberley? Are we convincing enough?"

"I think Mr Manners might recognise us."

"He's not here on Thursdays, is he? His wife looks after the place in his stead. That's why I chose today."

"Oh yes, of course. Perhaps you should have left your handbag in the office, though."

Churchill glanced down at it. "Yes, I suppose I should have. Let's hide it inside the trolley." She placed it in a bucket, then looked up at her assistant. "I'd say that you're quite recognisable with your spectacles on, Pembers. You'll need to take them off."

"But I won't be able to see a thing without them!"

"It'll only be for half an hour or so. I tell you what, how about *I* wear them? They'd be a good disguise for me. No one will think it's me with your spectacles on, and no one will think it's you without them."

"That's a good idea. But you'll need to look after them carefully."

"Of course I will! Now, hand them over and let's get on with it. A simple transfer of spectacles should be enough to complete our disguise. Good grief! How do you manage to see anything out of these things?" Churchill squinted in a bid to see through the blurred lenses a little more clearly. "Right then, let's go. Lead us to the door, Pembers."

"Where is it?"

"It must be just in front of us somewhere. Is that it?" Churchill lifted the spectacles to get a better view. "Yes, that's it. Follow me."

The museum's interior was dingy and silent.

"Mind where you're pushing that trolley, Pembers. You'll knock an exhibit over if you're not careful."

"You can't call me by my real name, remember?" whispered Pemberley.

"Oh, that's right. You're Miss Newell."

"And you're Mrs Stringer."

"Correct."

"Oh, good morning. Are you the cleaning ladies?" A figure in a blue blouse and a floral skirt stepped into view.

Churchill squinted slightly and deduced that the blur must be Mrs Manners.

"We are indeed."

"Good morning, I'm Mrs Manners. I must say that my husband Barnaby and I were very disappointed to discover that our museum had been reported as being dusty. I try to give everything a good going-over each week, but it appears not to have been enough. Please pass on my sincerest apologies to Sir Waffleton-Jones, and I'm so sorry that you two dear old ladies will have to do all the work."

"Please don't apologise, Mrs Manners. We're merely doing our job."

"Oh, thank you. It's marvellous that you're still working at your age. It must be so tempting to stop and put your feet up!"

"It's not very tempting at all, Mrs Manners. May we begin with the Sir Morris Buckle-Duffington exhibition? No doubt that section of the museum is attracting the greatest number of visitors at the moment, so we'd better ensure that it's looking spick and span."

"Yes, absolutely. Let me lead the way."

Churchill followed Mrs Manners as best she could considering that she could see very little through Pemberley's spectacles. And when Pemberley drove the cleaning trolley into her heels she bit her tongue to prevent herself from emitting any curse words.

"Here's the exhibition on Sir Morris," said Mrs Manners proudly. "And here's his portrait. This was painted in 1862 by an artist who—"

"We're here to clean, Mrs Manners, not to examine all the fine treasures."

"Oh, of course. Shall I leave you to it?"

"That would be marvellous, thank you."

"How about a nice cup of tea to help you get started?"

"Perfect. Thank you, Mrs Manners."

"I'll put the kettle on."

Churchill watched as the blurred form of Mrs Manners retreated, then lifted her spectacles to check that she had actually gone.

"Right then, Pembers. Let's get to work."

Churchill eyed the key on the wall and the chest that sat beneath it. The palms of her hands began to feel damp as she considered what she was about to do.

"Oh, I don't know about this, Mrs Churchill," whispered Pemberley. "Do you really think we should break the moratorium?"

"We need to find out whether Sir Morris left a large pile of money to Darcy in his will or not," she hissed in reply.

"But who would have inherited it if she'd died?"

"I'm guessing it would have been old tortoisehead Sprockett."

"It doesn't look like he's spent any of it if he did."

"It's not immediately obvious, is it? But for all we know he mooches off to Monaco several times a year and lives it up over there."

"He doesn't look like someone who likes to live it up in Monaco."

"Maybe not, but that's rather beside the point. First of all we need to establish whether Darcy Sprockett was rich. A little rummage in this chest will hopefully help. We won't know until we've tried, will we?"

"But what if the curse is real? You remember Mr

Manners' words don't you? He said: '*It has been said that the key is cursed, and that anyone who touches it before the first hour of 1962 will suffer a terrible fate.*'"

"You certainly have a good memory for conversations, Pemberley."

"Yes, I do."

"Don't tell me you've succumbed to the superstitious way of thinking in these parts."

"I can't quite help it when I'm faced with this locked chest. It's lain here undisturbed for twenty years! The thought of having a look inside was all well and good before we arrived, but now that we're actually here I'm getting cold feet."

"Cold feet are of no help to a detective, Pembers."

"I realise that, but I can't help it."

"It's just as well that I'm made of sterner stuff, isn't it? Let's get on with it."

"What if Mrs Manners notices?"

"Just keep an eye out for her, Pembers. We can quickly close the chest again and busy ourselves with our dusters."

"How can I keep a lookout when I can barely see a thing?"

"Good grief, Pembers! I'm sure you're making this more complicated than it needs to be. I just want to have a quick butcher's in the chest."

"Butcher's hook... Look! I do like a bit of Cockney rhyming slang."

"Jolly good."

"Apples and pears... Stairs."

"Indeed."

"Barnet Fair... Hair."

"Yes."

"I'm off to have my barnet done."

"Could we open the chest first, please?"

"Have a butcher's at my barnet."

"Pembers, that's enough!"

"I must say that I enjoy visiting London. We always used to take rooms at the Savoy. They don't speak in Cockney rhyming slang there, that's for sure, but I quite like the idea of being a Cockney."

"If you can stomach the jellied eels, be my guest. Can we get on with this for now?"

"I'm sorry, Mrs Churchill. I become terribly talkative when I'm nervous."

"I'm going to unlock the chest now, so please keep a lookout."

"I'll need my spectacles."

"Fine!" Churchill snatched them off her face. "But hand them back to me if Mrs Manners reappears. They're a crucial part of our disguise."

Relieved that she could finally see without Pemberley's glasses, Churchill reached up toward the key and felt her fingers tremble as she lifted it off the hook.

"Any sign of Mrs Manners?" she whispered to Pemberley.

"None."

Churchill's hand shook as she tried to push the key into the lock. *Did curses really exist?* She glanced over at the Egyptian treasures in the cabinet close by and her mind wandered to the curse of the pharaohs.

"That Lord Carnarvon chap," she whispered to Pemberley. "He died of an infected mosquito bite, didn't he?"

"No. It was the curse after he opened Tutankhamun's tomb that did him in!"

"Don't say that! It was a mosquito bite."

"But that only occurred because of the curse."

"Oh, stuff and nonsense. Let's get on with it."

The key turned in the lock quite easily considering that the chest hadn't been opened for twenty years. Churchill paused, then lifted the lid.

Pemberley gave a nervous gasp as she did so.

"Keep a look out!" instructed Churchill.

Inside lay a pile of important-looking papers.

"Is that all there is inside?" asked Pemberley.

"It's what I expected. Now, where's the will?" Churchill lifted some of the papers out and began to leaf through them. "Most of these pertain to Sir Morris's business affairs," she muttered. "They look incredibly dull to me. Did he want people to think he was harbouring some sort of fascinating secret? It seems as though the man was full of hot air and nothing much else."

"It's not good to speak ill of the dead," whispered Pemberley. "His portrait is watching you."

"I don't think there's any harm in saying that the man was full of hot air. It's quite common among the upper classes; many of them are little more than gas and gaiters. I'm sure the great man wouldn't mind me saying that."

"His portrait looks quite cross with you."

"Oh Pembers, you do talk a lot of nonsense. Have a leaf through some of these papers and tell me if you find anything interesting."

"I'm supposed to be on lookout."

"Just have a quick riffle through while I take care of this next lot."

Pemberley took the bundle of papers from Churchill and glanced through them. "I can't understand why all this has been locked up in a chest for donkey's years. There's nothing of any interest here at all."

"My sentiments exactly. I think we're wasting our time here. We can only hope that Sir Morris's last will and testament is here, as that will tell us what Miss Sprockett inherited from him, if anything."

The two ladies spent a few minutes looking through the papers.

"I do hope Mrs Thonnings looks after Oswald properly," whispered Pemberley.

"Of course she will. Mrs Thonnings knows how to look after animals. She has a pet cat, remember?"

"Oh dear, so she has. Oswald will chase it!"

"I'm sure the cat will outwit him. They're usually cleverer than dogs."

"But not cleverer than Oswald. He's a particularly intelligent dog, you know. Just the other morning I was talking to him, and he understood every word I said. I can't think of a single human who could do the same."

"Neither can I, Pembers. He must be very clever indeed."

"I can hear someone coming! Quick, shut the chest!"

Pemberley hurled the papers back at Churchill, who threw them into the chest and quickly closed the lid. She pulled Pemberley's spectacles off and pushed them onto her face. She had only just managed to grab her feather duster when Mrs Manners reappeared with a tea tray.

"Is everything all right, ladies?"

"Oh yes, Mrs Manners, thank you for asking. We've just about finished with Sir Morris's treasures now."

"Jolly good. Here's your tea. I'll place it here by the ceremonial mask Sir Morris took from a tribe in what is now the Southern Nigeria Protectorate. He first journeyed to Africa in 1841—"

"Thank you for the tea, Mrs Manners, but we must be getting on. There's a good deal of dusting to do!"

"Yes of course, don't let me stop you. I wondered if you wouldn't mind paying particular attention to the seventeenth-century plough next. Having just examined it I've come to realise that it truly has become quite dusty. The plough has an interesting history, though. We think it originally fell into the hands of the Moldspit family, who lived in—"

"We shall certainly dust the plough, Mrs Manners. Don't you worry."

"Thank you."

Churchill buried her head in the chest again as soon as Mrs Manners had left.

"How odd! I can't see anything in here now."

"That's because you're wearing my spectacles."

"Oh yes, so I am. Here you go. Ah, that's better. This looks rather more interesting now... What's this? I must say this is extremely interesting indeed, Pembers. I do believe I've found Sir Morris's will!" Churchill pulled it out of the chest. "It runs to several pages." She skimmed her eyes over each page. "There's a lot of detail about all the items he bequeathed to the museum. The spear and the shield get a mention, as do the Egyptian artefacts."

"*Stolen* artefacts, you mean."

"Let's not get into all that now. Good grief, Pembers, here it is! Here is Miss Darcy Sprockett's name, and it states there that Sir Morris left her the enormous sum of—"

"Mrs Churchill?"

The voice startled her so much that the will fell out of her hands and landed on the floor. Mr Manners's eyes remained fixed on Churchill as she stooped to pick it up. She quickly threw it back into the trunk before fumbling the lid shut.

"Oh, good morning, Mr Manners. And how are you today?"

Chapter 35

"CAN'T you find anything at all, Inspector?" fumed Mr Verney as Inspector Mappin sat at his desk leafing through a hefty tome. Churchill and Pemberley sat opposite him, still wearing their cleaning uniforms. Mr Verney and an angry-looking Mr Manners stood to the left of the inspector's desk with the cleaning trolley.

"I can't find any arrestable offence that relates to the opening of a chest with a fifty-year moratorium on it," stated Inspector Mappin.

"It's quite simple," said the solicitor. "It has to be breaking and entering!"

"But nothing was broken," replied the inspector.

"Fraud, then," interjected Mr Manners. "They gained unlawful access to the museum!"

"The museum always has its doors open to the general public," said Churchill. "That's not unlawful access."

"But you fraudulently entered as cleaning ladies rather than as normal ladies."

"Cleaning ladies are normal too, you know!" remonstrated Pemberley.

"We merely wore disguises as part of our investigation," said Churchill. "It's what any self-respecting detective would have done in a similar situation."

"But you fooled my poor wife!" raged Mr Manners.

"I'm not sure how," said Inspector Mappin. "Any halfwit could see that these two ladies are Mrs Churchill and Miss Pemberley in ill-fitting cleaners' uniforms."

"Are you calling my wife a halfwit, Inspector?"

"No, I didn't mean that at all. I do apologise, Mr Manners. It's just that these so-called 'disguises' the two ladies are wearing aren't terribly convincing."

"I'd like to see you do better, Inspector," said Churchill.

"This isn't a costume competition, Mrs Churchill," said Mr Verney. "It's a serious matter of larceny."

"But I haven't stolen anything, Mr Verney."

"Ah, but you would have if Manners here hadn't stumbled upon you."

"I certainly wouldn't have. I merely intended to look at Sir Morris's last will and testament, and then place it right back where I found it."

"Inappropriate handling of private property!" announced Mr Verney. "Is that in your handbook, Inspector Mappin?"

"I wouldn't have thought so."

"Can't you check?"

"I've never heard of such a thing," muttered the inspector as he started leafing through his book again.

"Either way, these two women should spend a night in the cells to teach them a lesson," said Mr Manners.

"Two elderly ladies in the cells?" said Churchill. "I thought you were such a nice young man when I first met you, Mr Manners."

"And I thought you were a nice old lady," he retorted.

"How wrong could I be? It has to at least be an act of vandalism, Inspector. Detain these women for vandalism!"

"But we didn't vandalise anything," said Pemberley. "We simply opened a silly old chest, and I'm rather regretful now that we did. Will you let us go on our way if we sincerely apologise, Inspector?"

Inspector Mappin gave a snort. "If every criminal were let go after *sincerely apologising*, we'd be up to our necks in crime in this village!"

"How can one be up to one's neck in crime?" asked Pemberley. "Crime is a completely intangible thing. Up to one's neck in something that physically exists, such as mud, is understandable, but crime?"

"There's a good punishment," boomed Mr Manners as he pointed his finger at them. "Bury these two old ladies up to their necks in mud!"

"Now you're just being barbaric, my good man," said Churchill. "I'd venture to say that being confined to this room and listening to the nonsense you lot are spouting is punishment enough. Can we be on our way now, Inspector? We really need to return the trolley to Mrs Thonnings."

"But I'll have to detain you for something," he huffed as he looked even more earnestly through his handbook. "There's no doubt that the pair of you have done something wrong. I just need to pinpoint the relevant offence."

"Fraudulent impersonation," stated Mr Verney, "and the unauthorised opening of a vessel that is of exceptional importance to the populace of Compton Poppleford."

"It's just a mouldy old trunk," said Pemberley, "with woodworm in it."

"Filled with the dull papers of a man who had an over-inflated opinion of himself," added Churchill.

Mr Manners gasped. "You do realise you're talking about Sir Morris Buckle-Duffington, don't you?"

"Of course I do, though he could be the cat's mother for all I care," retorted Churchill. "I missed elevenses this morning, and it's left me feeling rather short-tempered and out of sorts. Perhaps, Mr Manners, you'd like to explain what your thoughts were when you learned that Darcy Sprockett had inherited a large sum of money from Sir Morris."

"My thoughts? I don't recall any of my thoughts from twenty years ago!"

"Weren't you a little tempted by the idea of getting your mitts on the cash?"

"Absolutely not! Miss Sprockett's affairs were entirely her own."

"But it was a large sum of money, wasn't it?"

"I really wouldn't know. And besides, it was none of my business."

"Is that why you serenaded Darcy Sprockett with your trumpet? Were you hoping she would marry you, and then the wealth would also become yours?"

"Not at all. I had no intention of marrying Miss Sprockett!"

"If marriage wasn't your plan, perhaps you persuaded her to leave you a bit of money some other way."

"How so?"

"I don't know. You tell me!"

"What are you getting at, Mrs Churchill?" asked Inspector Mappin.

"Miss Sprockett inherited a great deal of money from Sir Morris, Inspector. Whoever murdered her did so for her money."

"Nonsense!" growled Mr Manners.

Inspector Mappin chewed the end of his pencil

thoughtfully. "Mr Colthrop happens to live in a large house. I wonder whether he took her money."

"His wealth was all *Mrs* Colthrop's," interrupted Mr Verney.

"Oh I see."

"Mr Colthrop is not a murderer, Inspector Mappin," said Churchill. "Mr Manners, on the other hand, is far more suspicious."

"What utter rot!" protested Mr Manners.

Inspector Mappin rested his head in his hands. "I need time to give this some further thought," he moaned.

"Wonderful, Inspector," replied Churchill, getting up from her seat. "In the meantime, Miss Pemberley and I will return to our office for a cup of something and a slice of something else. You can come and arrest us for whatever it is you need to arrest us for whenever you're ready."

"You're not just going to let them walk free, are you?" fumed Mr Manners.

Mr Verney shook his head with disapproval.

"No. He's going to arrest us as soon as he's found something relevant in his police book," replied Churchill. "We won't be going far, will we, Miss Pemberley?"

"No. I don't really want to go anywhere ever again."

"Apart from the haberdashery shop to return Mrs Thonnings's trolley and collect Oswald."

"Oh yes, apart from that."

"This isn't justice!" barked Mr Manners.

"Can't you see that the inspector has a lot on his plate?" said Churchill. "He's got Mr Colthrop downstairs in the cells, and now there's you to consider as well."

"Me? But I've done nothing wrong!"

"That's what they all say, Mr Manners."

Chapter 36

"It seems we've annoyed Inspector Mappin again," said Pemberley as she took a sip of tea.

"I don't consider it a productive day unless we've angered that inept officer of the law," replied Churchill.

"Mr Verney and Mr Manners are angry with us, too. I don't like it when everyone's angry."

"You have to shake the tree to make the fruit fall, Pembers, and our little sojourn to the museum was very fruitful indeed. We have finally confirmed the fact that Sir Morris left a vast portion of his fortune to Darcy Sprockett. His intentions may have been kindly, but his generous gesture ultimately led to her downfall."

"Someone wanted to get their hands on her money."

"Exactly. Now, it could be old Mr Sprockett, but there's little to no evidence of any profligate spending on his part."

"Unless he's spent it already. He may have gambled it all away."

"That's a possibility, I suppose. But would he have murdered his own daughter?"

"Oh no. I can't imagine him doing that."

"Then there's Great-aunt Betsy," said Churchill as she selected a currant bun from the plate in front of her. "I consider her to be really quite suspicious. And she's also terribly rude, isn't she?"

"I don't think we should try telephoning her again."

"Me neither, but if needs be we could pay her a visit up at Walton-on-Thames. Then we also have Mr Manners and Mr Pentwhistle, both of whom claim some vague romantic attachment to Darcy Sprockett, which may or may not have been founded upon the knowledge that she was about to be left a large sum of money."

'But she wouldn't have left it to them, would she?"

"She might have done. Perhaps she was madly in love with one of them and expected a marriage proposal."

"In which case, why didn't the supposed murderer wait until they were married and then do the deed?"

"That's a good point. Perhaps she was so blinded by love that she promised him the money before they were wed."

"She may have done, but how would he have got his hands on it after she died?" Pemberley asked. "Do we know if she made a will?"

"No will has been mentioned so far, and she was rather young for that sort of thing, wasn't she? No one considers writing a will when they're only twenty years old."

"But it would be the sensible thing to do if one expected to inherit a lot of money at that tender age."

"You're right, Pembers, it would indeed. We'll need to investigate whether she had a will. She must have banked her fortune somewhere, so maybe she shared the account details with the man to whom she believed she was betrothed. She may even have made him a signatory."

"Yes, she may have done. And then once she was

deceased he might have cleared out the bank account. Hang on, what's Oswald eating?"

"He's eating something, is he?"

"Yes! He's just finished it, in fact, and now he's licking his lips. You didn't give him a currant bun, did you, Mrs Churchill?"

"Of course not. How many banks are there in Compton Poppleford, Pembers?"

"Just the one."

"Let's go and pay it a visit."

"Shall we change out of our cleaning lady costumes first?"

"I'd completely forgotten I was wearing mine. They're rather comfortable, aren't they?"

Chapter 37

THE BANK WAS an austere-looking stone building sand-
wiched between the butcher's shop and the barber's.
Inside, a bald, bespectacled man sat behind a window
mounted high on a polished walnut counter.

"Hello up there, bank teller!" said Churchill, standing
on the tips of her toes in order to see him properly.

His gaze remained impassive.

"I'm Mrs Churchill and this is my assistant, Miss
Pemberley. We're from the local private detective agency.
You may have noticed our offices above the bakery."

"I think I have, yes," he replied.

"That's a good start. Now, we happen to be investigating the sad demise of Miss Darcy Sprockett. We believe
she came into a large sum of money, which she may have
deposited at your fine bank here."

"And?"

"Well, we happen to think that the large sum of
money acted as a motivation for someone without any
scruples. We're wondering whether Miss Sprockett
unwisely shared the details of her bank account with this

unscrupulous person, who then helped himself – or herself – to the money once Miss Sprockett was deceased."

The bald man gave a shrug.

"Can you tell us whether that is indeed the case?"

"I'm afraid I'm not at liberty to share the details of our customers' accounts."

"I realise you're merely executing your duty in a professional manner, and that your superiors would no doubt be very proud of your conduct. However, these circumstances can hardly be considered the norm. For a start, this particular customer is no longer alive."

"In which case I could only share pertinent information with the next of kin."

"May I ask your name, sir?"

"Mr Burbage."

"You seem to be a very pleasant fellow, Mr Burbage, and the sort to quite rightly call a spade a spade."

"What exactly do you mean by that?"

"That you're the professional, pragmatic sort who takes pride in his work."

Mr Burbage straightened his tie. "I certainly do."

"That is very reassuring to hear. As a personal customer of your bank I'm encouraged to hear that my money is being looked after so proficiently."

"It is."

"I can't tell you how pleased I am to hear it, because, if I may be quite frank with you, some banks these days leave rather a lot to be desired."

"Indeed they do. We like to do things the old-fashioned way here."

"I'm delighted to hear it, Mr Burbage! Old-fashioned ways are always the best. Don't you agree, Miss Pemberley?"

Her assistant gave this some thought. "I'm not sure, really. Sometimes modern methods can be better."

"Do excuse Miss Pemberley, Mr Burbage, she has the odd wayward notion. Sometimes I have the crazy idea that she likes to disagree with me on purpose! Anyway, where were we? Oh yes. Perhaps there is one little thing you could do for us, Mr Burbage, as the professional and accomplished bank teller you are."

"What's that?"

"Simply tell us whether the account that was opened in Miss Darcy Sprockett's name remains open."

"What will you do with this information if I give it to you?"

"I shall use it to inform my knowledge-gathering in this case."

Mr Burbage sighed, got down from his stool and disappeared through the door behind it.

"Good grief! He's hardly a laugh a minute, is he, Pembers? One can only hope that he cheers up a little when he's at home, otherwise his poor wife must have a lot to put up with."

"Perhaps she's equally humourless."

"She must be."

"Or perhaps he doesn't have a wife."

"That's the more likely scenario, wouldn't you say? I can't imagine the miserable donkey persuading anyone to... Oh! Hello, Mr Burbage."

The bank teller glowered at them.

"I was just telling Miss Pemberley here about Farmer Drumhead's miserable old donkey. Thoroughly downcast, he is. Any luck with my query?"

"I've found an account in Miss Darcy Sprockett's name."

"Oh, marvellous! Is there any money in it?"

"The account was closed twenty years ago."

Churchill gasped. "Goodness, really? Then what happened to the money?"

"It was withdrawn."

"By whom?"

"I don't know."

"Good gracious! You know what this means, Pembers. It means that Miss Sprockett gave her account details to one of those rats, and after her death he or she scurried in and gobbled up all her money! Disgraceful! I'm surprised your bank would allow such a thing to happen, Mr Burbage. Were you not suspicious when someone who was not Miss Sprockett came into this branch and took out all her money?"

"I can't say that I recall it."

"You don't recall someone making off with Miss Sprockett's money? It would have been quite a vast sum."

"I don't. I was probably working at the Heythrop Itching branch that day."

"But don't you think that whichever colleague of yours was working here that day should have trapped the rat?"

"He would have seen no reason to if everything appeared to be above board."

"How could it have appeared to be above board?"

"If the person happened to be a signatory on the account or the next of kin."

"Do the records for the account show who withdrew the money?"

"No."

"Darn it! Someone got their grubby hands on Miss Sprockett's money, and we must find out who! Thank you Mr Burbage, although I must say that you weren't of great help to us given that we know nothing more than we did when we first walked in."

"You know that someone withdrew the money and then closed the account."

"I suppose we do, yes. It has merely served to confirm our worst fears, hasn't it, Miss Pemberley."

"Sadly, it has."

The two ladies left the bank and made their way back along the cobbled high street in the direction of the office.

"Oh no," groaned Pemberley as a familiar-looking lady in a blue blouse and floral skirt walked toward them. "We're going to have to face Mrs Manners again."

"Well, if she wants to be cross with us we'll just have to endure it for a few minutes."

"I hate it when people are cross with me. It makes my eyes go watery."

"She doesn't look that scary, Pembers, I'm sure it'll be fine. Oh, hello Mrs Manners!" Churchill gave the lady a wide smile. "I must apologise for that little incident this morning. We both feel quite terrible about tricking you into thinking we were cleaning ladies, especially after you made us such a nice cup of tea. It was all part of our investigation, you see, and it was quite important that we were able to look at Sir Morris's papers. We realise we upset a plethora of people by opening the chest when we weren't supposed to, and I apologise profusely for that. I hope you're not too upset by our behaviour, and please rest assured that we have incurred the wrath of a number of local personages as a result, the local police inspector being one of them."

"Thank you for your apology, Mrs Churchill, but it really isn't necessary."

"Oh, but I'm sure it is. After all, we tampered with an important museum exhibit and broke the moratorium that applied to the opening of a vessel of most distinguished importance to the populace of Compton Poppleford."

"Oh, don't worry about that," she replied with a smile. "I've seen Barnaby rummaging about in that old thing a number of times over the years."

Churchill felt her mouth hang open. "Mr Manners opened the chest?"

"Yes. Curiosity got the better of him, you understand. The temptation was always there with the key hanging from the hook right above it."

"I see." Churchill felt her fists clench. "And he had the gall to scold us in front of that dull lawyer and inept police officer!"

"Oh, please don't tell him I told you. I was sworn to secrecy, and I only told you because I didn't want you to feel so bad about it."

"All right, fine. Well, thank you for imparting the information to us, Mrs Manners. At least we feel a little better about our actions now."

"And you're both very good at dusting, by the way. The museum is looking much better now. When will you be back to finish it off?"

"We're not really cleaning ladies, Mrs Manners. It was a disguise."

"Oh right. Perhaps I've got myself a little confused."

"It *is* rather confusing, I'm afraid. Very confusing indeed."

Chapter 38

"WHAT A SILLY MAN MR MANNERS IS," said Pemberley once they had returned to the office.

"His actions make him even more suspicious if you ask me."

"I think they rule him out as a suspect."

"What makes you say that, Pembers?"

"Perhaps he opened the chest because he wanted to find out who Sir Morris had left his money to. Perhaps he did so because he hadn't realised Darcy Sprockett was the recipient. If he knew she'd inherited all that money from Sir Morris he wouldn't have needed to look at the will. The murderer must already have known that she'd inherited the money."

"Oh, I see what you mean. What excellent logic, Pembers. The alternative, however, is that he's just a nosy sort who wished to see what else was in the chest."

"There is that, I suppose."

"How funny to hear that the old chap has been digging about in the accursed trunk as well. All that scorn poured over us for opening it, and I'd be prepared to wager that half the village has stuck its proboscis in there at some time or another."

"At least we were honest about opening the trunk."

"Exactly. We may have been caught *in flagrante*, but at least we didn't pretend we hadn't done it. That makes us far worthier than the likes of Manners or any other chump who's had a delve about and then denied it afterwards."

As Churchill drained her cup of tea the book on her desk caught her eye.

"I haven't had a single moment to read *Wuthering Heights* recently. It's difficult to find the time, isn't it?"

"Not really. I always manage it."

"Do you? You must be far less busy than me in that case. I must say, they're all rather serious in *Wuthering Heights,* aren't they? You'd think they'd have developed a dry strain of humour to cope with daily life on those cold, rain-sodden moors, but no! Mr Burbage would have fitted in very well up there. Oh wait, I hear footsteps on the stairs. I believe we have a visitor."

Oswald began to bark.

"Can we stop him doing that, Pembers?"

"Stop him? But I've deliberately trained him to do it!"

"You trained him to deafen us? Why?"

"So he can be our guard dog, Mrs Churchill!"

"That scrappy little water thing? A *guard dog*?"

"Hullo?"

The brown-whiskered face of Inspector Mappin peered around the door, and Oswald greeted him as he stepped into the room.

"Hello, Inspector. Have you finally found an appropriate charge in your little book yet?"

"I'm afraid not, Mrs Churchill." He placed his hat on the hatstand and sat down. "I'm here to issue you with a warning instead."

"Oh no, not another one. Would you like a cup of tea before you get stuck into it?"

"Thank you, that would be nice."

Pemberley fetched an extra cup and saucer, and Churchill poured out the tea while Inspector Mappin officiously cleared his throat.

"Now then. I must warn you against any more of this dressing-up-and-pretending-to-be-someone-else business."

"We were working undercover, Inspector. It's what detectives do."

"It wasn't particularly successful, though, was it? You were found out."

"I'll admit that we may need to make a few revisions to our method of disguise in future."

"No revisions, please. No costumes at all, in fact."

"Inspector, you cannot possibly place such curbs on my business. I'm a private detective, and I must therefore use established investigation techniques."

"Mr Atkins often used to disguise himself," added Pemberley.

"There's a difference between a disguise and a costume," replied the inspector.

"How so?" Churchill probed.

"A disguise ensures that you cannot possibly realise that the person has disguised himself. A costume is merely different apparel worn by an easily recognisable person."

"An interesting distinction, Inspector. I must say that I'm impressed with your powers of observation. So from this point forward we will agree to disguise ourselves but not to wear costumes."

"Must you disguise yourselves? It will invariably end up creating extra work for me. Can't you just do some simple investigating? You're both getting on in years, you know, and it isn't very becoming for older ladies to be gallivanting about in fancy dress."

"We'll gallivant about in whatever we like!"

He sighed. "There's gallivanting and then there's *gallivanting*, Mrs Churchill. And the sort of gallivanting I don't like you doing is the sort that forces me to fill in countless forms."

"Then you need to speak to your chief inspector about all the bureaucracy."

"The bureaucracy works just the way it should, Mrs Churchill. The problems arise when certain individuals create *unnecessary* bureaucracy."

"You should speak to Mr Manners, in that case. He's the one who called you, not us. I didn't feel that it was a police matter at all. And we know for sure that it wasn't now because you couldn't find a relevant charge in your handbook."

"Why, oh, why must you make everything so difficult for me, Mrs Churchill? All I'm trying to do is issue you with a simple warning, and then I'd like to get on with the rest of my day. Won't you just accept the warning so we can put an end to all this?"

"That's a good point, Inspector. Yes, I accept it. Do you accept the warning, Miss Pemberley?"

"Yes."

"Jolly good. That's that done with, then." Inspector Mappin sipped his tea.

"What's happening with Mr Colthrop?" asked Churchill.

"Ah yes, him." The inspector wiped a dribble of tea from his moustache with his sleeve. "I've had to let him go."

"That is interesting news indeed. May I ask why?"

"I couldn't find any evidence against him."

"That's a shame, but not altogether surprising. I don't think there is the tiniest shred of evidence that Mr Colthrop had anything to do with Darcy Sprockett's disappearance. It was rather a surprise to hear that you had arrested him."

The inspector gave an awkward cough. "Well, if truth be told, Mrs Churchill, I was somewhat misled."

"Really? How so?"

"It's more a case of *by whom*."

"By whom, then?"

"By yourself, Mrs Churchill."

"Me? What on earth are you talking about?"

The inspector pointed to the incident board on the wall behind her.

"I saw Mr Colthrop's photograph up there and assumed he was your chief suspect in the Darcy Sprockett case."

"Oh, good grief! The poor man was arrested because he was up on our board, was he?"

"It's only because you just happen to have solved a few cases before now. I thought I could stay one step ahead of you if I went out and arrested him."

Churchill shook her head in disbelief.

"Out of interest, why is he on your board?" asked the inspector.

"As part of a completely unconnected case."

"Has he broken the law in some way?"

"Not that I know of, Inspector. But he doesn't know that we're investigating him, so I'd prefer it if you didn't mention it to him."

"I see."

Churchill took in the inspector's uncomfortable expression and sighed. "Oh dear. You've already mentioned it to him, haven't you?"

"Only in passing."

"Inspector Mappin! The cases we work on are confidential!"

"Then why do you keep everything pinned up on a ruddy great board for all to see?"

"Take your eyes off our board, if you please. In fact, we're quite finished here. It's time for you to shoo!"

"You can't tell an officer of the law to shoo," he replied, standing up and retrieving his hat from the hatstand.

"Who says? Does it say that in your special little book?"

"No, it doesn't."

"Goodbye then, Inspector Mappin."

Churchill waited for the police officer's steps to descend the stairs before speaking again. "It's only a matter of time before Colthrop marches himself up here, Pembers, mark my words. Let's fortify ourselves with a large slice of fruit cake."

Chapter 39

"So THIS IS your eyrie then, is it, Mrs Churchill?" asked Mr Colthrop as he stood in the centre of the office and glanced around.

"Eyrie, Mr Colthrop? I'm not a squirrel!"

"Eagle," corrected Pemberley.

"I'm sorry, what?" asked Churchill.

"You're not an eagle."

"No, I'm not an eagle, either."

"An eagle lives in an eyrie and a squirrel lives in a drey, Mrs Churchill."

"Well, good for them. And good for you for knowing such things, Miss Pemberley. Are you all right there, Mr Colthrop?"

"Yes, I'm just looking for something, you see," he replied, squinting up at the incident board.

"A squirrel perhaps? Or an eagle?"

"Oh… er, no… not at all. Are there any in here?"

"No. You were the one who brought them up in the first place, remember? I must say, Mr Colthrop, that I feel quite tempted to ask you to leave the room and then reenter so we can start all over again. I think we're all terribly confused."

"The wall there…" he pointed to the incident board.

"Yes? What of it?"

"You've got a map and various notes and photographs all pinned up there and linked together with string."

"Yes, that's right, Mr Colthrop. It's there to provide us with a useful visualisation of the Darcy Sprockett case."

"I see. Yes, well, I suppose it does rather, doesn't it? It's just that…"

"Just that what, Mr Colthrop?"

"This may sound rather silly when I say it, but Inspector Mappin mentioned to me that my photograph was up on the wall of your office, you see."

Churchill gave an exaggerated laugh. "Did he now?"

"Yes, and I must say that I was initially quite flattered. But then when he told me you'd linked my photograph to the terrible Darcy Sprockett case I was quite dumb-founded, to be honest with you."

"Inspector Mappin was completely mistaken," said Churchill.

"But why would he tell me that my photograph was on your incident board if it wasn't?"

"Because the man is a buffle-brained clot, Mr Colthrop."

Churchill felt increasingly relieved that the photographs of Mr Colthrop and his six sisters were safely at rest within the drawer in her desk.

"But he must have had a reason."

"No reason other than his own beetle-headed foolish-ness, I imagine."

"Strewth! You really don't like the man, do you?"

"On the contrary, I do quite like Inspector Mappin, but

he's hopeless at his job. Oswald the dog would make a better police inspector."

Mr Colthrop scratched his head. "I suppose the old inspector must have got his wires crossed."

"Not for the first time."

"No, I suppose not."

"You must be enormously relieved to have your freedom back, Mr Colthrop. Congratulations."

"Thank you, Mrs Churchill. Thank you." He grinned. "Are you sure you don't have a photograph of me somewhere in here?"

"Quite sure, Mr Colthrop."

"I rather liked the thought of you admiring my picture, you see."

"I'm much too busy to sit around admiring anything, Mr Colthrop."

"How terribly sad."

"Isn't it just?"

"I shall be dining at the French bistro this evening. You know, the little place I mentioned to you that time."

"Have a lovely evening there, Mr Colthrop. Good day."

"Ugh," said Pemberley once Mr Colthrop had departed. "He's taken a real shine to you, Mrs Churchill."

"It's enough to make one's toes curl, isn't it?"

"I don't feel as though I can eat any more of this fruit cake now. I've entirely lost my appetite."

"Let's forget about him for the time being, Pembers. We've got this case to crack for now. We know that someone emptied Darcy's bank account around the time she died, but who was it?"

"Pentwhistle, Manners, Munion, Sprockett or Great-aunt Betsy."

"I've had quite enough of Manners for one day. Shall we pay old saltybeard Pentwhistle another visit tomorrow and quiz him on the anomaly in his testimony?"

Chapter 40

Mr Pentwhistle was standing in the front garden of his cottage on Hibiscus Lane, half-covered by a large sheet of white canvas, when the two ladies arrived.

"Mr Pentwhistle?" ventured Churchill.

"Ahoy there!" He emerged from beneath the sail. "My spinnaker took an unfortunate battering in a katabatic williwaw."

"Oh dear. Have you seen the doctor about it?"

"No, it's my sail."

"The willy whatsit?"

"No, that's a type of wind."

"I'm afraid I'm not au fait with sailor talk, Mr Pentwhistle. You'll have to speak English with me."

"I'm just giving this sail a quick once-over, Mrs Churchill," he clarified. "All time on land must be put to good use, repairing and preparing."

"Indeed."

"How can I help you this afternoon?"

"Ah yes. We were wondering whether you could settle

the little contradiction in your account of the night Darcy Sprockett went missing."

"Oh, I see. We're still focusing on that, are we?"

"Yes, and we shall be until we've found out exactly what happened to Miss Sprockett that fateful night."

"Isn't it sorted now? The last I heard, Bertrand Pockleswathe was behind it."

"I think that was some random notion of Inspector Mappin's. He also arrested Mr Colthrop and then promptly released him again, so that demonstrates just how much he knows about the case."

"Didn't Colthrop do it, then?"

"No, I don't think so."

"Who was it, then?"

"Exactly! You told Mr Atkins you went to the pictures in Dorchester the night that Darcy Sprockett went missing, whereas you told me and Miss Pemberley here that you couldn't remember what you did that night."

"It was a long time ago."

"Indeed it was. However, Mrs Agatha Munion née Byles, says that she saw you in Poppleford Woods that evening."

"Oh yes, so she did."

"You can confirm it?"

"Yes."

"What was all this business about going to the pictures in Dorchester, if that's the case?"

"I probably got a bit muddled."

"Don't you think that seems rather suspicious?"

"What does?"

"The fact that you've changed your story about your whereabouts on the evening in question more than once."

Mr Pentwhistle sighed. "Look, Mrs Churchill, we're

talking about the events of twenty years ago, and I've sailed—"

"Around the globe by way of the Three Capes twelve times since then."

"Yes! How did you know that?"

"You told us before."

"I did, did I?"

"So in summary, Mr Pentwhistle, you now maintain that you *were* in Poppleford Woods the evening that Darcy Sprockett went missing?"

"Yes, because I remember seeing Agatha there."

"Did you speak to her?"

"We had a brief exchange and then went on our way."

"What were you doing in the woods to begin with?"

"Now that I simply cannot recall. But I used to take a shortcut through there to the Wagon and Carrot, so that's the most likely explanation."

"You'd hazard a guess that you were on your way to the pub when you saw Agatha, would you?"

"Most likely, yes."

"Did you see Miss Sprockett in the woods that evening?"

"I didn't, no."

"Can you remember what time you reached the Wagon and Carrot?"

"Haven't a clue, I'm afraid."

"Can you recall whether it was before or after sundown?"

"I couldn't tell you specifically, although I'm fairly sure it would have been before sundown. I certainly wouldn't have walked through the woods in the dark, and it must have been fairly light given that I was able to see Agatha Byles."

"Munion."

"Whatever she calls herself these days. I'd hardly have seen her in the dark, would I? Neither of us would have been wandering about the woods in the dark; not with the rumours of goblins and so on floating about."

"Don't tell me you believe in all those silly superstitions."

"I'm a sailor, Mrs Churchill! You don't get anyone more superstitious than us seafarers. Never set sail on a Friday and all that."

"Really?"

"And never take bananas on board," added Pemberley.

"What?" questioned Churchill.

"Definitely no bananas!" said Mr Pentwhistle. "And no whistling, either."

"Why ever not?" Churchill asked.

"It's bad luck."

"How do you know about not taking bananas onto a boat, Miss Pemberley?" asked Churchill.

"From my days on transatlantic steamships, Mrs Churchill."

"Of course, I should have known. Where were we, Mr Pentwhistle? Ah yes. You're certain, then, that you were safely ensconced within the confines of the Wagon and Carrot public house by sundown on the evening that Darcy Sprockett went missing?"

"Yes."

"And you definitely weren't at the pictures in Dorchester?"

"No."

"And you weren't doing something else?"

"No."

"Jolly good. And how much do you know in regard to Miss Sprockett's private affairs?"

"Nothing! What sort of chap do you think I am?"

"Were you aware of her financial situation?"

"All the money Sir Morris left her, you mean?"

"How do you know about that?"

"I read it in his will."

"What were you doing reading his will?"

"It's in that old chest down at the museum."

"You opened Sir Morris's chest?"

"Of course."

"But it has a fifty-year moratorium to prevent it being opened!"

He gave a cynical laugh. "No one pays any attention to that. I can't think of a single person in the village who hasn't had a riffle through Sir Morris's trunk."

Churchill felt her teeth clench as she thought about the telling-off she and Pemberley had been on the receiving end of at the police station.

"The trick is not to get caught," added Mr Pentwhistle, as if he were somehow reading her mind.

"Evidently. Suffice to say, then, that you were aware Miss Sprockett had inherited a large sum of money."

"Yes. We all knew Sir Morris was flush with funds, and as he died without an heir we wanted to find out who would inherit it. Blow me down if it wasn't Darcy Sprockett!"

"And if you'd married Miss Sprockett you would have benefitted from the money yourself."

"Yes. She would have made some fellow very rich indeed."

"You, perhaps?"

"I didn't want to marry Darcy; I wanted to sail the high seas. Besides, I think she preferred dusty old Manners over me."

"You could have bought a tidy little boat with all that cash."

"Come to think of it, I could have. It's not worth marrying someone just for that, though."

"Or you could have asked her to lend you the money to buy a boat."

"I never would have done that."

"Or you could have stolen it."

"What? Stolen Darcy's money? Never!"

"Do you know whether anyone else might have stolen it?"

"Absolutely not! Apart from Bertrand Pockleswathe, perhaps. That's the sort of thing he'd have done."

"Did she make anyone else a signatory on her bank account?"

"I really couldn't tell you, Mrs Churchill."

"It wasn't you, then?"

"No! Why on earth would she do that?"

"Perhaps you persuaded her to share some of the funds so you could buy your boat."

"I made my boat, Mrs Churchill. Why are you trying to pin this on me all of a sudden?"

"I'm merely asking you the same questions that must be put to everybody."

"You should ask Bertrand Pockleswathe."

"He's in prison, isn't he?"

"Yes, I believe so. Please excuse me now, I must get on with fixing my sail. The old leg's almost better, and with a strong wind I could be off to sea again by next Tuesday."

Chapter 41

"I REALISE what I'm about to say may be tantamount to treason, Pemberley," ventured Churchill as they made their way to the bakery, "but I don't feel as though Atkins did a very thorough investigation on the Sprockett case."

Pemberley gasped. "But of course he did! He was thorough in the extreme!"

"Then why didn't he take into account the vast sum of money Sir Morris bequeathed to Darcy Sprockett? It doesn't receive a single mention in his case file, yet everyone in Compton Poppleford knew that he'd left her the fortune in his will."

"Perhaps he didn't consider it relevant."

"Of course it's relevant! But even if it wasn't, you'd think he would at least have mentioned it and explained why he didn't think it relevant. To ignore it altogether strikes me as sheer incompetence."

Pemberley pulled a crumpled handkerchief from the sleeve of her cardigan and began dabbing at her eyes with it.

"Oh dear. What now, Pembers?"

"Mr Atkins wasn't incompetent. He was a very good detective!"

"I'm sure he was... most of the time, anyway. Perhaps just not on this occasion."

"I don't like it when you say such things about him. It's not his fault he's dead!"

"I realise that's not his fault. While there can be no doubt that he must have accepted some degree of risk when he chose to row a canoe down a crocodile-infested river in Africa, one could never expressly say it was his fault that he died."

"It was the crocodile's fault."

"Yes, it was. Although one cannot blame the animal's natural instinct for taking advantage of an easy lunch once the canoe had capsized."

Pemberley let out a terrible wail.

"Oh, Pembers, control yourself! I'm sorry I mentioned Mr Atkins, and I didn't intend to speak ill of the dead. I'm merely pointing out that perhaps he wasn't completely perfect at his job on this occasion. Perhaps he had the odd day when he wasn't feeling quite up to it and just happened to miss one important clue in all of this. He was entitled to make a mistake here and there. He was only human."

Pemberley emitted a quiet sob and Churchill let out a bemused sigh.

"Perhaps there was some subtlety to his investigation that I somehow overlooked, Pembers. Maybe I'm mistaken. I expect that I shall look through the case file another day and find that he had mentioned the inheritance after all. Come along, now. Let's cheer ourselves up with a few custard tarts from the bakery."

. . .

No sooner had the two ladies sat back down to eat their custard tarts than Mrs Colthrop arrived.

"Congratulations on your husband's release from the cells," said Churchill. "I trust he wasn't too upset by his ordeal."

"He doesn't seem bothered at all. It was only one night in the end, and I think he considers it a good story to tell down at the club."

"All's well that ends well, eh, Mrs Colthrop? It seems Inspector Mappin got himself in quite a muddle."

"The inspector has a very important job to do. He was only doing his best."

"Indeed."

"And now that Peregrine's free to do as he pleases, the important matter of identifying his lady friend looms once again."

"Absolutely, Mrs Colthrop, but are you quite certain that he has a lady friend? Miss Pemberley and I have only ever seen him with male acquaintances or with his sisters. There has been no indication at all that he has strayed to date."

As she spoke, Churchill thought of the unpleasant proposition Mr Colthrop had made beside Sir Morris's statue and tried to push it to the back of her mind.

"I'm quite sure there is someone, Mrs Churchill. As I told you before, it's the whistling that gives him away."

"Ah yes, that. Have you noticed anything else at all? Lipstick on his collar, perhaps?"

"No, just the whistling."

"Perhaps the whistling is due to something else; his being in a particularly good mood, for example."

"Are you telling me that I don't know my own husband?"

"Not at all, Mrs Colthrop."

"Then please find this lady he's been dallying with or I shall have to ask someone else."

"No need to ask anyone else. We'll do everything we can to find her."

"Good. Within the next few days?"

"We'll do our best, Mrs Colthrop."

"We don't have to spend the next few days following Mr Colthrop around again, do we?" complained Pemberley once Mrs Colthrop had departed.

"I suppose it's the only way to discover the identity of his fancy lady, though I'm still not convinced that there is one. There can be no doubt that he tries it on with other women, but I'm not sure that he's enjoyed any real success."

"You're probably not the only one he's propositioned, Mrs Churchill."

"Of course not, there will almost certainly be others. You might be next, Pemberley."

"No, not me."

"I wouldn't be so sure."

"But I *am* sure. I've mastered my withering stare, you see."

Churchill laughed. "Oh, Pembers, I can't imagine that would work at all!"

Pemberley glared at Churchill with piercing eyes that were enlarged by the lenses of her spectacles.

"Oh, gosh! Is that your withering stare?" Churchill felt a chill run down her spine. "Crikey, Pemberley, I see what you mean." She distracted herself with a custard tart.

"It even works on Oswald," said Pemberley. "He's trying to squeeze behind the filing cabinets as we speak."

She got up from her desk and tried to coax him out with a biscuit.

"Now then, Pembers, we've got a lot on our plate," said Churchill.

"Haven't you just eaten the last custard tart?"

"Not *that* plate. Our metaphorical plate."

"That's my favourite type of plate. You don't need to wash it!"

"What? Oh, I see. Don't distract me, Pembers, I'm trying to come up with a plan. Now you heard old sea dog Pentwhistle, he's hoping to sail next Tuesday. How long does it take to sail around the world?"

"I don't know. About a year?"

"Well, if he's the murderer he'll be able to evade justice for a whole year, or even more if he decides never to come back. It's crucial, therefore, that we nail this Darcy Sprockett case before next Tuesday."

"But today's Friday."

"I realise that."

"And we've just told Mrs Colthrop that we intend to follow Mr Colthrop about for the next few days. How are we going to fit it all in, Mrs Churchill? Oh, I hate it when there's too much work to do. I feel so overwhelmed!"

"Calm yourself, my trusty assistant. Where there's a will there's a way."

"That's just a meaningless saying, Mrs Churchill!"

"Doesn't it help you feel better at all?"

"No. Wills and ways do nothing for me when there's a lot of work to be done."

"Well, the best we can do is make a start, Pembers. Let's rearrange our incident board and give this case a little thinking time."

Chapter 42

THE TWO LADIES spent the next hour or so moving the pictures, pieces of string and pins around the incident board.

"This isn't a particularly flattering picture of Mrs Munion," commented Churchill.

"That's one of the better ones."

"Some people don't photograph well, do they? It's most unfortunate."

"Do we still need her picture up on the board? Can she really be considered a suspect?"

"Well, let's see now. She was in Poppleford Woods the night Darcy Sprockett went missing, but she says that she returned home before sundown. And in Atkins's case file he mentions that both of her parents provided an alibi for her."

"Darcy was last seen at a quarter to ten that evening, wasn't she?"

"Yes. Great-aunt Betsy stated that Darcy arrived at her cottage at half-past nine and left at a quarter to ten. It would have been quite dark by then, and Mrs Munion née

Byles would already have been at home, according to herself and her parents."

"In which case she can't have harmed Darcy."

"It doesn't seem likely. And what would her motive have been, anyway? I suppose Darcy's wealth would have been a motivating factor for rather a lot of unscrupulous people. The only other motive I can think of is that the two girls were rivals in the Compton Poppleford May Day Fair All Girls' Triathlon. Perhaps their little spat turned into something more deadly."

"But when? Agatha was at home before the last sighting of Darcy."

"According to the Byles clan, she was, but family members quite often provide false alibis. In many cases I'm not surprised that the nearest and dearest speak up on their behalf. They don't want to believe that a loved one has done anything wrong, do they?"

"Shall we leave Mrs Munion up on the board, then?"

"I think we should for now, Pembers."

"What about Barnaby Manners?"

There was a sharp intake of breath from Churchill. "My estimation of him has plummeted ever since he lambasted us for opening Sir Morris's chest when his own grubby mitts had been rummaging about in there all the while. What a disgrace! He portrays himself as a mild-mannered, trumpet-playing, learned man of local history, but I think he's a little more sinister than that, Pembers."

"Surely he's too dull to be sinister."

"The dullness is all an act. If you've been up to something you shouldn't have, what better way to cover your tracks than to be so inordinately dull that no one stops to give you the time of day?"

"He's hiding behind a featureless wall of tedium, you mean."

"Oh, I like that, Pembers! I like that a lot. It sums Mr Manners up perfectly. His picture must absolutely remain on the board. And what's more, do you recall that he couldn't exactly remember what he was doing the night that Darcy went missing? He tried to distract us with talk of *What a Lark with Tommy Briggins* on the wireless. Very suspicious, if you ask me. He paid Darcy a visit earlier that day, and who's to say he didn't return and follow her through the woods that night?"

"Ugh!" Pemberley gave a great shiver.

"And then he lurked outside Great-aunt Betsy's cottage until she came out again."

"Ugh!"

"I'm afraid it's the sort of thing sinister people do, Pembers."

"He doesn't deserve to be curator of the Compton Poppleford History Museum or chairman of the Compton Poppleford Local History Group."

"He certainly doesn't. That's another thing sinister people do. They manage to worm their way into positions of authority and respect so that no one would believe they had ever done anything wrong."

"Ugh."

"Must you keep making that noise?"

"I can't think what else to say; it's all so horrible. Are you planning on asking Inspector Mappin to arrest Mr Manners?"

"We don't have quite enough proof as yet, but his motive must have been Darcy's money. There's no doubt about that."

"What's he done with it all, do you think?"

"Who knows? Spent it on the conservation of that old plough, perhaps. There's another reason I suspect the man as well."

"What's that?"

"He wears those dreadful daywear bow ties. There's nothing quite like a bow tie to suggest that its wearer wishes to appear more innocuous than he really is. I'm not talking about the smart evening wear bow ties of black or white, but those awful patterned ones that are usually over-sized and brightly coloured. They hint at the fact that the wearer is a jaunty, jocular fellow who enjoys a bit of banter and repartee, and that he doesn't take himself too seriously. We, on the other hand, know that he undoubtedly has something to hide."

"Isn't that rather a sweeping statement?"

"I have yet to see it disproven."

"But Mr Manners isn't jaunty or jocular, and I've never seen him enjoy any sort of banter, and—"

"Let's not overanalyse everything, Pembers. There's still our sailor friend Timothy Pentwhistle to consider, of course."

"Ah, yes. The man who's changed his story more times than I've changed my vest."

"There's no need to bring your personal hygiene into this, Pembers."

"But he's incapable of sticking to a single story. One moment he said he'd gone to the pictures in Dorchester and the next he'd walked through the woods to the Wagon and Carrot and seen Mrs Munion along the way."

"And he argued with Darcy Sprockett on the day of her disappearance. He appears to have conveniently forgotten what the disagreement was about, but there's no denying that it happened because Atkins found witnesses."

"Does the case file mention alibis for Manners and Pentwhistle on the evening that Darcy went missing?"

"Manners's alibi was his mother, so that doesn't mean much. As for Pentwhistle, I don't think there was an alibi for him at all that night. We could ask in the Wagon and Carrot whether anyone saw him there that evening."

"Ask if anyone saw him there *twenty years ago?*"

"It's worth a shot, wouldn't you say?"

"I think it would be a struggle to believe anyone's word twenty years after the event."

"You're right, Pembers, it would be." Churchill sighed. "Some people are able to recall distant events very accurately, while others struggle to remember anything that happened before last Thursday."

"And even then it's a question of whom to believe."

"Indeed. I still think it's worth asking down at the Wagon and Carrot. I can't imagine the clientele having changed much over the past few decades in a place like Compton Poppleford."

"What makes you say that?"

"For a start, there's nowhere else for the menfolk to have a drink of an evening, is there?"

"There's the Pig and Scythe."

"That public house full of smock and clog-wearing rustics? I can't imagine Pentwhistle and his ilk frequenting the place."

"The Wagon and Carrot it is, then."

"When it comes to motive, I'd say that Mr Manners or Mr Pentwhistle could have been driven by greed. It's fair to say that there was a vague romantic association between both men and Miss Sprockett."

"Very vague, I'd say."

"Yes, but precise enough that one of them may have tried to charm his way into her bank account."

"I can't imagine Mr Manners charming anyone."

"Neither can I, Pembers, even if he wore his best bow tie! My suspicion is falling rather heavily on Pentwhistle now. I don't think it can be any great coincidence that he's planning to set sail next Tuesday. He's obviously beginning to feel the heat of our investigation!"

"Do you think so?"

"Oh yes. He can't get his ropes and sails repaired quickly enough."

"Or his leg."

"Exactly."

"Why don't you ask Inspector Mappin to arrest him?"

"Proof, Pembers! We need more proof. Besides, there's someone else we haven't discussed yet."

"Bertrand Pockleswathe?"

"I really wish people would stop mentioning that man to me. If we eliminate all other options I'll have a think about Bertrand Pockleswathe. I'm talking about someone else altogether. Great-aunt Betsy herself!"

"Oh no, not her."

"She has to be considered a suspect, Pembers."

"But she was eighty-one when Darcy went missing! She couldn't possibly have harmed a young woman who was athletic to the point that she had come second in the Compton Poppleford May Day Fair All Girls' Triathlon the previous day. Darcy was made of strong stuff."

"Perhaps Great-aunt Betsy incapacitated her in some way. She told Atkins they had a tot of brandy together when Darcy arrived to collect the eggs. Perhaps she put some poison in the brandy."

Pemberley considered this for a moment. "It's possible, I suppose, but how did the elderly lady subsequently transport Darcy's body to the field where it was found?"

"Hmm. We discussed this once before when Mr Bingley visited, didn't we? That's rather a tricky puzzle to solve, and there's really only one way to find out."

"And how's that, exactly?"

"By visiting her in person."

"What? All the way up in wherever it is?"

"Walton-on-Thames in Surrey. I know it well."

"I told you the name she called you when I telephoned her, didn't I? She said you were an interfering cockalorum."

"I care not a jot about that. It's merely the response of a woman who is feeling the heat of our investigation."

"I thought Mr Pentwhistle was feeling the heat of our investigation."

"They both are. People lash out like wounded foxes when they're under threat."

"I feel a little confused, Mrs Churchill. Who is our chief suspect: Mr Pentwhistle or Great-aunt Betsy?"

"They're both equally suspicious, as far as I'm concerned, though I'll have to meet this Great-aunt Betsy before I can make up my mind on that score."

"But we're running out of time. Mr Pentwhistle sails in four days, and we also need to catch Mr Colthrop in the act, quick smart."

"He's not planning on sailing anywhere."

"No, but you told Mrs Colthrop we'd have the case solved within the next few days. And now that we're planning a trip to Surrey, how on earth are we going to fit it all in?"

"It's quite simple, Pembers. We'll have to split up."

"No way!"

"I'm afraid so. I know that we've become accustomed to one another's company, and I must say that I find you quite indispensable at times, Pembers. But sometimes we must spread our resources out a little."

"I don't want to do anything on my own."

"Needs must."

"What will you do and what will I do?"

"You'll visit the Wagon and Carrot to find out if

there are any witnesses to corroborate Pentwhistle's alleged presence there on the evening Darcy went missing."

"And you?"

"I shall visit Great-aunt Betsy in Walton-on-Thames."

"You're a braver woman than me, Mrs Churchill."

"Yes, I should think I am. But there's something else I need you to do, Pembers."

"Oh dear. What might that be?"

"I need you to catch Mr Colthrop in the act."

"Oh, must I?"

"Yes. Just continue with the surveillance programme we implemented before that jughead Mappin arrested him. If anything, it'll be more subtle than when there are two of us involved."

"I'm not sure I'm up to it."

"Of course you are. You've got Oswald the detective dog with you!"

"Oh, yes." Pemberley smiled. "So I have."

"And you also have your withering stare in case Colthrop gets any funny ideas."

"Yes, I suppose I have that too."

"I shall get myself on the early morning branch line service to Dorchester tomorrow, Pembers, then hop on the mainline service to Waterloo. I'll telephone you once I get there."

"Oh, but the branch line is so slow, Mrs Churchill."

"It'll be an arduous journey all right. I'll have to catch another train from Waterloo to Walton-on-Thames, and the sandwiches they serve in those buffet carriages leave a lot to be desired."

"You should take a supply of freshly baked eclairs with you."

"What a brilliant idea, my right-hand woman. I shall

pick some up on my way home and then settle down for an early night. Good luck, Pemberley."

"Good luck, Mrs Churchill. I'll miss you."

"I'll only be gone a few days, Pembers, enough of this nonsense. Oh, now I've gone and got something in my eye."

Chapter 43

"Now THEN, Pembers, how did you get on?" asked Churchill as the two ladies walked through Poppleford Woods the following Sunday evening.

The trees were busy with birdsong and there was a balmy, floral scent in the air. Oswald trotted alongside them, pausing to sniff among the nettles and snap at the butterflies.

"I want to hear how you got on first. How was Great-aunt Betsy?"

"All in good time, Pemberley. As I've already told you, I need to discuss something with Mr Bingley. Did you find an alibi for Mr Pentwhistle at the Wagon and Carrot?"

"I did and I didn't."

"Oh dear. What does that mean, exactly?"

"Well, as you predicted, a lot of the regulars there now were also regulars twenty years ago. Most of them could recall Mr Pentwhistle visiting the Wagon and Carrot back then, but none could be certain that they expressly saw him on the evening that Darcy Sprockett went missing."

"I suppose that's to be expected. In that case his

account is plausible because he was in the habit of frequenting the Wagon and Carrot, but we have some difficulty in pinning him down to that precise date. If only one of the regulars had kept a diary."

"And written down all the names of those they drank with in the Wagon and Carrot every day?"

"That would have been useful, wouldn't it? Never mind. Did you catch Colthrop in the act?"

"I'm afraid not, Mrs Churchill. The situation was quite hopeless. He was at the club for most of Friday, and then he spent all day yesterday fishing. Oswald and I tried to keep watch from across the riverbank, but when I allowed my concentration to lapse for a moment Oswald swam across and ate his sandwiches."

"Oh dear."

"This morning he went to church with Mrs Colthrop, and then they had lunch together at the French bistro."

"Oh well. Never mind, Pembers, you did your best."

"I did, but it wasn't good enough, was it? And now Mrs Colthrop will be cross because we still haven't found out who her husband's lady friend is."

"Do you know what, Pembers? Let's forget about her for the time being. I think she's mistaken about all that other woman business anyway. We'll do our best to get this Darcy Sprockett case solved by the end of tomorrow, and then we'll tell Mrs Colthrop we've decided not to work on her case any more. It's incredibly tedious spending one's weekend watching Mr Colthrop fishing and going to church and having lunch with his wife."

"It was the most boring weekend of my life."

"Well, I think you and Oswald did a sterling job. Don't look so despondent, Pemberley."

"Oh, and Inspector Mappin visited after you'd left for

Surrey. He had something he specifically wanted to discuss with you."

"What was it?"

"He wouldn't tell me."

"It can't have been that important, then. We'll catch up with him soon enough. Let's see what Mr Bingley has to say for himself."

A short while later the two ladies and their detective dog reached the white cottage with its rose-filled garden. Churchill gave a short rap on the shiny front door.

"Oh, hello," said Mr Bingley when he answered.

"I hope we're not disturbing you from your doctor studies," said Churchill.

"My thesis."

"Yes, that."

"What can I do for you?"

"We've come to ask a little favour, if we may. Will you be at home tomorrow?"

"Yes, I'm always at home."

"Perhaps you wouldn't mind us having a little gathering here at about three o'clock."

Mr Bingley frowned. "I don't really like gatherings as a general rule."

"I'll be in charge of it, Mr Bingley. You won't have to do anything other than turn up."

"My cottage is rather small for a gathering."

"We can hold it out here in this pretty little garden."

"Very well. What's it in aid of?"

"I need to update everyone on the Darcy Sprockett case."

"Have you solved it?"

"That would be telling, Mr Bingley."

"When do I get to find out?"

"At the gathering tomorrow."

"Oh, all right then. I'd better get back to Tolstoy for the time being."

"Please do. I happen to have finished reading *Wuthering Heights*. Helped me while away a long train journey, it did."

"Oh, wonderful! How did you find it?"

"I've read happier stories."

"Such as?"

"Ones in which people don't die quite so often, but instead go to nice dinner parties and dances."

"Perhaps you'd enjoy a bit of Jane Austen, Mrs Churchill."

"I'm sure I would. Who's that by?"

"Jane Austen is the name of the author."

"Of course it is, I knew that really. Well, Miss Pemberley and I had better be off. We have a lot of organising to do."

"Oh no, really?" asked Pemberley.

"Yes. Whoever said that Sunday nights were for quiet contemplation, eh? We'll see you tomorrow, Mr Bingley."

"I wish you'd tell me what's going on, Mrs Churchill, I'm beginning to feel rather left out," said Pemberley as they left Mr Bingley's cottage.

"Right, I shall. But you mustn't breathe a word of it to anyone else before the gathering."

Chapter 44

CHURCHILL AND PEMBERLEY spent Monday morning persuading a select group of people to attend the gathering in Mr Bingley's garden that afternoon.

"If another person replies with the word '*Why?*' I shall throttle them," said Churchill. "Surely it shouldn't be this difficult to round everyone up."

"I suppose they consider their time to be precious," replied Pemberley.

"Evidently."

"Mr Manners says he has no one to man the museum, and that he'll have to close it for an hour."

"I hardly think there'll be hordes of people feeling terribly upset about that, do you? I don't think I've ever seen another visitor in that dingy old place."

"Mr Pentwhistle says he needs to adjust his sextant this afternoon. It's out by a few degrees, apparently."

"Adjusting his sexton is more important than our gathering, is it?"

"Sextant."

"Did you tell him there'll be no need for one in a prison cell?"

"Good gracious, no. But that would have been a good reply, wouldn't it? I can only ever think of good replies once a conversation has ended, and even then I don't always think of a very good one. I'm not a natural conversationalist like you, Mrs Churchill."

"Oh, there's nothing to it. I just happen to say whatever comes into my head."

"Mrs Munion has had to cancel her game of tennis."

"What a shame, given that she probably hasn't found the time to play a game since, oh, probably yesterday."

"You can be quite scathing at times, Mrs Churchill."

"I can't abide hearing people's nonsense excuses, that's why. Do none of these people care about what happened to poor Darcy Sprockett?"

"It was rather a long time ago."

"Quite! Come along now, it's time to head over to Mr Bingley's."

To Churchill's relief, most of the chairs dotted around Mr Bingley's front garden were filled by three o'clock. Pemberley made cups of tea for everyone while Mr Sprockett helped pass around a plate of currant buns.

"We should 'ave more parties like this!" he crowed.

"This isn't a party, Mr Sprockett," Churchill said scornfully. "It's an update regarding the tragic events that befell your daughter in this very place twenty years ago."

"All right, all right. It ain't often I sees other people, yer see."

"Maybe you could venture out of your ramshackle home every once in a while, Mr Sprockett, and cheer on the Compton Poppleford cricket team or visit the Wagon and Carrot."

"Still goin', is it, the Wagon an' Carrot?"

"Yes."

"'Ow about the Pig an' Scythe?"

"Yes, Mr Sprockett. Why don't you take a stroll into the village once we've finished here and have a look for yourself? I have other pressing matters to concentrate on at the moment."

"Right you are. Curran' bun?"

"Thank you."

Inspector Mappin sidled up to Churchill in a conspiratorial manner. "I've brought my handcuffs with me, Mrs Churchill, to make any necessary arrests."

"Well done, Inspector. It's invaluable to have the strong arm of the… to have the constabulary present at these events."

"Who did it, then?" he whispered.

"Patience, Inspector."

The grey-looking solicitor, Mr Verney, took a seat next to Mr Pentwhistle. As Mr Bingley made himself comfortable in a deck chair, Oswald jumped up onto his lap. Mr Manners, Mrs Manners and Mrs Munion squeezed together on the white garden bench. The farmhands who had discovered the skeleton in the field had turned up, as had Mrs Higginbath, for no reason Churchill could determine other than out of sheer nosiness.

Churchill felt her hands tremble as she arranged her papers. She enjoyed public speaking once she got into the flow of it, but the anticipation always made her nervous.

"Right then!" she announced over the idle chatter. "Let's begin. Does everyone have a cup of tea and a bun?"

"I've a cup of tea but no bun," called out Mr Manners.

"Miss Pemberley, could you please furnish Mr Manners with a bun?"

Pemberley did as she was asked, then returned to her original position by Mrs Churchill's side.

"Am I allowed a second bun?" Mr Verney called out.

"Only when we can be certain that everyone present has had one," replied Churchill. "We'll return to the buns once I've finished saying what I have to say. Now then, let's get on with it. Our gathering here today is to conclude a twenty-year-old case that was recently reopened following the discovery of a skeleton in Todley Field. The *Compton Poppleford Gazette*'s headline at the time stated: '*Mystery of Darcy Sprockett Solved*'. This was, however, a little misleading. Although the skeleton had been discovered, the case was far from solved.

"Darcy Sprockett disappeared twenty years ago from this very location, where she had just collected a basket of eggs from her Great-aunt Betsy. Elizabeth Earwold, as her great-aunt was otherwise known, lived in this cottage – which is now inhabited by Mr Bingley – at the time. We are indebted to him for hosting us here today."

Mr Bingley gave a polite nod from his deck chair and patted Oswald on the head.

"Twenty years ago, at a quarter to ten in the evening, Darcy Sprockett walked down this garden path, out through the gate and onto the path that led through the woods. No one ever saw her again. The basket of eggs was discovered at first light the following morning on the path about thirty yards from where you are all sitting now."

Heads turned and necks craned as the audience looked around and tried to picture the scene.

"Mrs Munion, then Miss Byles, took a walk in the woods that evening. She was a sometime friend and sometime adversary of Miss Sprockett. They were rivals in the

Compton Poppleford May Day Fair All Girls' Triathlon. Is it possible that they met in the woods that night and exchanged angry words? Did an argument escalate out of control?"

"No!" Mrs Munion called out. "I've already told you I wasn't out that late!"

"I only have your word for it, Mrs Munion."

"But it's the truth! There's no need to point the finger at me just because I beat you in a game of tennis."

"I'm merely presenting an objective view, Mrs Munion. Tennis games won or lost matter little to me. Now then, where was I? Oh yes. Mr Manners visited Miss Sprockett on the day of her disappearance and tried to woo her with his trumpet-playing."

"I wouldn't describe it as *wooing*, exactly," Mr Manners said, his cheeks flushed.

"That's a fair point. The words '*trumpet*' and '*woo*' don't really sit well together, do they?"

"Violin and woo sounds better," said Mr Pentwhistle.

"Indeed. I think most other instruments would sound better when it comes to wooing. However, Mr Manners chose a trumpet."

"There was no *wooing*!" interjected Mr Manners. "It was just *trumpeting*!"

"You recall the trumpeting very clearly, Mr Manners, but your recollection of the remainder of the evening is rather vague. Why is that?"

"Because it was twenty years ago!" he retorted.

"Indeed. How often have we heard that excuse used over the past few weeks, Miss Pemberley?"

"Very often," her assistant replied with a roll of her eyes.

"Mr Pentwhistle finally remembered what he did that evening, and it turns out that he was also out walking in the woods. In fact, he and Mrs Munion happened upon one another. And after exchanging pleasantries with Mrs Munion, Mr Pentwhistle may also have happened upon Miss Sprockett."

"But I didn't!" he piped up.

"I wouldn't expect you to admit it if you did."

"But I actually didn't."

"So you say, Mr Pentwhistle. But I'm told you had a disagreement with Miss Sprockett beside St Dustin's Well earlier that day."

"So people have said, but I can't recall it."

"That's rather convenient, Mr Pentwhistle."

"I'd say it's rather inconvenient that I can't recall it, otherwise I'd be able to clarify what was said and done that day and avoid this infernal finger-pointing that's been going on for the past few weeks."

"Hear, hear!" Mr Manners called out. "I've had enough of the finger-pointing, too! Awful business."

"It's a complete nonsense," added Mr Pentwhistle. "The sooner I set sail tomorrow the better!"

"Now, let's introduce another rather important factor in the disappearance of Darcy Sprockett," continued Churchill, "and that is the large sum of money she inherited from her former employer, Sir Morris Buckle-Duffington. The local dignitary died just a few short months before Miss Sprockett vanished."

"That money was supposed to have been a secret," interrupted Mr Verney.

"It was never going to remain a secret in a place like Compton Poppleford, was it?" replied Churchill. "Besides, Sir Morris practically invited people to look at his will by leaving it lying in a trunk at the local museum and decreeing that no one was to look inside it for fifty years. If that's not a red rag to a bull I don't know what is. The fact of the matter is that Miss Sprockett was rich, and everyone around here knew about it. There can be no doubt that someone wanted to get their hands on her money."

Everyone looked around at each other, as if wondering who the culprit might be.

"Marriage would have secured access to her fortune, wouldn't it, Mr Manners?"

"Erm, would it? Er, yes, I suppose it would have done."

"Were you interested in Miss Sprockett's money, Mr Manners?"

"No."

"Really?"

"Well, I suppose it made her a little more interesting."

"Did you ever propose to Miss Sprockett?"

"I..." He gave his wife a sidelong glance and his face reddened once again.

"This was twenty long years ago, Mr Manners. You may as well come clean."

"I, er... Yes, I did."

There was an audible gasp from around the garden.

"And what was her reply?"

"She declined me."

"How about you, Mr Pentwhistle? Did you propose to...?" A movement in front of Churchill caught her eye. "Oh, we have a visitor."

Chapter 45

A SHINY GREEN motor car bounced slowly along the track toward the cottage and stopped on the other side of the gate.

"Who on earth is that?" asked Inspector Mappin.

"I recognise that car," said Mr Bingley.

The driver got out and opened the rear door. Silence fell as an elderly lady stepped out of the car and walked slowly, with the support of a stick, toward the gate. She wore a rose-coloured dress and a set of cream pearls. Her hair was white, her gaze cold and steely.

Mr Bingley lifted Oswald down from his lap and stood to help the old lady through the gate.

Churchill cleared her throat. "Ladies and gentlemen, may I present to you Miss Elizabeth Earwold, otherwise known as Great-aunt Betsy."

The old lady walked through the garden and Mr Verney rose to offer her his chair. She gave him a civil nod and slowly sat before glancing around with mild disdain.

"Thank you for joining us, Miss Earwold," said

Churchill. "I'm so pleased that you accepted my invitation to return to your former home."

The old lady gave a wan smile.

"Great-aunt Betsy!" said Inspector Mappin with a grin. "Well I never! Long time no see."

"Miss Earwold has joined us at just the right moment," said Mrs Churchill. "After all, I gathered you here today to identify the person responsible for the disappearance of Darcy Sprockett. Now I ask you, who was the last person to see Miss Sprockett that fateful night?"

"Miss Earwold!" chorused several voices.

"Exactly. Miss Earwold was the last person to see her great-niece here in this very place at a quarter to ten that evening. And there you have it." Churchill started folding up her papers.

"Have what?" queried Mr Verney.

"Miss Earwold did it?" asked Mr Manners. "Impossible!"

"An old lady?" questioned Mrs Higginbath.

A general muttering began.

"There has to be some mistake, Mrs Churchill!" whispered Inspector Mappin. "I can't handcuff an old lady. I can't even believe she's still alive! How old is she?"

"A hundred and one."

"You want me to handcuff a one hundred and one year old lady? Ridiculous! I mean, I know she's a murderer, but I have to draw the line somewhere. It simply cannot be done. Surely some clemency must be shown to the elderly and infirm."

"Let's hear what Doctor Sprockett has to say, shall we?"

"Doctor Sprockett? Who on earth is he?"

"*She* is just getting out of the car now."

Churchill cast her gaze back toward the car in time to

see a fair-haired woman in a smart navy dress clambering out. She walked up to the gate and gave the puzzled audience an awkward wave.

"Thank you for joining us, Doctor Sprockett," said Churchill. She noticed flashes of recognition on a few of the faces. "Shall I introduce you to everyone as Doctor Darcy Sprockett?"

"Darcy?" Mr Pentwhistle jumped up from his chair. "You're a doctor now?"

"I am."

"You're alive!" said Mrs Munion, her jaw hanging loose.

"Well I never," Mr Sprockett muttered to himself. "I ain't never thought I'd see the day!"

After everyone had greeted Darcy Sprockett warmly, the bemused lady took a seat in Mr Bingley's newly vacated deck chair.

"Would you like to explain all this, Doctor Sprockett, or shall I?" asked Churchill.

"I imagine you've already done a very good job, Mrs Churchill, so I'll allow you to continue," she replied with a smile.

"Very well. Ladies and gentlemen, you will have noticed by now that the girl you once knew as Darcy Sprockett is alive and well. She is now living and working as a doctor in Walton-on-Thames, Surrey. I stand by my previous assertion that Miss Earwold was responsible for Darcy's disappearance, because that's the truth, albeit not in a nefarious manner. I have recently returned from Walton-on-Thames, where I spent a day in the company of these two ladies. The true story behind this case is really quite a simple one.

"Twenty years ago, Doctor Sprockett was a twenty-year-old woman who toiled day and night for her family and for her employer, Sir Morris Buckle-Duffington. Her dreams of becoming a doctor seemed impossible to realise, having been born into a family of limited means. Furthermore, she was aware that neither of her parents would have approved of her choice."

Mr Sprockett gave a loud sniff.

"Inheriting Sir Morris's wealth was a curse as well as a blessing. Although Darcy felt that her future had become a little more secure, she was pestered on a daily basis by people who wanted a slice of the pie. Potential suitors regularly called at her door, and proposals of marriage were made on an almost daily basis."

Mr Manners shuffled uncomfortably on the bench.

"Every member of the Sprockett family put their feet up and sat back waiting for Darcy to supply their every want and need, it wasn't long before she'd had enough. Therefore, she concocted a plan with the family member she was closest to: Great-aunt Betsy. They planned Darcy's supposed disappearance, so that she would never be pestered again. Miss Earwold had a friend in London who was a doctor and helped to secure a place for Darcy at the School of Medicine for Women.

"There was understandable upset over Darcy's disappearance," continued Churchill, "but Miss Earwold felt confident that it would gradually die down. She came up with a story about goblins, hoping that people would either believe it or dismiss her as a batty old lady. When my predecessor, Mr Atkins, investigated the case he cleverly discovered the truth behind it. However, when Miss Earwold begged him to keep his discovery a secret he acquiesced."

"Atkins knew what happened all along?" barked Inspector Mappin.

"He discovered it during the course of his investigation. His supposed failure to find out what had happened to Darcy Sprockett wasn't a failure at all. He simply agreed to keep his findings quiet."

"He never breathed a word of it to me."

"He was thoroughly professional, Inspector." Churchill noticed Pemberley giving her a proud smile.

"Miss Earwold remained in correspondence with her great-niece, and when Darcy invited her to come and live in Walton-on-Thames she agreed."

"There was nothing down here for me any more," the elderly aunt piped up.

"And everything would eventually have been forgotten about, had it not been for the recent discovery of a skeleton in Farmer Jagford's field," said Churchill. "Everyone leapt to the conclusion that Darcy Sprockett's remains had been found."

"Who is it, then?" Mrs Munion called out.

"That's a very good question, Mrs Munion."

"Funnily enough, Mrs Churchill, I paid a visit to your office on Friday to impart some news," said Inspector Mappin, "but you weren't there."

"Indeed I wasn't. Was that piece of news relevant to this conversation we're having here today?"

"Exceptionally relevant. I received the report back from the bone expert gentleman in Dorchester. The one who examined the skeleton found in the field."

"The osteologist," stated Pemberley once again.

"Yes, him. It turns out the skeleton is not that of a young woman, but of a man aged between seventy and ninety years old."

"What?" Mr Manners cried out.

"The current theory is that the bones are the skeletal remains of old William Boskerworth," said the inspector.

"The chap who got lost in the terrible blizzard of 1872?" asked Mr Manners.

"Yes, that's the one," confirmed Inspector Mappin.

"He went out in that blizzard sixty years ago and never came back," Mr Manners said sadly. "It was before my time, but I still remember my father telling me the story."

"I hear the Boskerworths are arranging a funeral service for him," added Inspector Mappin, "and all are welcome to attend."

"I'll be there," said Miss Earwold. "I remember poor Mr Boskerworth well."

"Goodness, that is a sad tale," said Churchill, "but there's no denying that it clears everything up rather nicely."

"Thank you, Mrs Churchill," said Doctor Sprockett, rising to her feet. "For many years I had no interest in returning to this place, but seeing the cottage and these beautiful woods again reminds me how perfectly lovely Compton Poppleford is. I should have returned much sooner. I apologise to everyone gathered here if my sudden departure caused any upset. I really didn't think anyone would miss me."

"I missed yer," said Mr Sprockett.

"Thank you, Father."

"The 'ouse got pretty dirty after yer left."

"You didn't fancy picking up a broom and giving it a good sweep yourself?" she asked.

"Me? Do women's work?"

"You might want to have a conversation with your father about why your mother left him at some stage, Dr Sprockett," said Mrs Churchill. "Now, I think my work here is done. Do you feel as though your work is done, Miss Pemberley?"

"Oh yes, and I'm feeling rather tired." She picked Oswald up and he licked her face.

"What will you do now, Mrs Churchill?" asked Mr Bingley. "Have a well-earned rest?"

"Just for a few days, perhaps. I quite fancy putting my feet up and reading a bit of Jane Austen."

"Which one?"

"Is there more than one Jane Austen? I wasn't aware of that."

"No, there's only one. I meant which book?"

"Her most famous one, I should think. What's it called again?"

"*Pride and Prejudice.*"

"That one, then. Come along, Pembers, let's leave these people to it."

Chapter 46

AFTER A FEW RESTFUL days away from the office, Churchill and Pemberley met in Poppleford Woods to enjoy a short stroll together.

"Oswald has learned to play dead," said Pemberley. "Watch this. Play dead, Oswald! Oswald, *play dead!*"

The little dog lay down on his side with his tongue hanging out.

"You can see that he's still breathing, Pembers."

"He has to, Mrs Churchill. He's a dog, not an actor!"

"Well, he's a very good dog actor."

"Isn't he just? Jump up, Oswald!"

The little dog sprang to his feet again and gave a loud bark.

"Oh, he's quite adorable, isn't he?"

"He really is. He's like the son I never had."

"A very hairy son."

"What's wrong with having a hairy son?"

"Nothing at all, it was just an observation."

The two ladies walked on.

"Great-aunt Betsy was all right in the end, wasn't she?" said Pemberley. "She didn't call you an interfering cock-alorum again. In fact, she was quite polite after all that."

"Yes, we established a good rapport from the off up in Walton-on-Thames. That's what happens when you meet person to person, you see. So much can be misconstrued over the telephone. She was obviously rather protective of her great-niece and not at all keen for the truth to be revealed. That's why she was so rude about anyone who happened to ask questions. I explained to her that enough time had passed for the truth to be known without causing any harm to either Darcy or herself. Fortunately, the two ladies were eventually persuaded of that. It was all rather a pleasant relief to everyone, wasn't it?"

"Fancy Atkins keeping his knowledge of Darcy Sprockett's whereabouts a secret. It shows that he knew about the inheritance all along."

"There were definitely some purposeful omissions in that case file, Pembers. It was very considerate of him to comply with Darcy's wishes."

"I always knew that Atkins was faultless."

"He does appear to have been, doesn't he? I'm sure there must have been something he got wrong once. It happens to the best of us. Oh, good grief!"

Churchill stopped suddenly, her heart in her mouth.

"Did you see *that*?" Her voice trembled.

"No! What?"

"A flash of white, Pembers, just up ahead. It can't be... No, please don't tell me it's the White Lady of Poppleford Woods!"

Churchill's knees felt weak.

"It can't be," replied Pemberley, her voice wavering. "Everyone said that Darcy Sprockett was the White Lady, but she can't be because she's still alive. Besides, I thought you didn't believe in those silly superstitions, Mrs Churchill."

"I don't! Not really, anyway. Not unless I actually see something, as I'm sure I did just then. Shall we turn back?"

"We're on a circular route, Mrs Churchill. If we turn back now it'll take us longer to get out of the woods than if we simply carry on."

"But I don't want to carry on. There's definitely something… Oh, I'm all of a quiver!"

"What exactly did you see, Mrs Churchill?" Pemberley's voice was becoming equally tremulous.

"A flash of white dress on the path up ahead. It's the White Lady, I'm telling you!" The back of her neck prickled.

"It does sound rather like her. It's certainly similar to the sight Mrs Higginbath and I saw in the woods a few years ago!"

"What did you do?"

"We ran away, screaming."

Churchill gave a shiver. "I can't say that I blame you. I'm close to doing something very similar myself!"

"If it is the White Lady," ventured Pemberley, "she's fairly unlikely to be malevolent. I imagine she just appears in front of a person and then walks off again. I'm sure she won't harm us."

"Just glimpsing her is enough, Pembers, I didn't want to see her at all! I don't want to be exposed to any more of the dreaded ghost. Oh, help!"

"Oswald! Come back!" shrieked Pemberley.

"Oh no!" Churchill felt a surge of dread run through her as she watched the little dog scamper down the path in the direction of the White Lady. "Oh, stop him, Pembers!

He doesn't know what he's doing! She'll bewitch him and then we'll have a ghost dog in the office. Pembers! Where are you going?"

"To fetch Oswald!" she called back over her shoulder as she dashed off down the path.

Churchill glanced around at the menacing woods that encircled her and decided she would probably be safer with Pemberley and Oswald than on her own.

"Wait!" she cried out. "I'm coming with you!"

Churchill hurtled down the path after her assistant and the disappearing dog.

A moment later she heard barking and laughter, and then she almost careered straight into the back of Pemberley, who had stopped abruptly.

"Not in front of the dog, Peregrine!" said a woman's mirthful voice.

"It's only Oswald," cackled a man in response.

"Oh, hullo?" said the woman.

Churchill peered past Pemberley to see a man wearing plus fours and a pith helmet just as he was releasing himself from an embrace with a red-haired lady wearing a white dress.

"What ho!" he said, doffing his pith helmet.

"Mr Colthrop," said Churchill sternly. "And *Mrs Thonnings*?"

"Hello, Mrs Churchill," Mrs Thonnings said coyly as she smoothed her dress. "This isn't what it seems."

"I see."

"We meet again, Mrs Churchill!" said Mr Colthrop jovially. "This *really isn't* what it seems, you know."

"No? Well, I must thank you kindly for your help, Mrs Thonnings."

"Help? What did I do, Mrs Churchill?"

"You've always wanted to help us with a case, haven't you?"

"Oh yes, indeed I have!"

"Well I do believe you have just solved one for us."

The End

Thank you

~

Thank you for reading *Puzzle in Poppleford Wood*, I really hope you enjoyed it!

Would you like to know when I release new books? Here are some ways to stay updated:

- Join my mailing list and receive the short story *A Troublesome Case*: emilyorgan.com/a-troublesome-case
- Like my Facebook page: facebook.com/emilyorganwriter
- View my other books here: emilyorgan.com

And if you have a moment, I would be very grateful if you would leave a quick review of *Puzzle in Poppleford Wood* online. Honest reviews of my books help other readers discover them too!

Get a free short mystery

~

Want more of Churchill & Pemberley? Get a copy of my free short mystery *A Troublesome Case* and sit down to enjoy a thirty minute read.

Churchill and Pemberley are on the train home from a shopping trip when they're caught up with a theft from a suitcase. Inspector Mappin accuses them of stealing the valuables, but in an unusual twist of fate the elderly sleuths are forced to come to his aid!

Visit my website to claim your FREE copy:
emilyorgan.com/a-troublesome-case

Trouble in the Churchyard

A Churchill & Pemberley Mystery Book 4

Who's been tampering with the graves in St Swithun's churchyard? Elderly detectives Annabel Churchill and Doris Pemberley are asked to investigate by Mr Grieves the sinister sexton. Meanwhile the sleepy English village of Compton Poppleford is rocked by the murder of its favourite philanthropist, Mr Butterfork. Who could have possibly wished to harm him?

When the murderer leaves clues in the churchyard, Churchill and Pemberley are keen to solve the case. But Churchill finds herself distracted by the charms of debonair Mr Pickwick and his art gallery. A night-time fright in the churchyard brings her to her senses and the ageing detective duo are soon convinced of their suspect. The trouble is, they could be completely mistaken...

Find out more at: emilyorgan.com

The Penny Green Series

~

Also by Emily Organ. A series of mysteries set in Victorian London featuring the intrepid Fleet Street reporter, Penny Green.

What readers are saying:

"A Victorian Delight!"

"Good clean mystery in an enjoyable historical setting"

"If you are unfamiliar with the Penny Green Series, acquaint yourselves immediately!"

Books in the Penny Green Series:

Limelight
The Rookery
The Maid's Secret
The Inventor
Curse of the Poppy
The Bermondsey Poisoner

The Penny Green Series

An Unwelcome Guest
Death at the Workhouse
The Gang of St Bride's

Find out more here: emilyorgan.com

Made in the USA
Las Vegas, NV
26 December 2020